It's Not All Rocks and Roses

Anthology

Volume 1

Authors Round Table Society

Stories by:

J. J. Aarons
Edmund J. Asher
Miracle Austin
Natalie Clountz Bauman
Susie Clevenger
Gabrielle DeMay
B. Ellen Gardner
Thomas Fletcher Grooms
Rita Ownby Holcomb
John M. Moody
James William Peercy
Claudette Stacey Peercy
Elizabeth Silver
Gary Smithers
Cynthia Vannoy
Kelly Willbanks

AuthorsRoundTableSociety.com

All characters in this book are fictitious. Any resemblance to actual persons, living or dead, is purely coincidental.

It's Not All Rockets and Ray Guns

Published by arrangement with the authors.

Copyright © 2019 Authors Round Table Society

All rights reserved. Reproduction or utilization of this work in any form, by any means now known or hereinafter invented, including, but not limited to, xerography, photocopying and recording, podcasting, and in any known storage and retrieval system, is forbidden without permission from the copyright holder.

For information contact:

Three Sided Coin Publishing

ThreeSidedCoin.com

Manufactured in the United States of America

Library of Congress Control Number: 2020901282
ISBN: 978-1-937491-05-5

DEDICATION

To all the wonderful Authors Round Table Society members who believe in their dreams and have chosen to make them a reality.

To the love and support we give each other.

To the readers who enjoy great stories.

Contents

ACKNOWLEDGMENTS i
WHAT THIS IS ABOUT ii

DYSTOPIAN 1

FOLLY OF AN EMPIRE 2
   by Cynthia Vannoy 2

FANTASY HORROR 27

GAUNT 28
   by Edmund J. Asher 28

FOLKLORE / FAIRY TALES 42

FREDDIE THE RED FROG 43
   by Gary Smithers 43

HISTORICAL FICTION 52

QUEEN OF MY HEART 53
   by Rita Ownby Holcomb 53

LITERARY FICTION 78

BREAKDOWN 79
   by Kelly Willbanks 79

DIARY OF A MAJIK USER 88
   by James William Peercy 88

LIGHT OF LOVE 98
   by B. Ellen Gardner 98

REPLACED 110
   by Elizabeth Silver 110

PARANORMAL 118

OLD SOULS AT THE ANTIQUE MALL 119
   by Natalie Clountz Bauman 119

LADY SCARLET 127
   by Susie Clevenger 127

PARANORMAL HORROR 150
WAKE 151
   by Miracle Austin 151
SCIENCE FICTION 166
ALREADY DREAMED 167
   by Claudette Stacey Peercy 167
DREAM PHASE 181
   by John M. Moody 181
ILLUSION 199
   by J. J. Aarons 199
RED EAGLE 225
   by Thomas Fletcher Grooms 225
SCI-FI HORROR 233
FLYING BROKEN 234
   by Gabrielle DeMay 234
ABOUT THE AUTHORS 246

ACKNOWLEDGMENTS

We wish to express sincere appreciation to all the Authors Round Table Society members who have submitted stories for this anthology. It is an honor to work with such good and loyal friends in the spirit of writing. They have given of their hearts and souls to be a part of something so special.

To all of you, highest commendations.

WHAT THIS IS ABOUT

We believe in artist helping artist. Whether it is education on marketing or practice on story composition through writing, music or poetry, it is the Authors Round Table Society's mission, A.R.T.S., to aid their fellow wordsmiths.

A.R.T.S. invites everyone to be part of our group, whatever artisan they are. All intertwine into the cosmos known as 'creativity,' regulated by the stars of 'logic,' and laid out on a spatial canvas of 'thought.'

For this anthology, we have focused on the color *red*. The word *red* will be found in each story at least one time.

We have divided the stories into genres for readers who like specific types of adventures. For those tales which we felt did not precisely fit in one of the listed genres, the genre of Literary Fiction was chosen.

Read. Enjoy. Share with others. When you find a story you truly love, please let us know. We would love to hear from you.

James William Peercy

DYSTOPIAN

Dealing with an imagined state or society where there is great injustice, dystopian confronts the frightening possibilities in a world of malcontents. While it means 'bad place,' it can also reach out for the goal of good in a dark, foreboding world.

A subgenre of fantasy, dystopian allows the reader to not only explore this new world but also take a critical eye to their own. Let the journey begin!

James William Peercy

DYSTOPIAN: STORY 1

FOLLY OF AN EMPIRE

by Cynthia Vannoy

The sky bleeds above the desert. The sunset burns bright on my mother's red felt tent. The tent is a vast, multi-splendored tribute to the men and women who gave their lives on the battlefield, today. I regret I won't live to see the finish of the war or see the face of my beloved leader one last time.

I'm content. I gave my life to her long ago, when I was but a girl and she was the one who lay bleeding like a sunset into the cooling sand.

My sword arm aches, yet my body is quiet now, much like the surrounding battlefield. I lie on my side where I fell after the last wrenching blow. Warm sand cradles me as if the Mother Herself holds me in Her outstretched hand. Moving seems such an effort. Cheek pillowed in warmth, I try to watch the sunset, but I am drowning in memory.

"*Takama.*"

As if from across a vast plain, I hear my name.

A dream? The wind? No, only the past, coming like a thief to steal me away, back to where it all began, lifetimes ago with *her*.

***

"Takama, what is it?"

I didn't look away from the strange, bright star pinned against the night sky. "Don't know. One of the Caliph's dirigibles, probably."

"No, *that*," my younger brother said.

Only then did I realize my younger brother had stopped somewhere behind me. Abruptly leaderless, dozens of bewildered, sleepy goats milled about my legs. Turning back, my eyes followed his pointing finger.

As far as the eye could see, the desert stretched. Long fingers of sand seamlessly melded under wind-stunted trees and scrubs, only to waterfall over the next layered riser of rock.

We both knew this area as well as the face of our mother. Our tribe has lived here for generations. I knew the low formation of sandstone to which Iken, my younger brother, pointed, but I didn't recognize the extra shape within its moonlit shadows.

My brother looked hesitant, so I crept closer. Here on the Plateau of Rivers, moonlight is nearly as bright as sunlight, but it robs life of color, painting everything in shades of gray and silver. Yet, I could see a woman lying there although only a partial profile showed through tangled hair. Unlike our sun-darkened skin, hers was the pale pigment of strangers seen on soldiers from distant lands as they passed through the *souk* looking for wine, women, and food.

I stopped and said, "It's *her*. The priestess."

Only then did Iken barge up beside me, breathless with excitement, eyes huge in the moonlight. "That crazy woman whose been wandering around and scaring the herds for a month? Is she *dead?*"

Anger rose in me at his unseemly avidity. "Don't call her crazy. And no, of course she's not dead–I don't think."

Iken shrugged, unrepentant. "She's no priestess. I've heard her raving. Everyone knows she's sun-struck." Despite his brash words, he remained rooted in place as I moved closer to her.

Annoyance made me bold, but even as I drew near enough to touch her shoulder, I smelled the reek of spilled blood. "Iken, give me your *cheich*."

"What?" he said. "No. Mother'll stripe my hide."

I strode back to him, ripped the long tangle of fabric from around his head and shoulders, and then returned to the unconscious woman. With the knife from my belt, I worked at sawing the dark linen into strips while Iken's squawks of outrage buzzed like a gnat in my ears.

"Go wake First Mother," I ordered as I tightly bound the woman's gore-sticky wrists in turns of fabric.

She wasn't death-cold, though her pulse couldn't be felt to a cursory touch. I knew the feel of dead flesh. She only lay close to the Hag's door, the door of death, not over the threshold.

"What're *you* going to do?" Iken demanded from a safe distance.

"I'll carry her back and lead the herd with me. But I need you to rouse the Elders, so they'll be ready before I get there. Tell First Mother this one's lost a lot of blood."

He hurried off without another word. I shook my head, knowing nothing had sunk in. He'd arrive in camp bellowing like a cut lamb about his stolen *cheich* and have everyone in an uproar. Perhaps First Mother could slap pertinent information from him. As the tribal healer, she'd know what to do.

I knew little of the mysteries of healing. I'd grown strong from hauling water and hefting sheep or goats. Unlike the many daughters in our matriarchal tribe, I had no gift for the more esoteric ways of womanhood.

Boys leave to become men. Girls stay to become women. But what about those caught between? The Caliph's army doesn't take women, and I've no love for motherhood, cooking, and weaving. Where do I go?

The stranger sprawled at my feet might have an answer, if she survived.

The priestess's body felt malnourished, all long gangly limbs and jutting ribs. Although her robes were ragged, her bare feet shredded,

I could see no other injuries aside from the ragged gashes down her forearms. It appeared she had managed the deed with a very sharp bit of flint I found tangled in one sleeve.

With a sigh for my foolishness, I hefted her pitifully, bony form across my shoulders and began the long trek home.

**

After the initial uproar of excitement, life settled back into tedium while the priestess called Leila recovered. But barely a month later, had she upended our insular world.

Fierce argument drew my attention one night. It spilled from the red tent, a woman's sanctuary normally reserved for laughter, singing, and the celebration of newborn babes.

"This is madness," Atty Herma said with her usual bluntness. "We will *not* fight the Caliphate armies for some fool tale!"

"Then you will die," Leila said in the common tongue of the Empire, not in Tamazight, my native language. Fortunately for her, we understood.

"We'll certainly die if we fight," Herma continued. "We have swords, knives. His soldiers have *weapons,* not just guns, but scatter-wave projectors and chemical bombs."

I huddled outside the tent, riveted to the silence of the pregnant pause.

Atty Herma said, derision filling her powerful voice, "You think us ignorant sheep-herders who don't know a musket from mutton? My sons are in those Hag-ridden armies. My sons, her sons, and *her* sons, too!"

Without seeing, I knew my aunt pointed to the women in the tent.

"Most are already dead from the endless fighting," shouted Herma. "We may not own the weapons that shred our children's bodies, but we *know* them!"

Quiet certainty came from First Mother Magwen, the eldest, as she said, "If the Empire was not led solely by men, they would have our daughters as well."

Although not blood mother to any still living among the Tribe, First Mother stood as mother to us all when decisions were made.

Her blood sister, *Atty* Herma, and the other *Attys* blustered. First Mother had laid down the law.

But Leila, whom First Mother had brought back from the Hag's bony grasp, had words of her own. "The Empire will take your daughters in due time, if it is not stopped."

"Oh ho," Atty Kweller joined the fray. "First it was the Caliph, and now it's the Empire!"

"Do you not see what is happening?" Leila's worn voice rose above the squawking of the many mothers. "Piece by piece, your world is being dismembered. The largest piece you see is your sons. But think of the world itself. How large are your lands now? Shrunken? And your flocks? Your grain?"

Aside from mumbled assent, silence fell behind the felt walls.

"Has the Caliph demanded you buy only Empire grain for sowing? Yet his merchants give less every season for your harvest?" asked Leila.

That brought vigor back into the dissenters. The voices rose in such volume, I could no longer discern one from another. Leila knew it was a sensitive subject.

Our tribe lived closest to the edges of the Empire's *civilization*. We saw more Caliphate influence creeping into our lives. I'd already heard many of my *Attys* complain that since our seed grain was no longer derived of our mother's mothers, the results were not as rich or plentiful. Empire wheat grew with less water, which was good in a place of annual droughts, but at what cost? What alchemy had been wrought on the seed?

"*Enough,*" First Mother Magwen shouted.

I jumped.

"The world changes, but the Tribes remain," she intoned. "We will move on as our mothers' mothers have done since the Goddess birthed the Moons. The Empire of Men will do to themselves as they wish."

"The Empire of Men will destroy *everything*," replied Leila into the ringing quiet. "I offer the matter of water and grain only as an example from your own experience. Far worse happens all across Her Face. In the cities, smog from engines of commerce spoils the air. Diseases breed in overcrowding and filth. Water sources are depleted. What remains is fouled in sheer disregard of nature. Outside the cities, entire forests larger than this desert are felled to build ships and fuel their machines of war.

Leila continued, "You know the Emperor's alchemists have mastered the ability to detonate chemical bombs from impossible heights, far higher than any bird can soar. With these, his Caliphates decimate entire cities, poisoning the air, killing human and animal alike with wasting diseases. This I attest to personally."

A wave of murmuring followed.

My belly clenched as I thought, *So the rumours are true?* Memory of her emaciated frame made me wonder. *Malnourished or ill? my thoughts continued.*

Leila's voice dropped, forcing me to lean closer. "But all of this pales to what I saw as *scriptorae* to Imperial Defense. There are plans to make a weapon to destroy the world. Not just cities, not just continents, the *planet*."

In the shocked silence which met this announcement, I was startled to notice Iken had snuck up beside me. His dark face was crimped in wicked glee at the chance to expose my spying, but something in my own expression must have convinced him otherwise. Blank with dread, he nestled in beside me to listen.

"How is such possible?" *Atty* Herma groused, but even I could hear the uncertainty in her normally brash tone. "How can one kill a world?"

"Imperial Defense has mastered the building blocks of life and created a weapon," said Leila.

I knew none of my family present recognized that concept any more than I did, but none raised her voice in question.

"If unleashed on the armies of the West, this weapon will spread unstoppable poison across Her entire face. Those unlucky enough to survive the initial detonation will die of sickness and starvation within a season," continued Leila.

"Why would anyone employ a weapon which would kill the user as well?" someone choked out.

"Infinite control," came the quiet answer from Leila. "Would *you* dare bluff such a ploy after what's already been unleashed in smaller doses? But I've heard the talk. Some think the Emperor is unstable enough to do it."

"How can you know any of this?" *Atty* Herma scoffed into the panicked murmurs. "How could a lowly *scriptorae* learn the secrets of alchemists?"

Leila sounded regretful and weary. "The Goddess brought me to the knowledge," she answered with the same simple conviction she used any time she spoke of her connection with the divine. "I *shouldn't* have had access, but the scrolls came to me by unknown means. I shouldn't have been able to comprehend their meaning. I'm no alchemist! But She gave me to understand. She's spoken to me in dreams ever since."

Atty Kweller sneered and said, "Yes, all of us have heard you for weeks as you wandered about our hills, raving about prophetic stars and end of times. Why here? Go tell this to the people in the cities."

"I have," quietly said Leila. "They won't listen. I was whipped in the *Praetorium* for speaking against the Empire. Even those who would listen were shamed into disavowing me." She sighed. "I begged the Mother to give me the right words, but She told me to follow the signs. She said I'd find reason among the Daughters of Tinan."

Gasps followed.

Iken and I exchanged shocked looks.

"What signs?" asked First Mother Magwen with quiet gravity.

"There would be a new star in the heavens by which to set my path. That the Daughters of Tinan would understand my words. And that true believers would join me here, in this place of safety."

"Here?" someone asked in disbelief.

Iken huffed as if he, too, could not believe such a statement.

"You claimed to come from Byzantium," Magwen said.

I know I must have shared the amazement of everyone in the tent. Byzantium, the great Capital of all the Emperor's lands, was the seat of power to which even the mighty Caliph owed allegiance.

I thought, *Why would someone from the Capital come here, to a lonely bit of land in the desert?*

But I already knew Leila's reply. It was her answer to everything.

"The Mother told me to come here," said Leila.

More argument followed with no answers decided. I learned that a similar stalemate had occurred among the men. And yet, the discussion from the red tent had been transformative to me. It was the night I realized Leila would be my key to a new life.

Byzantium!

The time-honored tradition of hosting guests, even begrudged company, fell to elder sisters and cousins, not grubby herders like me. Yet, I managed to finagle my way into the women's red tent at least once the next month, when my own moon blood flowed, and I'd earned my few days of rest. Leila remembered me.

"You're Takama," she said.

Somehow, I mustered the courage to look into those amazing eyes: light gray as a dove's wing. By the sunlight slanting through the open tent flap, I marveled at the pinkness of her skin, her odd, flaxen hair. It was so unlike my own plain, brown eyes and black curls.

"Yes," I politely agreed when I realized I'd been staring. I forced myself to look away, even though this, too, seemed rude.

We were the only two in the tent. There was so much I wanted to ask, but where to start? I didn't have the skill of First Mother Magwen or the boldness of *Atty* Herma. I knew sheep and goats. I knew how to shear, slaughter, and birth them. I knew a little of the sword, thanks to my older brothers. They had returned once on leave from the army and took pity on me when I begged for instruction.

"Thank you for bringing me to safety," Leila said.

I blushed when I realize I'd been staring again. The horrible slashes on her wrists had healed to thick, pink scars, but my eyes went to her soft, unblemished hands. It was so obvious she'd been a city-born scribe. By comparison, my sun-dark hands bore scars and callouses aplenty from working with livestock or beating wool into felt for tents. My *Attys* and cousins were no different.

"I had to," I was horrified to hear myself say. Of course, I'd been thinking about how vulnerable she seemed, but it sounded as if I'd answered her gratitude with flippancy. "I couldn't just leave you out there," I awkwardly finished.

"I cannot repay you or your family for rescuing me," she replied, "but I'm afraid it's time for me to go. First Mother knows I'm ill, and I heard the men of the Tribe arguing with her last night."

I couldn't dispute that. The Tribe had decided its guest needed to move on. It was exactly what I needed. But, now I had to convince her to return to the cities, not wander, raving in the desert until she died. After a moment, which stretched out for years in my mind, I ventured. "What will you do?"

She sighed and gazed through the open tent flap with an expression which might have been wistful but was also despairing. "Go back out and try again."

"Try to sacrifice yourself again?" I asked, dumbfounded.

"Oh," Leila laughed, "Goddess, no. I meant, try to convince people of Her Word."

'Oh," I echoed. We both laughed in shared embarrassment.

Hearing us, others returned, and my moment alone vanished. Not until days later did I have the chance to tell her of my decision.

"When you leave, my Lady, I will go with you," I said.

She looked confounded. "Takama, w*hy?*"

I smiled and hoped it looked convincingly virtuous instead of gleeful. "Because the Mother told me to."

***

At this point in her life, Leila was little more than a beggar, a status which I shared the moment I left our grazing lands. I owned my clothes and a dagger. Our tribal money came from wool, meat, and crops, none of which I could take with me when I fled. We survived on what little travel food Leila had been gifted and what I'd smuggled out myself, as well as, the kindness of the neighboring tribes who did not yet know I was apostate.

The moment we reached Baalt, however, we were at the mercy of the Mother. Evidently, She had determined I would learn the folly of my dishonest departure by harsh example. I should have made my intentions known to the tribe, but I'd feared the expected denial.

Compared to great cities like Byzantium or Asturias, Baalt was a filthy little harbor town. But to me, fresh from the desert and wide-eyed as a newborn lamb, it seemed a metropolis. Though confident in the security of her Mother Goddess, Leila tried to warn me that the denizens of Baalt's underbelly had already sniffed us out.

My naiveté died an early death. My enthusiasm had faded with the warmth of the day and the growlings of an empty belly. True hunger was as new an experience to me as the effluvia of city life. This was *not* how I'd imagined things back in the desert. I determined I'd leave Leila just before dawn while she slept. She was crazy, just as Iken had said.

The very first night they surrounded us like hyenas where we'd tried to bed down beside a public fountain. As the shadows of the three brigands detached themselves from the darker shapes of nearby buildings, I lay wide awake in the moonlight. Until this point, I'd agonized over my ability to get back home. Now, I curled on my side around a hard knot of fear.

The fist with which I gripped my dagger shook. I couldn't catch my breath. At the first touch of a hand on my shoulder, I came upright with a panicked bellow followed by wild slashing and stabbing.

My blade made contact. A baritone yell rang out over my own shrieks. Movement blurred under the moon's silver light. I couldn't distinguish features, only the brightness of eyes and flash of metal.

Something caught me at the shins. I stumbled, landing hard on my knees and the heel of my left hand, but I never lost my dagger. I rolled, instinctively shying away from the coming blow, but not far enough.

A boot caught me, a glancing blow in the ribs. A male voice cursed in irritation. Another kick stung my right hand, loosening my hold on the knife. I flailed out with my left hand even as I curled in and tucked my chin against my chest to avoid a face strike. I'd wrestled with brothers. This at least was familiar.

Grabbing an ankle, I yanked with all my strength and felt the concussion through the ground when my opponent's head hit the fountain. My other hand rammed the dagger into the bulk of his thigh, but he was unresisting. He lay sprawled beside me, already dead.

His sword, a military *gladius*, tumbled from one relaxed fist.

A sword which should have killed me, I thought.

I was crouched there, panting and blank with shock, when Leila cried out.

I'd got to my feet, around the fountain, and lifted the *gladius* in both hands over the exposed back of the man atop her. The blade plunged in along his spine with little resistance, but I lost my grip when he spasmed like a speared fish and fell sideways against me.

I reached for Leila, unable to tell by moonlight if she had been wounded.

"Takama, you're hurt," Leila exclaimed.

I saw only superficial wounds: shallow scratches across one palm and wrist. I held my hand against my filthy tunic and tried not to think about infection.

A scuff behind me startled us both. I pulled the blade out of the man at our feet and turned.

Another beggar woman rifled through the clothing of the man I'd killed on the fountain. I dashed forward to reclaim my dagger. The woman recoiled from the *gladius* in my right hand but returned to untangling the man's money belt.

I left her to it.

Only then did I notice the additional person sitting on the fountain's edge. The bearded man chuckled when I lifted both weapons with a snarl.

"Fierce little thing," he grunted in amused gutter-Latin. "Put those down before you stab yourself. I don't hurt children."

When I brandished the *gladius* instead in half-remembered lessons, the stranger shook his head. One long leg stretched out to prod the dead man in the face with a booted toe. "I'm not one of these scum. I ran off the third one. Keep the pig-sticker, but you'll need his scabbard."

With a grunt, he stood and strolled over to Leila. I hurried around the other side to put myself between them.

"Takama, I think he means well," Leila cautioned.

But I didn't trust her judgment. The man was bigger than either of us, lanky but muscled. I had no doubt he had honest training with the *gladius* at his hip.

"Heard those three talking about you in a tavern," he commented. "Knew who they meant, but didn't know where you were, so I had to follow at a distance." Moonlight illuminated his sardonic grin as he looked at me again. "I didn't know your desert rat had teeth."

"Neither did I," Leila sounded amused.

Glancing over at her, I realized she'd already removed the second dead man's money belt and now tugged on one of his feet.

"Here," she tossed a boot at me, "see if it fits."

"Robbery?" I croaked, surprised at how much my throat hurt from screaming. As if I were padded with wool carding against the world, everything felt distant. "What does your Goddess say about that?"

Leila looked at me.

To my astonishment, I thought I read derision there.

"She says *survive*," she retorted. "He tried to rape, kill me. Perhaps not in that order. I'll take what the Goddess offers."

"Good survival rule," the stranger commented in a jest. "Don't waste time being squeamish."

A sigh came from Leila, her amusement gone. "I suppose *you* want his money?"

"What? No. I didn't come to rob anyone. I came to see if you were hurt." The man sounded offended, and I wasn't surprised when he turned away. "I'll leave you to it. Be a little more careful, for gods' sake."

"Mother bless you. Please forgive my rudeness." Leila stood now to offer a hand in friendship.

I tsked in disapproval.

"I am Leila. This is Takama."

Our would-be benefactor wore a wry expression above his unruly blonde beard. However, he took her hand.

I didn't offer mine.

"Kervis. Look, priestess, you need to find a better place to sleep. Port Guard doesn't even patrol here."

"I'm not a priestess. I just speak for the Mother," said Leila.

Kervis glanced from Leila to me and back again, before shrugging. "I know a pot-shop that opens before dawn with the bakeries. After that, I'll show you a safer place to sleep, assuming your desert rat doesn't skewer me."

I blinked, surprised by the weight of the sword I'd forgotten I still held. It felt natural in my hand. "I'm of the tribe of Amazigh, not a rat," I muttered to no-one in particular as I bent to try on the boot. It fit. "And I'll need that sword belt."

***

Near dawn and fed, thanks to the Empire coin from the dead bandit and outfitted with stolen boots and a sword, we followed Kervis to the safer interior of an unused boatshed. I still expected treachery, but so far he had shown only concern. I felt even *Atty* Herma would wonder at the motives behind his friendly demeanor. Did he consider us helpless idiots? I couldn't argue with this imagined assessment.

To my dismay, there in the quiet with a full belly and the honeyed light of sunrise gleaming through slatted walls, I began uncontrollably shaking. When Leila reached for me in concern, I choked, horrified to find tears coursing down my cheeks. My throat felt stuffed with the wool carding which had seemed so comforting right after the fight.

"Takama?" asked Leila. "Have you taken ill?"

I couldn't answer for the longest time, but she seemed to understand. Kervis handed over a skin of mead, and I managed to swallow past the rock in my throat. When Leila's arm comfortingly squeezed around my shoulders, the dam burst, and I could do nothing but shudder and sob with my head against my knees.

"Battle-shakes. She'll be fine," I heard Kervis comment. The humiliation of weeping only redoubled my tears.

He exchanged more quiet words with Leila, and then left the shed.

"There's a first time for everything," Leila murmured once the storm had passed.

I shook my head and wiped snot on my sodden sleeve. Shame burned me as if I stood in front of an open forge, both for my emotional display and my thoughts.

"You saved me, Takama," she insisted. "At least, take comfort in that. Actually, you probably saved us both."

"I was going to *leave!*" Horrified at the disclosure, I put my head back down on my drawn-up knees.

I thought, *Why did I need to explain?*

But I felt again the fear when I'd thought her to be wounded, the terror of losing her.

During the night, I'd been ready to desert her to her lunacy, run back home like a whipped dog. Instead, I'd stayed, fought, and killed to protect her.

"I see," Leila said above my head now. When I ventured nothing further, she sighed, yet the arm around my shoulders remained. "But you didn't. Why is that?"

"Don't know," I gasped.

"I do."

I was surprised enough to sit up and peer at her through swollen eyes. "You do?"

Leila's smile was tired but kind. "She touched your heart. The Mother guided you--still does."

I swiped at my eyes, angry with myself as much as with her impossible faith and said, "I don't believe in all that nonsense. I only came with you because I thought you were the way out of my useless life, that you'd be a good guide in the cities. Instead, you've reduced me to beggar, thief, and murderer. Why would She allow that?"

"Are birds beggars? Bees? The lion who takes what he wants from the herd?"

"What?" I asked and thought, *She was back to talking nonsense. Had she heard a word I said?*

"It's just a trial, Takama. It will pass. Have faith in the Mother."

Have faith, this was Leila's litany for any situation, one which I found very difficult to follow so blindly.

Leila believed. Even before she'd opened her veins in an insane attempt to gain the Goddess's attention, she'd been a devout believer. There was no messy pantheon of Empire deities. Wherever we went, whomever we met, she exhorted the Word of the Mother and of a return to a sustainable, agrarian life. Small wonder she'd been whipped and banished.

From town to port to island and back, we tramped for months. Charity and a few odd jobs along the way elevated us just above beggars. Spring faded to summer and then to autumn. I was not alone in my worries we would soon be following our rootless leader through snow drifts.

During our travels, a few of the nomadic Tribes and the gentler townsfolk agreed with her message. A handful joined our strange fellowship. However, the majority of listeners, even some who agreed, were not inclined to fight the Caliphate and Empire to end technology.

Suicidal, they claimed. *It would take an army or intervention from the Mother Herself.*

Leila always smiled and stressed how the latter would be made true all too soon. That calm premonition never failed to unsettle listeners. I'd heard it times beyond counting, and it still unsettled me.

"I thought the star over the Plateau of Rivers was a sign of peace," I once said, early in our journey.

Leila shook her head. "It signifies safety, a safe haven for believers when the Final War happens."

"But what if people listen? Won't that stop the War?"

She sighed. "War was ever a certainty, Takama, but I made a bargain with my sacrifice. Believers will survive the Fall of the Empire to usher in a New Age."

Even patient Kervis, who had stayed with us since Baalt, seemed taken aback by her certainty.

Prognostications of doom, as our learned companion, Avitus, called them, were not what soldiers and their families wanted to hear. For every sympathetic ear she reached, twenty cursed her. At least, we'd only been run off and not assaulted for such inflammatory talk. I learned to be grateful for Kervis' looming presence, even if his sarcastic humor annoyed me.

Seeing I was determined to become competent with the sword I carried, he and another follower, Huran, decided to give me lessons. Like Kervis, dark-skinned Huran had been a sailor for the Emperor's navy. People might smile behind their hands at a skinny Berber girl carrying a sword, but the two ex-mariners made them think twice.

***

Despite my initial impatience, by early autumn when we at last came to *the* city, the Capital of the Empire, Byzantium, I was both jaded and terrified. Only there did I truly realize my own insignificance in the world.

It was too big, too crowded, and too much. How could a place be flawless yet filthy? With its smell, noise, and impossible crowds, no one seemed to mind being shoulder-to-shoulder. No one took notice of the unbearable weight of buildings, which left everything below in perpetual shadow. The people appeared deaf to the clanking, hissing machinery, braying street-corner barkers, and the shriek of factory sirens.

At first, sleep completely eluded me. Everyone else seemed overjoyed to be sleeping indoor, but I found the chosen traveler's hostel to be dingy and smelly. It was definitely too bright and too loud at any given hour. Artificial light left me anxious and irritable.

I shuddered every time one of the bloated monsters, known as dirigibles, hissed overhead. After my first sighting of the air machines, Caecilia, who was experienced with such things, took me to the airfields to prove people entered the monstrosities and lived to tell the tale.

On our third day in the Capital, I suffered an emotional breakdown.

Our group of eleven rested by a fountain in a city square. Drained, both physically and emotionally, I tried to relish the gift of sunlight on my face. If Leila suggested we stay one more day, I would throw myself from the top of a building.

Kervis, who'd expected me to enjoy my first visit to Byzantium, couldn't understand my sudden distress. Another Tribeswoman, Zeğiga, tried to enlighten him.

"Byzantium is everything the desert is not. There is no peace here," she said.

"In the desert, you can *feel* the Mother," I added, privately surprised to remember that connection. "Even in the silence, there's balance. *Especially* in the silence."

"Sounds nice," replied wizened little Avitus. He'd lived all his life in a suburb of Byzantium. "Why'd you leave?"

Memory of my original gullibility rose with a pang. "Travelers' tales painted a picture of prosperity, wealth, hygiene, and advancements in medicine and commerce. But they lied."

Or, I thought, *at the least, misconstrued reality.*

Thanks to Leila's teachings, the trap of this unsustainable life seemed glaringly apparent. What good were the supposed luxuries if steam technology powered most of the miracles? Its invention had birthed the Age of Technology, the very antithesis of the Goddess's message.

Our leader seemed to grasp my inner struggle and said, "There *are* advancements which harmonize with the Goddess. For instance, bioluminescent algae illuminates the streetlamps, not gas or coal. Some of the smaller-scale farms still practice permaculture, which links them to the land. And the cities do exercise *some* reclamation."

"Caliph Cartaeus is studying a form of power in solar emissions," Avitus added, but younger Aelius snorted.

"He's lucky to be considered mad and not disloyal to the Empire!" the young man declared.

An argument ensued between the two as to how many ancient aqueducts had been replaced by steam-powered pressurization. Kervis, erstwhile lieutenant to Leila's erratic leadership, shushed them with a glare.

I knew my companions meant to console, but my eyes, now open, could not be closed to reality. Technology ruled with an iron fist, and that iron came from mining the Mother Earth. Commodities of iron ore, coal, metals, even salt, fueled the wars. The Empire subjugated everything in its ravenous, ever-reaching borders, but within those boundaries, the Caliphs fought one another for access to what fueled their armies.

To me, it strengthened the certainty the Emperor was mad. Why else allow his own people to war amongst themselves? But most Byzantines found it completely normal.

"That's life." They'd shrug, disinterested, as Leila tried to speak the Word of the Goddess. They were cynical, hidebound, and completely unwilling to open their eyes to Leila's message.

I saw myself in their displayed attitudes, but I saw the futility in it, too.

"I see the truth," I said now in despair. "The lives of city dwellers are no less brutal, meaningless, or short than any of the Tribe. Technology's only made them less content with what they've been given."

As if to prove my point, a four-person, steam driven car clanked past us on the paved roundabout. Pedestrians stepped aside with no more concern than if it had been a horse and cart. Oblivious to the miracle of transportation, two passengers inside heatedly argued.

"This is your second trial, Takama," Leila sadly murmured once the clamor died away. "You've come full circle."

I considered her remark and said, "I left the Tribe thinking I wanted civilization. But now I can see its gold is actually dross."

Our companions murmured appreciatively, and Leila nodded with a sympathetic smile. "Well said, my friend."

"This is what people are to see?" Black-haired Lin asked in her accented, far-eastern lilt, "Their lives have no meaning?"

"Of course not," Leila waved a hand at the sterile city. "I want them to see there is a better way to *live*. This is not sustainable. It's killing the Mother."

I looked on in silent despair as the inevitable talk of conversion rose. Here, in a metropolis teeming with the world's most intelligent minds, only eleven of us had gained enlightenment. How could the Mother possibly build a New Age?

***

We didn't tarry more than a week in the Capital. Leila had been banished once, and as she was incapable of silencing her convictions, we couldn't risk drawing the ire of the local Guard. Instead, we bartered quick passage back across the Bosporus to Anatolia and then across the Mediterranean to Alexandria.

"Too dangerous," Leila complained when Kervis told her he'd booked passage on a merchant ship.

"Traveling overland past the Sasanian Caliphate is *far* worse," he warned. "Two Caliphs have been at each other's throats over Damascus for years now. No-one but the armies travel that coast, and even they're wary. Don't fret. It's a good time for sailing, hardly any storms."

"What is so special about Damascus?" she persisted obliquely.

With a glare for Kervis's error in judgment, Avitus was quick to reply, "Nothing. Nothing *we* care about."

We all knew Leila well enough to know she would have considered traveling overland had we not stopped her. Places of extreme danger drew our prophetess like a magnet. I also doubted Leila's notion that her Goddess was an omniscient protector. Somehow, we had all come this far without serious injury. However, I was not about to risk the whims of a deity I knew to be fickle. Naturally, the Mother took my doubt as a challenge.

***

Leila collapsed on deck one fine afternoon, half-way through our voyage. It happened so unexpectedly, I thought she'd been struck by something unseen.

Kervis carried her below decks as if she weighed nothing at all. In reality, she was desperately underweight, but I'd grown so accustomed to it, I'd forgotten how she'd once alluded to illness.

"She's never shown signs of sickness before," I exclaimed as he laid her in an empty hammock. By now, Leila was completely unconscious. We all milled like lost goslings.

Hesychia, our unofficial healer, felt Leila's forehead, pried back her eyelids, and read her pulse. "No fever, thank the Mother. Kervis, fetch water. If anyone asks, she was overcome by the heat. They can't think she's ill, or they'll toss her overboard out of fear."

I cursed in Tamazight as a chill crawled up my neck. "How long before we reach Alexandria?" I asked after Kervis' departure.

Huran closed his eyes to hide his despair. "A week, at best."

***

To our intense relief, Leila roused a day later. She remained desperately weak and disoriented but could at least string words together in comprehensible sentences.

"Oh, my friends, our time has run out," she said.

We frowned at one other in the lamplight. Leila's voice was little more than a thready whisper. I was thankful most of the crew and passengers were up on deck.

"Something terrible has happened," she continued. Ignoring the water I proffered, she rolled her head against the rough netting of the hammock, her eyes closed. "The tide of war has changed. A great evil . . . death will spread . . . such death."

"The prophecy?" whispered Avitus.

"Mad to have done this . . . he is insane," came her whisper.

"Who?" Kervis questioned.

I shushed him and said, barely breathing the words, "She's talking about the Emperor."

Beneath us, Leila tossed in increasing anxiety.

I continued, "They'll throw us *all* overboard if she's heard."

"Blood and iron," Kervis swore in the soldier's patois, and by the flickering candlelight he looked haunted. "Cenaeus loosed his warhead?" he continued, his fists clenched. "If this were a military ship, it'd have communications. We could know."

"To what end?" I protested through numb lips. "You've heard her. This weapon will destroy the earth."

Kervis roughly shook his head. "I won't just give up." Taking Leila by the shoulders, he cradled her upper body against his chest. "Leila, tell us what you see. What does She want us to do?"

Unlike our more devout companions, I couldn't recall the tall man ever speaking of the Goddess as a trusted deity. He occasionally called Leila "priestess" in jest, but never prayed with her or beseeched the Mother on his own. We both had merely centered on Leila like human lodestones, following in her wandering footsteps as she preached to the masses.

"She will rise . . . ohh." Briefly, Leila buried her face in Kervis's broad chest like a child before she returned to agonized tossing. "She is wroth indeed. All will be torn asunder and the unbelievers brought to task." Her murmurs died away as she faded out again.

"We need to get home," I whispered. My eyes were fixed on Leila's face, so I didn't immediately notice the group's reaction.

"*Your* home? The desert?" Huran asked.

I nodded. "That's where she followed the Star. To the Daughters of Tinan on the Plateau of Rivers."

Avitus shook his head. "I've never heard of it."

"We'll need horses." Even under such circumstances, it warmed me that Zeğiga understood.

Kervis did not sound so optimistic. "That's assuming we reach Alexandria alive."

***

Kervis's pessimism was well-founded. A day later, a faster ship came alongside, pausing long enough to pass shouted details and exhort us to greater speed.

The Emperor had loosed his threat. As the days crept on, a poisonous-smelling grey cloud eventually blocked the entire sky. Compass navigation became unreliable. Lacking even starlight to navigate, our carrack blindly wallowed in what the captain hoped was southwest, but the Aksumite coastline found us first.

How we survived the wreck, I cannot fathom. While the others prayed in rapturous gratitude, Kervis, Huran, and I took charge. We stole horses, raided deserted houses for food, and drove the others to match our pace as we rode like *ifrit*-possessed madmen. Leila had to be tied to the saddle in front of Kervis. Reduced to a hollow-eyed specter, our leader raved the entire way.

Darkened skies rained ash. The air turned sour then stale. Small animals died in catastrophic numbers. Humans and other larger mammals developed sores in their mouths while some swelled as if struck with plague. The latter died within hours. We began to consider them the fortunate ones.

"She will cleanse the folly of Man with a great Reckoning," Leila warned in tones of prophecy. "There is safety in the desert. Safety in nothing. She counts towards Her moment by each species' death."

She spoke of what we experienced, but not in a manner which suggested she understood it was happening. She had become a mouthpiece for her Goddess. Every time I woke, gasping and gripping my sword in whatever shelter we'd managed to secure, I expected to find her cold beside me. If not dead from the holy fire which stormed through her ravaged body, then she should be dead from the same sickness which had taken us all. But every day, she was still there, incoherent, yet alive.

"Do your people have a stronghold?" Kervis asked me once, days after we'd come ashore.

I shook my head. It hurt to speak.

"No stores of food," he continued. "No shelter? Did she give them any instruction before you left?"

"Same as everyone else," I irritably replied. "To go there. To wait."

He pulled at his beard in desperation. "We're all going to die."

I tried to rest my head on my knees. My joints ached as I said, "Then I'll die in the tent of my mothers." But it was not to be, not yet.

Even the devout were stunned at what greeted us when we arrived on the Plateau of Rivers. People as far as the eye could see, a veritable tent city of survivors.

"Impossible," groaned Kervis. "How will we feed and shelter this many?"

None of the rest of us had answers. I couldn't even find the tents of my Tribe in this mass of humanity.

Someone recognized Leila. "Priestess!"

"The Priestess! She's come!"

"Blessed be! We're saved!"

Like guests late to a feast, we were coaxed down from our horses by gentle hands and led to shelters. We were given clean water, food, and a secure place to rest. I made sure Leila lay nearby, and then I fell into a black sleep.

An immeasurable time later, I woke to find everyone in the tent gathered around our pallet. A wan, waxen effigy of herself, Leila lay propped against Kervis, speaking in such low tones her words had to be passed from mouth to mouth like a child's game.

"Fear not what comes, my friends. She will protect us. All who remain in this sacred place will survive to see life anew in Her image. Fear not the coming darkness."

Barely a day afterwards, the sky blackened to pitch. Cook fires faded as if robbed of oxygen and could not be rekindled. Where we, eleven, huddled inside the tent, Leila's fingers felt cool in my fevered grasp.

We all reached for one another in some way. Kervis gripped my shoulder. Zeğiga held my opposite hand. Tiny Lin curled against my chest like a mouse. I heard Caecilia murmur to a sobbing Hesychia.

Everyone screamed when the thunderous tremors began. A rising gale ripped away the tents and stole the breath from our lungs. Such fear could not be maintained. As flotsam on the swells of an earthly tidal wave, we could do nothing more than cling to one another with eyes clenched shut and pray.

Dawn brought me awake with a start. Others stirred from cramped positions to gasp at the panorama revealed beyond camp.

Landmarks around us appeared unchanged, but we beheld them under sunlight from a radiant blue sky, breathed air so fresh it tasted sweet on the tongue. I'd gone so long without honest light that a nearby clump of grass appeared impossibly green.

Everyone turned at Kervis' cry, "Leila!"

Our leader smiled, albeit weakly, from the curve of his arm. "Welcome to the New Age," Leila softly proclaimed.

"Survival comes with a price," Leila announced much later that same, miraculous day.

As the camp of thousands had roused to find themselves still alive, everyone sought out Leila. Fearing for her safety, I moved us all to a natural amphitheater nearby: a stony basin which sloped gently down to an open "stage" of sand and rock. There, Leila sat on a boulder, Kervis at her shoulder. Like the rest of us, she was still desperately weak, even sick, but alive.

"The Mother has taken into Herself all the poisons of the Empire's folly," she explained. "The machines of war, the mines and cities, and all of the putrefaction which Man wrought on Her Face in the name of *progress* are gone. In its place, She has created new lands, new oceans. Some flora and fauna we will find the same, others reinvented. It is up to us, *all* of us, to maintain this precious gift."

Gasps, delighted laughter, and praise greeted this announcement, but Leila was not finished.

"This is a time of transition, and possibly, a time of reckoning. We are not alone on Her Face."

Those of us listening wore identical expressions of horror.

"Not all survivors made it this far. And not all still out there are believers in the Faith. They no longer have Empire technology, but they *will* try to take this new civilization from us. We must organize ourselves, build a refuge here, and be ready to defend it at all costs. *We* are the beginning, my friends, the founding of a New Age in Her Grace."

Thus, the true Final War began. Their technology now useless, their factories and cities gone, unbelievers formed marauding bands to take by force whatever they could find.

It wasn't long before they found us. The Goddess had given us a fighting chance. Now, it was up to us to hold what we'd been given.

The End

For more of Takama's story, watch for future serialized editions by author Cynthia Vannoy. Also, in the works are tales after the New Age, a series of full-length novels detailing the life of the Temple Guard and the fight against new enemies of the Faith.

Find snippets of archaeology, photo references, and music relatable to the work-in-progress on the author's Facebook page: Ravens Words.

About Cynthia Vannoy

Cynthia Vannoy is an expatriate Yankee currently residing in what was once Mexican territory with two cats and a devoted husband who doubles as her go-to R & D man. After receiving a Fine Arts degree in the late 20th century at the University of Steven F. Austin, she labored in the less-refined arts of management, real estate, and retail advertising, all while attempting to distill the spirit of a dream in novel format.

Having more recently retired to the slightly less dreadful world of medical correspondence, she carves out time to write while occasionally pausing to dabble in art, living history reenactment, full-contact sword combat, Middle Eastern dance, gardening, and sustainable living.

She also enjoys taunting her beta readers on her Facebook page: Ravens Words with snippets of archaeology, photo references, and music relatable to the work-in-progress.

https://www.facebook.com/Chaim2017/

FANTASY HORROR

Fantasy includes the elements of a story, which may or not be explainable by science and/or proven fact. The events are set in places, about people, and concerning things removed from our everyday lives by some detail, no matter how minor. This in no way means the difference in the detail cannot exist, it simply means we have never discovered their existence or do not believe they do.

Horror is the attempt by the writer to disturb the reader, shaking them from their everyday existence and allowing them to step into another. It can be appalling, macabre, or simply the worst side of human nature. It can be used to wake people up to the reality of what could happen if we continue traveling our chosen path.

Together, these two create a genre of dark fantasy, eerie steps around the corner, and a moment that never leaves the mind.

James William Peercy

FANTASY HORROR: STORY 1

GAUNT

by Edmund J. Asher

It was the perfect night, not so much as a cloud in the sky to obscure the light of the moons, both of which were full. The shine was so bright a vampire would think twice about heading out for a bite. The only thing brighter, on this particular night, was a lone boy overflowing with optimism for his adventure.

"This is more than an adventure," he would tell you, were you to ask. This adventure was to be his proving. He was every bit of seven years old, or so he would claim, and the Emperor had chosen him for this task. More accurately, the Emperor had chosen a representative, his Lore, and not the boy in particular, though a Lore the boy was.

But that made no matter to him. If it made any matter to anyone else, it wouldn't after he returned successful in his proving. The boy's thinking was that, once proven, the Emperor would have no choice but to make him a member of his Loyal.

For such an undertaking, it was only fitting the boy carried his family sword. The very one all sons of the Lore family carried into battle to metamorphose into men. As compliment to the blade, he wore silver armor with a blue cape, the colors of Vrist, the kingdom of the empire.

Though small even for his age, made to appear smaller by his armor, he stood every bit of his height with shoulders back and chest puffed out.

Pride was visible in his posture for all to see, though there was no one else present: pride from wielding his family sword, though it took both hands, and pride from bearing his countries colors, though his cape dragged the ground.

But he bore the weight of it all, as his brother did before him, their father before them, and back as far as the boy dared to imagine.

The scale of the boy's daring and imagination was larger than life, as one would expect of a son of Lore. The latter, his imagination, showed him a long line of his ancestors, extending from his brother back to the beginning of Vrist as an empire. The former, his daring, pressed his imagination beyond. Surely, his was a lineage of bravery born with the world, a place called Nyth.

Of his lineage, there had never been greater than his brother. The boy believed this with everything he was. He had no dream other than to be as brave a man as his brother, and now was the time.

The castle, which he would enter as a boy and exit as a man, stood before him. Between boy and castle stood a wall, torn apart by the hands of time. Between wall and boy ran a dark moat, daunting even had he known how to swim. Spanning the moat was a drawbridge, down as if to say, "Come on in!" The drawbridge would be welcoming, were it not collapsed, a perilous path suspended by a single chain that added, "But watch your step."

Heeding the warning of the drawbridge, the boy crossed, careful of his footing, but not with so much care as to prevent a pebble plunging into the moat. With his eyes, he traced the descent of the pebble to the water below. The surface thrashed as the pebble vanished, something wildly moving beneath it.

The boy swore he saw a tentacle reach up for him. His imagination raced with his breath, let him feel the slimy appendage wrap around his ankle and squeeze, let him hear the sound of his bone crushing and the whooshing in his ears as he was yanked into the ominous waters.

How brave this boy was! All that was needed to pull him from his fear and return his attention to his crossing the drawbridge was a simple, childish thought.

I'm up here, and it's down there!

Efforts refocused and intent on keeping his thoughts true, his feet moved once again. Triumph flowed through him upon his successful crossing. He glowed brighter when he met his next challenge with little difficulty, picking his way over the rubble which had once called itself a wall.

Beyond the once-wall was a courtyard, barren except for a great tree at its center. The boy tried to imagine the tree full of color, beautiful, as it must have once been.

However, the reality before him was pervasive in his mind's eye. Crows perched in the twisting dead branches of the tree, cawing and flapping at his intrusion as he passed beneath them. If asked, he would tell you he had heard the message of "leave" croaked from amidst their racket.

Imagined or not, it would take far more than a bird to keep him from his destiny. Silently, he swore it would take Aegrym, the God of Death, himself to turn him away...

He tripped, the catching of his boot on a hollow-something coinciding perfectly and eerily with his swear at the God of Death. The boy picked himself and the hollow-something up, gave it a look, and discovered it looked back.

Little imagination was needed to know it was a skull, a skull no larger than his. With a shiver, he tossed it away. The great imagining here was convincing himself it had only been a rock, a rock which had yet to lose its last baby teeth, but a rock all the same.

Leaving the rock behind, the boy followed a broken path on which he made a game of hopping from stone to stone, all the way to castle's door. The castle itself was in a better state than its surroundings, appearing timeless, apart from the occasional absent stone.

It wasn't hard for him to imagine what the castle must have been centuries ago, before life had fled its halls. He allowed that bright vision of the castle to pass almost as quickly as it had arrived in his thoughts, for his goal awaited him. He would not find his proving in happy pasts.

Standing at the base of the double doors to the castle, his already small size was dwarfed, further still, as he imagined two giants easily walking through the door, side by side with room to spare.

The boy inhaled deeply as the weight of his quest came to bear on him, the enormity of his undertaking reflected in the enormity of the doors. Had he thought to turn back, he wouldn't tell you even if you had asked. A Lore is much too proud for that.

As best a boy can, he steeled himself feeling his clammy palms. Somewhere in the halls of the castle turned crypt, beneath its towering twin spires, waited his proving.

Then, when he needed it most, his father's words came to him, and the boy's voice gave the words life.

"A Lore lives in war, thrives in battle, and never dies there."

The words gave him courage. He tried to stop his memories at that point, but his thoughts carried on.

"Where does a Lore die?" the boy asked.

His father's smile was quiet. Sad? Reminiscent? The boy didn't know how to describe it.

His father's reply finally came. "The only place Death finds a Lore is in his bed, fast asleep after a life well fought."

The boy had never liked that part, but he felt safe in knowing he had much fighting left to do. As he reached for the door, the castle yawned, doors opening inward. If this struck him as the least bit odd, he didn't show it. After all, it was like every scary story he'd ever read.

And if the castle was yawning, then the door was a mouth. If the door was a mouth, then the red carpet that met him was its tongue. As he crossed the threshold, onto the castle's tongue, he wondered how it liked the taste of his boot bottoms. His laugh echoed through the massive hall as he marched its length.

On its walls hung rows of small gargoyle figures spaced at regular intervals, serving as sconces for orbs of flame, which they held reverently above their stone heads. Unlike anything he had ever seen, the orbs, created by demon magic, inspired awe. With guilt as his weapon, he battered his amazement into submission and buried it, albeit in a shallow grave.

Sarim, the magic of demons, was forbidden, both in his country and for him as a Lore. With dangerous curiosity squared away, the next demand on his attention was the towering statue of a man, standing at the red carpet's end between twin staircases that turned to meet each other on the landing above.

The boy stood in the man's shadow, scrutinizing the statue. The man stood upright, regal and tall; sword sheathed at his waist. Whichever king of old the statue embodied was a mystery, its face chipped away and scattered about the base of the statue.

The boy passed through the statue's shadow, scooping up a piece of its face and stowing it in his pocket. As he climbed the right staircase with the statue on his left, he felt a growing unease creep over him, its gaze upon his back.

It's all in your head, he told himself as he kept an even pace upward. How could it watch me without eyes?

It was purely imagination which was the source of his anxiety. When he could no longer convince himself of this, when he could no longer endure the imagined eyes on his back, and with only a few steps remaining, he quickly skipped to the top of the stairs. He then turned and attempted to catch the statue out of place . . .

But it stood perfectly still, in its original location and facing its original direction, as most, the boy included, would desire of statues. Had you asked him about the sword of the statue, he would more than likely tell you, "It was sheathed, of course!" He would say this not because of any lack of imagination, but because he failed to recall or refused to accept that it ceased to be true.

Nonetheless, satisfied to falsely find the statue had stayed put, his attention returned to what waited before him.

Three choices became clear: a hall that curved out of sight to his right, a hall that curved out of sight to his left, and a door made of ashen wood to his front, opposite the balcony, which looked out over the entryway to the castle.

The boy deliberated over his choice of path much longer than necessary until an onlooker might feel compelled to shout, "Choose! One path is as good as another."

This, the boy would ignore, while heavily considering the ashen wooden door. Scarred deep into the wood were what looked like letters, letters that enthralled him while he attempted to decipher their meaning.

It was done for such a long time that an onlooker watching the boy watch the door would reach the end of his patience and would drag the boy down one hall or the other himself.

But no such onlooker existed, so there was no choice but to wait until one thing or another came along to interrupt the boy's enthrallment. What eventually ended the spell of his unrelenting curiosity?

Metal cacophony met his ears. He thought it echoed from the hall to his left, now from the hall to his right, and so his feet carried him to the right hall.

When his mind caught up with his feet, he hesitated. Quick to correct his fear, he was steadfast in reminding himself of his duty.

A Lore doesn't know fear, he thought. You're here for a reason, to prove yourself and be made Loyal, to bring this wicked Sarimist to justice at or on the tip of your sword.

He moved in the direction of the racket. It helped to remember his sword. He drew it from its sheath and with it found his courage as well. Courage in hand, he traveled the hall as silently as he could manage.

Jarring sound poured unending from around the curves in the right hall and soon came to be accompanied by a shrill voice. "No, no, no!"

The boy peeked around a curve to see the corridor straighten out. Halfway down the length of the corridor was the owner of the voice, a mottled green creature with a scrawny rag-clad body and a large sideways oval for a head.

The goblin tried desperately to place a helmet on top of a collapsed suit of armor. Once satisfied, it stepped back to admire its work. Amid its admiration, the helmet fell from the armor, clattered against the stone, and rolled toward the boy.

The goblin winced, pulling down on its floppy tattered ears as the sound the helmet made echoed down the hall. Its fearful red eyes followed the path of the helmet and came to rest on the boy peering into the straight hall. Both were startled.

"Human? What doing here?" demanded the goblin.

The boy stepped out of hiding; his courage boosted by the sword in his hand. As he approached the goblin, he said, "I need to find the Sarimist who has made these ruins his home."

"No, no," the goblin shook his floppy ears, "Why want do that? You don't want do that!"

The boy stepped closer. "I do."

"No!" The goblin stepped back.

"Take me to him." The boy made his point with the point of his sword, holding it out toward the goblin.

It whimpered, not for the sword, but for the hall behind the boy. "Is coming! Run! Run!"

The goblin heeded its own advice. It turned and sprinted deep into the hall, as fast as its little legs could carry it, around a bend and out of sight.

The boy turned to see what had severely frightened the goblin.

A short distance away, and growing closer, was a shadow. The gargoyle-ensconced lights died as the shadow passed. The shadow twisted into the form of a man, draped in robes of darkness.

"Will you be the one?" A voice like a whisper crept into the boy's mind. The shadow stretched out its enshrouded hand.

The Sarimist, thought the boy.

The boy finally stood before his proving. Whether his composure shattered, or he simply understood the shadow's touch would hold a fate worse than death, didn't matter. The result was the same. He turned and ran the way of the goblin.

Another whisper welled up, spoken in his head as though it were a thought of his own. "Where does a Lore die?"

The boy ran faster, trying to escape the answer. Still, the answer came. "In his bed."

He dared to glance over his shoulder. The hall was empty but still he ran. The passage curved up and to the right and went on forever. It went on so far he believed he would die if he didn't stop running . . .

He didn't stop running.

Then came a long stretch of hallway with a door at its end. The

34

door grew larger as he rushed toward it, giving him a slight hope and a second breath because of its appearance.

When his small hands grasped the doorknob, the door resisted, though he forced it open. The door fell shut after he stumbled through. Only then did he stop running.

He stood on a bridge, which spanned the towers of the castle. The Great Moon, Orison, hung large in the sky beside the bridge, seemingly close enough to touch. He looked to the sky for the smaller Odius Moon, grasping for familiarity, only to find it had vanished below the horizon.

Opposite his side of the bridge was the goblin, suspended in the air by a long, snake-like whip of a tail. The tail led from the goblin-neck to a crouched, black demon with a body both bony and slender, its face devoid of features.

The demon had yet to notice him, too taken with watching the goblin struggle for air.

Helpless and breathless, the goblin struggled as the boy watched. A wet crack cut through the night air and the goblin's struggles ceased. The boy found himself alone in his hopeless plight, facing the demon in front, and the shadow coming from behind the door.

The boy released his held breath with an unintended gasp.

As if the boy's voice held sway over it, the monster lurched to a stand like a whittled-down puppet on strings. Despite the demon's hunched form, standing tall it would have easily looked down on a tall man. Had it been over the boy, it might as well have been a large tree.

The demon crept toward him, cocking its head like a cat, curiously flicking its still-limp-goblin-grasping tail. With its arms as long as its body, it dragged its spiked nails across the stone bridge.

The boy stood still, his sword raised, a dilemma both before and behind him.

Which direction held the greater terror? He knew the answer. To turn back would be to face his worst fear, to stand before the shadowed man.

Had you asked, the boy couldn't have explained why he felt this way. It was better to face a dozen faceless beasts than to stand in the shadowed man's presence.

The demon's arm shot out for the boy like an arrow from a bow. The boy, nearly knocked over by the impact alone, batted the arm away, becoming a passenger to an instinct he didn't know he possessed.

Resolved to go forward, he met the gaunt demon with all the ferocity a child could muster. The boy charged with a tiny roar and wild swinging. Guided by Luck, his blade connected with the demon's arm, severing the demon's appendage at the elbow.

The demon recoiled, a harsh trilling emanating from somewhere within.

A gleeful shout rose from the boy as newfound confidence drove him in for the kill. But before he could close the distance, black ooze gushed from the wound on the demon's stump. The ooze snaked its way to the fallen forearm and raised the forearm as a shield against the boy's attack.

With confusion and revulsion, the boy watched as the demon formed a mangled arm twice the length of its original. The fiend took the boy's pause as an opening, darting its spear-like fingers past the boy's guard and wrapping them around the boy's throat. Before the boy could do anything in response, the demon hoisted him into the air.

He frantically swung his sword, panicking as the demon's tight grip around his neck prevented breath and blood from reaching their destinations. The edges of the demon's fingers were sharp, as though they would cut him at any moment. His sword found its mark time and again, but if the swatting made any difference to the demon, it didn't show.

The demon plucked the boy's weapon out of the boy's hand and tossed it over the edge of the bridge. Then it pulled the boy close, faceless to face. The boy could see indentations where any other creature would have eyes, as if leather skin had grown over the sockets.

On the wind, the whisper of the Sarimist carried to the boy and the demon. "Bring him to me."

The demon dropped its head to the side, its eyeless gaze staring downward. Then, to the boy's mix of horror and relief, the demon loosened its grip, allowing him breath. The demon complied with the demand, carrying him toward the door from which the boy had escaped, back toward the shadowed man.

The boy's struggles and kicks served no purpose. In desperation or defiance, he spat on the demon. It stopped and growled. A seam appeared to reveal a mouth where before there had been nothing, horizontally splitting its face into a toothy smile.

The demon's orders were either forgotten or ignored as it dangled the boy over the side of the bridge and slowly loosened its grip.

The boy clung, fastening himself to any part of the demon he could hold on to. The demon let go, almost before he had managed to wrap his fingers tight around its claws. His full weight hung by his hands, gripping tight to what felt like knives. The demon wiggled its fingers, toying with him, expectantly watching for the boy to plunge toward the ground.

Finally, with the boy's hands wet with blood from the sharp razor-like claws of the demon, the boy slipped.

He plummeted toward the ground, closing his eyes, stretching his last seconds as far as they could go. Had he the time to think on it, had you the chance to ask him, he might have told you he was thankful for the demon's disobedience.

The boy thought, Better to die . . .

Flailing at his sheets and screaming for help, the boy jolted upright. He realized quickly enough where he was and quieted himself: in his bed, safe, and surprised that his foolish shouting had not stirred his brother. His lips shuddered as he nervously chuckled. Not wanting to bother his brother with his nightmare, he covered his mouth.

The boy peered across the room, straining to see his brother through the darkness. The moonlight, shining through the window between them, made the task no easier.

As the boy calmed, his fear, anxiety, and embarrassment subsided. He could hear his surroundings over his no longer pounding heart.

It was quiet. Then there was a wet squelching sound. He caught trace of a distorted silhouette against the blackness of the room. The silhouette bent over his brother's bed, gently jerking from side to side.

Frozen, the boy tried to call out to his brother, but the name caught in his throat.

Breathe, he thought. You're awake. You'll be okay.

The squelching stopped. He could no longer see the silhouette no matter how hard he tried. His eyes remained locked there until relief found him, sureness that his mind had played tricks on him, as it so commonly did. He collapsed back onto his pillow and closed his eyes.

Tap. Tap. Tap.

He reopened his eyes to see motion, a slinking of something across the floor between the beds. As the face of the faceless demon from his dream came into the narrow beam of moonlight, fear flooded him again, bringing with it the stink of nauseous leather.

His body screamed for him to move, but he couldn't because of his shaking. In the moonlight that washed his way, his cheeks shone with tears.

The demon hovered with its faceless face above him as it had on the bridge. It looked deeply into the boy's eyes as though its sockets held their own.

It tilted its head, gently catching the moonlight across its maw in a mockery of the boy's tears. Outlined in red, its mouth was otherwise invisible until it ripped open its indistinct face to show the boy its jagged smile and crimson-stained teeth.

The boy tried to scream for his father and mother, but a pitiful squeak came out, followed by a confused mutter. The muttering worked its way to his lips stopping him from reacting any other way. His terrified curiosity unconsciously desired to know, "How?"

The demon raised its hand from the darkness into the moonlight. The boy flinched as a sharp nail gently pricked his forehead, drawing the smallest bead of blood.

Struggling to understand, the boy came to a conclusion, which voiced itself in an uttered whisper of, "Me?"

The demon was merciful. It gave him an answer. The demon was cruel. Its answer was yes followed by a slight nod of its head.

It was unbearable for him to consider, impossible to understand, how he was responsible.

How did I conjure forth a demon?

He hid under a blanket of guilt which settled over all other emotions.

There, beneath his blanket, he sobbed and waited to be taken as his brother had been. He was helpless in a world where he had no brother, undeserving of life when this had somehow been his fault, where this monster had spawned from him.

The demon pulled back the covers, hid its full smile behind blood-stained lips, and stared, trilling happily, delighted in the boy's resignation as it fed on the boy's fear.

When the boy could take no more, he closed and covered his eyes and ears tight. He prayed to the Gods, The Child God most of all, that he still dreamt, caught in his nightmare.

Eventually, his sobs and prayers ran out. His rattled breathing filled his ears.

He didn't dare look again until morning's earliest light pried at his eyelids. Once his courage had built, he let one eye unseal.

The monster was gone! He jumped to his feet in a moment of relief and joy so brief as to hardly be worth mentioning. The floor was sticky beneath him.

His brother's bed was, mostly, empty. A trail of blood came from it, some dripping to the floor. A memory of the castle's red-carpet tongue was forced into his mind, a brief interruption to the boy's desire to cease existing, to escape a pain he couldn't describe as he looked at the room around him. The path of red trailed out the boy's open window.

He collapsed onto the macabre carpet and wept. He cried out again, pleading.

The Gods of Nyth didn't answer . . . or so the boy believed.

The End

Inspiration for Gaunt

Gaunt is a precursor to my upcoming novel, *The Sarimist Loyal*. While working on my novel, I was convinced I had created an original character who would introduce readers to the world of Nyth. While sifting through my old notes I happened upon a ten year-old child's early attempt at story writing—inspired by Lovecraft, it seems. I reread it, fondly and with much nostalgia, and realized the boy's struggle was the backstory of my novel's protagonist, Orym Lore. Orym, a character I believed I had thought up on the spot one day, had actually been with me for well over a decade.

As I was having trouble justifying the actions of the Orym in my novel, this discovery came with perfect timing. I persisted, growing less confident with each page that my writing was true to the character. With the rediscovery of the short story came the knowledge that I didn't know who Orym was or at least I had forgotten. The Orym I had been writing was true. He knew his story; it was just my job to write it down.

While Gaunt ended with a dark twist, it was a child's story compared to my usual, more adult writing—Orym grew up, and so did I. For this reason, in part, I used the third-person perspective in this story as opposed to how I usually write . . . in the first person. The children, both the one who wrote the story and the one the story is written about, are so distant from myself and Orym that they might as well be different people. It was difficult to walk in their shoes. For Orym, it was painful, and perhaps for me as well. I found myself remembering a time where Nyth was a boy's escapist idealization and not the dark world it has become.

I find it fitting that Orym is how I introduce the world of Nyth. He is, after all, its beginning, if not chronologically, then in the mind of a child. Because, in that child's mind, before there was a Nyth, there was a boy: a boy and a god.

About Edmund J. Asher

Edmund J. Asher is an author of dark fantasy and science fiction which revolve around the world of Nyth. When not living in his own mind, he resides in Nowhere, Texas with his beautiful wife and two children. When not writing about his world, his time is spent with them.

On the rare occasion he is left with time unspent, he pursues any one of a billion different interests. He then, more often than not, wanders from his library and back to his family, missing them after only a brief hour of solitude.

Sometimes he finds opportunity to sleep, during which he is regularly awakened for any of a myriad of reasons. Some examples of such being the voices of characters who demand recording, dreams which demand the same, or either of two small, shadowed figures, his children, whose whispered demands are varying.

Be awaiting his first novel, entitled *The Sarimist Loyal*. You can follow its progress, read other short stories, and anything else regarding the author and his world on his blog/website at EdmundJAsher.com. You can also keep up-to-date by following him on twitter (@edmund_asher) or on his barren and desolate Facebook page (Edmund J. Asher).

FOLKLORE / FAIRY TALES

Comprised of customs and traditions, stories passed down from word of mouth create much of what we know as folklore. Considered by some to be fairy tales, and like fairy tales, also containing truths of life, folklore helps to explain the unexplainable in a world that requires logic and thought.

Fairy tales, a subgenre of fantasy, deal with idealized circumstances of a potentially magical nature. In general intended for children, they are loved by children and adults alike containing exquisite beauty, ultimate perfection, and incredible luck. While some fairy tales do lean toward the darker side of life, their purpose is to entertain and perhaps educate in an unusual manner.

These two genres hint at truths in our world, guiding the minds of inquisitive people to explore what is around them.

James William Peercy

FAIRY TALE: STORY 1

FREDDIE THE RED FROG

by Gary Smithers

Going to Grandma and Grandpa's country house in the deep woods of Plaistow, New Hampshire, was something I used to look forward to at the end of each school year. I remember the strong scent of pine carried by the cool, sweet, gentle breeze rustling through the trees. It was everywhere around their house. Memories like these never go away!

Their old mill pond was my favorite place to spend time. The pond was less than a hundred yards from Grandpa's back porch.

Grandpa built a boat dock about twenty-five feet long to accommodate his little red dinghy which was badly in need of a paint job. Even I could see that, but as Grandpa used to say, "It floats."

We went fishing often in the summer. Sometimes we picked wild blueberries along the old winding path, leading down to the boat dock. Grandpa would always find the biggest night crawlers, I had ever seen, the night before we went fishing.

Grandpa treasured his shiny, red fishing rod with a shiny, silver and gray reel and kept it in tip-top shape. Before he went into the house, he wiped it down every time we were done fishing. I used an old bamboo rod with a hook tied to the end of the line.

One day, when I had gone down to fish by myself and sat on the dock with my feet dangling, almost into the water, I heard a frog around where I was fishing. It croaked a couple times, and I sort of knew whereabouts the sound came from.

It wasn't unusual to hear frogs or birds and sometimes crickets out there, so I paid it no mind and kept on fishing. I heard a woman's voice calling my name.

"Jake, Jake."

The voice came from about the same area as the frog.

"Jake, over here."

When I looked, there was a little red frog calling my name from on top of a lily pad. The frog jumped closer onto another lily pad near my right foot.

The frog said, "You are the one, Jake."

I was startled and said, "I didn't know frogs could talk."

"They can't, but I can, because I am special," said the frog.

I asked, still trying to make sense of what was going on, "What do you mean that *I'm the one*?"

"You are the one person in the world who can save me."

In that instant, it really dawned on me, I had been talking to a frog. I was shaken up a bit, jumped up, and ran to the house. I had to tell Grandpa and Grandma about my stunning adventure.

But even as I ran, I heard the voice calling me, "I need you. Come back."

The farther I got from the pond, the fainter the voice sounded. Should I tell my grandparents, or should I keep this my secret? I decided to tell them.

"You must have fallen asleep and dreamed about this," explained Grandpa.

"It must have been all the pollen," said Grandma. "It's bad this time of year, and it must have affected your thinking."

"I was fully awake Grandpa. And, I didn't see any pollen, Grandma, whatever I saw," I loudly said.

Grandpa told me he had never seen a red frog in all the years he'd lived here. They told me to sit down and eat.

It was Saturday night, and we had homemade baked beans cooked in Grandma's oven. We also had frankfurters (hot dogs) and warm, brown bread with butter.

I was really wound up when I went to bed that night, wondering if I had imagined it. It took a while, but I finally fell asleep.

The next morning when I woke up, my mind was spinning a mile a minute. Grandma called me to come down to breakfast. The smell of bacon was in the air.

I love bacon and couldn't think of anything else except getting down there as fast as I could. Before smelling the bacon, I was going crazy thinking about that little red frog talking to me. Had I just imagined it?

After the pancakes, fried potatoes, bacon, and scrambled eggs, I was full and happy. Grandpa asked me if I wanted to help him with some yardwork, and I said yes. So after a couple of hours of that, I was hungry again. We put all the tools away and went inside.

Grandma had some fresh apple pie and milk—oh, how I loved her apple pie. After I was finished, she invited me to go lie on the sofa, if I was sleepy, and I did.

I dreamed about that stupid red frog and the whole experience I had down at the pond. When I awoke, I jumped up and ran down to the pond.

Grandpa was already there with his fishing pole and a bucket of those big, fat night crawlers to fish with. My bamboo pole was on the deck beside him. I baited my hook and started looking around for that little red frog.

"Do you see your frog anywhere, Jake?" asked Grandpa.

"Nope, I don't see the frog anywhere, Gramps."

My pole bent down almost to the water. I thought I was going to lose my grip.

"Looks like you got a big one, Jake. Maybe it's Bubba, the fish that got away?"

I could hardly hold my pole as it continued pulling me toward the water.

"Yep, it's got to be Bubba. Hold onto him, boy," said Gramps.

Grandpa picked up the net, and he pulled the fish in. It was a great, big catfish which weighed in it at eight pounds, four ounces. He said it was Bubba, and he had been trying to catch him for years.

"Congratulations, Jake. You got him!"

I watched Gramps take up all the tackle, poles, and Bubba. He went back to the house.

I sat there and thought how great it had been catching that big fish. In midthought, I heard a loud croak. It was so loud I turned toward the sound and slipped right off the boat dock into the pond. When I came up out of the water, I confronted the red frog face to face. It kissed me on the lips twice.

"Yuk!"

With a big swoosh, this beautiful woman came straight up out of the water. She appeared like a ghost. She said she would see me again when I was older.

I must have passed out because I woke up on the boat dock on my back. I looked around to see if that beautiful woman was around, but I didn't see her anywhere. Was my mind playing tricks on me or did that really happen?

I ran to the house screaming, "I saw a woman. I saw a woman come right out of the water."

Grandma grabbed me and held me asking if I was okay.

"What did you say you saw?" Grandma asked.

"I fell into the water, and when I came up, a red frog kissed me on the lips twice. I saw a woman, or a ghost, come up out of the water where the red frog was. I must have fainted because I woke up on the boat dock soaking wet. The woman and frog were gone."

Gramps got up and went out the door. Grandma held me without saying a word.

When Gramps came back, he said he didn't see any red frog or any woman down at the pond and asked me if I was okay. I told him I was, but I really wasn't sure.

That year in school I told my class about the red frog and the beautiful "ghost" woman. They all laughed. I went on to the third grade and had a great year.

I tried not to think about the red frog or the woman, but it was always in the back of my mind. Somewhere along the way, I started to believe it really didn't happen at all.

I did look up "red frog" in the encyclopedia and found some information. References stated red frogs were rare, endangered species, and that some were poisonous. Scientists believe the poisonous species acquired the poison from around their environment by ingesting plants, ants and other insects. The only poison found around Grandpa's pond was poison ivy, but I didn't think the red frog ate any of that.

For several summers afterward, I went back to the pond, but I didn't see the red frog or the woman. I decided to name the frog Freddie with an 'ie' at the end of its spelling.

I fished with Grandpa during my summers, always looking for the frog and the woman. And though I enjoyed my time with my grandparents, the magic of visiting the pond disappeared little by little each time I couldn't find Freddie.

After high school, I joined the Navy. I got out after four years and came back home. My home of record, and my parents address, was the same as when I was living with them at 63 Varnum Street, Haverhill, Massachusetts. My girlfriend, when I had joined the Navy, had married my best friend while I was in boot camp, so I didn't have anyone to come back to after getting out of the Navy.

Within a few days of arriving in Massachusetts, I received a registered letter in the mail informing me that my grandparents had both passed away.

I loved them so much, and it made me very sad. In the letter, I was instructed to go see a lawyer in Nashua, New Hampshire to sign some papers.

When I got there, they said my grandparents, John and Evelina, had left their house, property, and all their savings to me, free and clear for my pleasure and use. I was taken back by their generosity, and in front of that lawyer, I busted out crying like a child.

I had no idea they had so much property around their house. Twenty-five acres in total, of which they only utilized the two acres I saw in the summers I went there. The rest of the property was undisturbed pine forest.

In my jeep, I headed over to check the old homestead. Memories of that red frog ran through my head as I drove toward their place. It had been so long ago, I had convinced myself it was a dream, even though a nagging doubt remained.

Arriving at their address, 3 Old Mill Pond Road, I pulled into their gravel driveway. I got out of the jeep and took in the fresh air filled with the scent of pine. The birds chirped around me, and I felt the peace I once had as a child come over me.

After going inside, I sat on the old couch I used to sleep on and took in all the smells which were so familiar. My grandparents had only been gone a couple of months, so it was still as pristine as I remembered. They died in a car accident on their way to church. I sat there, and again, I cried like a baby.

After a while, I got up and started toward the pond. It was summer, and the path was full of blueberries along the way. The blueberries reminded me of the many times Grandpa and I went down this same path to go fishing.

Everything was the way I remembered it. I walked down the dock and sat on the edge. It had been years since I had been there, and I had grown quite a bit. I had to roll my jeans up and take my shoes and socks off, because my feet touched the water when I hung my legs over the dock.

I closed my eyes for a second and a voice called out, "Jake, Jake, you came back!"

I turned toward the voice and saw Freddie the red frog. I got so excited, I fell into the water. When I came back up out of the water, there was Freddie, right in my face.

That red frog kissed me right on the lips. Boom. Out of the water came the most beautiful woman I had ever seen. But was this the same woman I had seen when I was a little boy?

I woke up on my grandparent's couch with this woman looking over me, holding my hand. I scrambled back from her and asked if she was the same woman I saw when I was a little boy.

She said, "Yes, it is the third kiss which has saved me from an old witch's curse."

Well, we had a lot to talk about because none of this made any sense to me. Witches and curses? These things I only heard about in books and movies.

"Where have you been, Jake?" Freddie asked. "I've been alone for many years waiting for you to come back."

She said her name was Frederica, Freddie for short.

How did I get that right?

Frederica said, "I was a princess and was cursed three-hundred years ago by an old witch from the Ottoman Empire. My father, King Stephan Batory, had been killed in the battle against the Ottomans. The witch turned me into a frog and sent me far away. She said I had to kiss a handsome boy or man on the lips three times to break the curse."

That was a lot of information for me. I asked her what she wanted to do now.

She said, "I want to marry you and live in this house forever."

I said, "I won't live forever."

She continued with a beautiful smile, "When I kissed you three times, the curse was lifted, and I was saved. I have a good feeling that we are going to live a little longer than we were supposed to."

Plaistow, New Hampshire was a very small township. That afternoon, Freddie and I went down to find a justice of the peace. Without any paperwork and a few bucks, he married us.

We moved into the old house. I had missed my grandparent's funeral because I was in Italy, during my tour in the Navy. The letter about their death wasn't sent to me until I came back home.

It took us about four years to get the house the way we wanted it. Some repairs had to be made and some painting had to be done. We even had the boat dock rebuilt, and I worked on the ten-foot skiff, painting it red like it was in grandpa's day.

At first, Freddie wasn't too keen on going near the pond, but eventually she went down there with me. We took the skiff out on the pond a few times and did some fishing.

We lived there for about twenty years and were very happy. Neither of us was aging, it seemed, and we thought it would be a good idea if we moved away before people started to notice.

Freddie and I moved to a small seaside town in Maine, just forty miles away. We found a small loft on Main Street over a specialty store. I hired someone to maintain the old homestead, back in New Hampshire, so it would be ready whenever we came back.

I had studied photography in the Navy and was a freelance photographer. My specialty was old covered bridges and barns in the countryside along with some seascapes and boats. My pictures were framed and usually sold for $150.00 or more, depending on the size. The specialty shop, downstairs, sold a lot of my pictures, and some were bought in restaurants and tourist venues.

We lived there for another twenty years, and again, neither of us was aging at all. Freddie suggested we move on to another place so people wouldn't notice. Every twenty years we moved for several more decades until we realized we had started to grow older.

It was time to move back to the old homestead, back to grandpa's house.

Note:

Quietly and sweetly holding hands, Jake and Freddie passed away one evening. This is their tale found on an end table next to their sofa. May they rest in peace.

The End

About Gary Smithers

Gary Smithers enlisted in the United States Navy at the age of seventeen. After twenty years, he retired and worked as a professional photographer, and then as a management analyst for government contractors.

He has written poetry, lyrics and a few short stories. His lyrics were published on an album as a BMI author.

Gary also builds custom birdhouses for a hobby and volunteers at a local hospice organization twice a week. He co-founded a coffee group ten years ago called *The Java Posse* at a local coffee shop and meets with that group in the mornings during the week.

HISTORICAL FICTION

We hear it all the time, fact is stranger than fiction. But what if the fiction is fact?

This genre of literature explores just that. Although the story is fiction, it borrows settings, characteristics, and the past to weave a tale which is both believable and plausible. It is always set in the past, be it one day or hundreds of years, one minute or an hour. And though it can use real things from that time period, it does not necessarily have to be.

James William Peercy

HISTORICAL FICTION: STORY 1

QUEEN OF MY HEART

by Rita Ownby Holcomb

June 1862

The summer sun beat down on the gentle, rolling, Tennessee hills as the procession of children wound their way down the tallest knoll.

After church, the family went to leave flowers on their mother's grave and then headed home to get Sunday dinner on the table. They resembled a gaggle of geese as they were led by the gangly Sam. Lizzie brought up the rear carrying baby Henry.

Eli Ownby had stayed behind for a few private moments at his wife's grave but was catching up to his children.

Pounding hooves could be heard and dust flew as the farmhouse came in view.

Wondering who it could be, the children stopped and stared. Around the curve in the road came a line of a dozen horsemen wearing the butternut uniforms of the Confederate Cavalry. The leader called a halt to the column just as Eli joined the group of awestruck children.

Dismounting from his big gray stallion, the tall officer offered his hand to Eli. "Lieutenant John Christopher, 10th Tennessee Cavalry, Sir. We are advancing into Murfreesboro to meet General Nathan Forrest and wonder if you might have some water for our horses and maybe a bit of food for my men?"

Eli shook the man's hand, introduced himself, thoughtfully nodded his head, and quietly said, "Certainly, lieutenant. Follow us up to the house and we'll see what we can find for you. That is a splendid animal you are riding."

"Thank you, Sir. I raised Shadow Dancer from a colt, and he has served me well. He's saved my life more than once."

That was the cue the two older boys needed to start plying the other soldiers with questions and to admire everything from their horses to the sabers in their yellow sash belts. Lizzie quickly shooed the younger children toward the house, while Eli and the lieutenant slowly walked and talked quietly.

As they approached the house, Lizzie told Craig to run to the smokehouse to grab a ham and instructed Mattie to check the storeroom for potatoes. She then settled the three littlest ones in the corner with a cookie and a picture book and put five-year-old Mack in charge.

A large hollowed-out log was tucked under the eaves of the porch roof for a horse trough. Moss covered and worn with age, it collected rain runoff. However, Sam and Jack knew it would need to be filled so they gathered buckets of water at the well, to accommodate the horses entering the yard.

Geese and ducks noisily scattered.

The dusty soldiers were tired, and by the looks on their faces, it was evident they were glad to be out of the saddle for a few moments.

Eli and the lieutenant stepped up on the porch as Mattie poked her chubby little face around the door jamb. Naturally curious, fun loving and gregarious, she perkily said, "My big brothers Watt and Ed are in the army, too."

Eli laughed, cleared his throat, and in a formal tone said, "Lieutenant Christopher, may I present my daughter, Queen Ann Matilda Ownby."

His brown eyes twinkling, Christopher squatted on the porch to bring himself face to face with the tiny girl. "It's very nice to make your acquaintance, but that's too many names for such a little girl. What shall I call you? I know. I'll call you Queen, because you are the Queen of my heart."

Instinctively, the little girl threw her plump arms around the soldier's neck, squeezed, and gave him a kiss on the cheek then turned and ran into the house.

Laughing out loud, Christopher looked up at Eli.

Eli shrugged and chuckled. "She's never met a stranger, and I hope she stays that way. Let's see what Lizzie has found to feed your men."

An hour later, after a hearty meal consisting of fried ham, potatoes fried with apples and onions, fresh sliced tomatoes, plenty of good fluffy biscuits, served with lots of sweet butter and some of Carol's peach preserves for dessert, the men were ready to join their comrades to the west. The lieutenant thanked Eli for his hospitality and complemented Lizzie on the best meal they'd had in a while. She blushed and thanked him shyly with the pride only an eleven-year-old can exhibit.

The lieutenant was impressed with this family and stirred by the young girl, still in short skirts and pantalets and charmed by the chubby little Mattie. The entire family were all neat and clean and well mannered.

Then just before he slid his foot in the stirrup, he stooped once more to take Mattie's hand. "If ever you are in need, send me a message and I will come as soon as possible."

"I wonder where the mother is," one of the soldiers commented to the Lieutenant.

"I believe she's up on yonder hill," was Christopher's reply.

As the soldiers rode away, Lizzie wearily turned and commented to her sister, "Come on, Mattie, let's clear up this mess."

Mattie flounced into the house and stated rather haughtily, "My name is Queen and that is how I will be called from this moment on!"

July 1863

"Nannie Taylor, Nannie Taylor," Queen, yelled as she ran up the path to the Taylor home.

Marthey came out the door; caught the girl and squatted down to her level. "Ma's not here, Queen. What's the matter? Is someone hurt?"

"It's Lizzie. She's bleeding, and I'm scared. Come help her, please."

Marthey turned back into the house and called to her sister, "Betsy, Lizzie's hurt so I'm going to the Ownby's. Send Ma when she gets home."

"Did she cut herself?" Marthey asked Queen, as they both hurried down the path.

"I don't think so. The bedclothes and her nightgown was all bloody this morning when we got up. She tried to hide it, but I saw and I'm scared. We can't lose her too." The little girl stopped running and started to cry.

Marthey stopped running also, and as she started to console the crying child, she chuckled. She realized what must be happening. The little girl, Lizzie, was becoming a young woman. She had noticed Lizzie's clothes fitting differently and her body changing. This was a time when a girl needed her mother.

Queen stamped her foot, doubled up her fist, hit Marthey on the arm and demanded, "Why are you laughing? Lizzie might be bleeding to death, and you're laughing. You're mean, Martha Jane Taylor."

Marthey tightly hugged Queen and said, "I'm not mean, Queen. Come on, let's check on Lizzie. I think she will be fine."

When they arrived, Lizzie was in the side yard stirring the wash kettle while Mack was playing with Maggie and Henry on the far side of the house.

"Queen tells me you are bleeding, Lizzie. Do you feel alright?" Marthey asked.

"Queen, why did you tell her?" She dropped the stir stick and sat down on the ground and started to cry. "I'm dying, Marthey. I'm going to bleed to death from one of those spatulas, just like Mama did."

Queen eyes were big, and she had a terrified look on her normally happy face.

"What do you mean, you have a spatula?" Marthey asked the sobbing girl.

Lizzie cried harder, "I heard Mama telling your mother, she said her spatula wouldn't heal and she was bleeding all the time from her private place. But I can't die. The little ones need me. The bleeding stops for a while, but it always comes back."

Marthey refrained from laughing this time and gently said, "That was a fistula, Lizzie, and it's from a tear during childbirth. Believe me, you don't have one. How long has this been happening?"

"Since early spring. This time is the worst. My belly hurts, and I feel like my insides are falling out. The bleeding is worse, and I don't know what to do." She cried harder. Queen came up behind Lizzie and hugged her around the neck.

"Get up, Lizzie. You aren't dying. Let's make some coffee, and I'll explain what is happening and what you need to do. You come too, Queen. I sure wish you had told me or Ma before now, so you didn't have to worry so much the past few months. Come on, you'll be fine."

Lizzie and Queen followed the older girl into the kitchen and Marthey patiently and lovingly started explaining the facts of becoming a woman to them both.

"The first thing you need to know is that this is natural, and all women experience it. Every month you will bleed for a few days."

Queen's eyes got bigger, and she pursed her lips together in a show of distaste. "NO! Not me. I'm not gonna do it."

Marthey chuckled and told the little girl, "You won't be able to stop it, Queen." She turned her attention back to Lizzie. "I'll help you make a belt to wear around your waist, and you can use Henry's old diapers to catch the blood."

Queen yelled as she stamped her little foot, "I'm not wearing a diaper again, Marthey. Ever. I refuse." She stormed out of the kitchen and ran off into the woods with the hound dogs following.

"Silly little girl," Lizzie said with all the maturity a twelve-year-old could muster. "Sometimes I don't know what to do with her."

Now that she was confident that she wasn't dying, she was striving to be grown up.

In a flash of recollection, she saw diapers sunning on the lawn at the Taylor home, even though there were no babies. With four women in the family, there would be a definite need for lots of rags.

December 1863

The sun was weak in the morning sky when Lizzie sent Queen looking for any late berries, roots, fruit, or vegetation they could eat for supper. The little girl had managed to find a few late berries. The old apple tree on the hill had a few pieces of fruit left, which the birds hadn't destroyed. There was a bit of watercress from the creek and a few wild turnips. Not much, but it would have to do. She was discouraged and was wandering down the path daydreaming when she found herself face to face with a big gray horse.

Startled, she let out a squeal. She turned to run off into the woods when a deep voice said, "Whoa, Shadow Dancer! Well, low and behold, if it isn't the little Queen of my heart?"

In one movement, he leapt from his horse and lifted the child in his arms. She giggled, dropped her basket, wrapped her arms around his neck, and cried, "Lieutenant John, I knew you'd come. You said you'd come. I've prayed that you'd come. I'm hungry and the babies keep crying, and I'm so tired."

She felt safe for the first time in weeks and, as she delivered her babble of words, she snuggled into his arms and simply drifted off to sleep.

John Christopher couldn't help but notice how she had changed since he last saw her. The plump little girl with shiny curls and a quick smile was so pitifully thin her clothes hung on her tiny frame. Her hair was dull and lank. He lifted her hand and noticed that her fingers and palms were scratched and bleeding. He put the tiny palm to his lips, and she whimpered in her sleep.

Her fragility and the dark smudges under her eyes tugged at his heart. A tear slipped from his eye as he contemplated the horrors of this cruel war. He motioned to one of the men to retrieve the basket and any edible bits of food, handed Queen to one of his men, and remounted his big gray horse. As he lifted Queen and settled the still sleeping child in his arms, he told the other soldiers, "Looks like we're just in time with these foraged supplies."

December 1865

It was the first Christmas the family had been all together in four years, and the first Christmas Maggie and Henry could remember a tree being lit with candles and shiny ornaments. Their eyes were wide with wonder.

While everyone was sipping cider, Watt produced a sack and started handing out presents. There was something for everyone.

Queen admired her pretty blue gloves crocheted by Lizzie, and Maggie was running a red hair ribbon through her hands.

Jack had carved a spinning top for Henry and showed him how to wind the string and make it spin across the floor.

Eli gave Craig his old Bowie knife with a new handle made by Jack from the antlers of the big buck Eli shot last year.

Eli and Lizzie both received new handkerchiefs. Eli's was a large square of cotton with his initials embroidered in one corner.

Queen pertly reminded her father, "That's for Sunday services only, Pa. Don't you be carrying it to go hunting."

Lizzie recognized Queen's clumsy needlework on her smaller linen hanky but smiled when she saw a golden halo over a bluebird in flight, painstakingly worked in the corner.

When Mack opened his parcel, he scampered to the corner without offering to share and sat with his back to the family.

Lizzie started to scold him, but Watt stopped her with a look and whispered, "Leave him be. It's Christmas."

So, Mack proceeded to try to eat the entire dozen sugar plums which was his gift this year.

Watt, Ed, Sam, and Jack had identical packages. They opened them to find new calico work shirts.

Ed looked puzzled. He knew there was no money to buy calico. Then, he recognized the fabric from one of his mother's old dresses.

After consulting with her father, Lizzie had finally taken the dresses apart and used the voluminous skirts to make new shirts for the older brothers. She and Queen had cut and stitched in secret for two months.

The men insisted on trying on their new garments. As each pulled the shirt over his head and inserted his arms in the sleeves, they got stuck. They were sputtering and wiggling and seemed to get nowhere. With their heads covered and their arms in the air, they looked like six-foot goblins stumbling around.

Queen laughed.

Maggie cried.

Lizzie frowned.

Lizzie approached the nearest brother and said, "What's wrong, Sam?"

"I don't know, but I can't get my head or my hands through the blasted openings," was his sputtered reply. Muffled words and lots of squirms were coming from the other three as well.

Lizzie took a close look at the collar of Sam's shirt and exclaimed, "Well, no wonder. The openings are sewn shut. QUEEN ANN MATILDA OWNBY!!!! What did you do?"

By this time, everyone was laughing, except Lizzie.

The men had managed to back out of the shirts with help from Craig and Eli.

"It's just a running stitch across the opening. See, it comes right out," Queen said through her snickers, as she pulled a thread and released the openings. The others followed her example and soon the men were wearing their new shirts, sipping more hot cider, munching the gingerbread from the tree, and admiring each other's presents. Maggie and Henry fell asleep sitting up. Mack dozed in the corner with sugar all over his face.

Watt walked to the door and opened it to find a foot of accumulated snow and more falling.

Ed joined his brother on the porch and watched as Watt fingered a tattered remnant of a tobacco twist.

"This is all that's left of the original twist Pa gave us when we left for the war. Think I'll keep it as a reminder."

Ed started humming a familiar tune as Eli stepped onto the porch and sang:

Hark! The herald angels sing.

December 1874

Near Christmas, Eli received a letter from John Christopher wishing everyone a wonderful holiday. He was living in Arkansas, married and had a baby son. They had a nice farm on Arbuckle Island in the Arkansas River, but he was considering relocating. Some of his cousins had moved to the Red River in Texas and the area sounded promising. John closed his letter with best wishes for everyone and a special regard for the little *Queen of my Heart*.

After the letter had been passed around and read by everyone, Queen snuck it into her pocket, slipped out of the parlor, and quietly climbed the loft stairs.

Lizzie and Jeff had come for supper, and Lizzie saw Queen leave.

Once in her room, Queen lay down on her bed and re-read the last sentence of the letter, "to the little Queen of my heart," and her eyes filled with tears.

She remembered that hot summer day, twelve years ago, when the dashing cavalry lieutenant rode into the yard.

Eli had introduced her as Queen Ann Matilda Ownby, but John Christopher had said, "That's too many names for such a little girl. I'll just call you Queen, because you are the Queen of my heart."

In that moment, Mattie had died, and Queen was born.

A year later, during the darkest days of the war and surrounding battles, John Christopher had returned, like a hero from a storybook on his tall gray stallion.

Queen dozed on the ride home and dreamed she was a grown woman, riding Shadow Dancer nestled in John Christopher's arms.

Lizzie opened the loft room door and found her sister asleep with the letter lying on her breast.

Queen awoke with a start and stuffed the paper under her pillow.

"What was that?" Lizzie asked.

"Nothing important. Just a list of things for Pa to get in town," Queen said, trying to hold back her tears. The tears won.

Lizzie removed the letter from under the pillow and sat on the edge of the bed.

"Oh, Lizzie, why couldn't he come back for me instead of going off and getting married?"

Her heart breaking for her sister, Lizzie reached out to take her hand. "You were just a child, Queen, and he was a grown man, being nice to a little girl. Did you really think he would come back for you?"

"I always dreamed about it. From that first day when he called me Queen of his heart."

Lizzie's practical side came through, and she lost her patience. "Well, he's married now and has a family. So, you had best forget about him and find someone else to dream about."

"But Lizzie, wives die. All the time. I can still dream. Besides, she's probably just some squaw or bar trollop."

November 1877

"We should take the northern route home, little brother, and stop in Arkansas to see John Christopher," Watt told Craig as they left Pilot Grove, Texas.

They had travelled from Tennessee to Texas to scout lands for settlement of the family.

"Wouldn't that take us through Indian Territory?" Craig questioned.

Watt answered, "I heard there's been no hostility for a few years. At least not to the east, where we're going. If you think you can shoot straight, we shouldn't run into anything we can't handle."

They arrived at Fort Smith, Arkansas nine days later and stopped at the General Store to see if anyone knew John Christopher.

"Go east along the river about four miles. When you come to a fork, follow the lower one. It joins back up with the river a little farther on, creating an island. You'll see a bridge crossing to the Christopher place. Tell him I got that calico his missus has been looking for and some pretty china buttons that match," said the proprietor.

"Why don't I just take it to him? How much for the calico and the buttons?"

"Let's see," the proprietor answered. "At seven cents a yard, there's twenty-two yards on the bolt, that's one dollar and fifty-four cents. And the buttons are fifty cents a card. That's a total of two dollars and four cents, but since you fellers are friends of Christopher, I'll let you take the lot for two dollars even."

"That sounds like a good price," Watt said as Craig dug in his pocket to find some change. They paid the man and stashed the fabric and buttons on the mule and took the road out of town to the east.

They found the bridge easily and crossed to the island. It looked to be about fifty acres with cleared fields and pasture surrounded by towering pine trees. As they approached the house, John was leaving the barn.

He was surprised and delighted to see Watt, and he remembered Craig as a youngster. John and his wife had two little boys and another child on the way.

Watt and Craig gave a descriptive account of Grayson County Texas, and the lieutenant was interested. He had been thinking about moving into Indian Territory, where his wife had relatives, for a while now.

Craig presented Mrs. Christopher with the parcel of calico, and John tried to pay him for the purchase.

Watt refused to accept payment. "It's small payment for all you did for our family during the war. Me and my brothers are much beholding to you for your help. Queen still speaks of you frequently."

"I didn't do anything any officer worth his salt wouldn't have done. But I'm sure Lucy is glad to get a new dress," John said and glanced at his wife who was smiling shyly.

Lucy said, "Thank you very much. This will make up nicely for a new Sunday go-to-meeting dress and maybe a shirt for John, too." Then, she turned back to the pot of stew on the fireplace hook.

The brothers slept in the barn where it was warm and snug, but they heard the wind howling outside. They planned to leave in the morning, but when Watt opened the side barn door, the wind almost blew the door out of his hand.

Blowing snow, like he had not seen since Fort Donelson, hit him in the face. He shut the door quickly and told Craig, "Looks like we're caught in a blizzard, brother. I'll make my way to the house to see what we can do to help John. You saddle the horses so we're ready if he needs us to ride with him."

Watt and John went out into the blizzard to check the livestock while Craig stayed to tend the animals in the barn. When they returned, they found Craig lying in the corner of a stall unconscious. There was blood on his forehead and trickling from his mouth.

Watt bent over and shook him as Craig began to groan and tried to sit. "What happened, little brother?" Watt asked with alarm.

Pointing to a cow with a nursing calf, Craig moaned, "That calf was lying down, and I thought he was dead. I picked him up. I guess he was just sleeping, and I scared him, 'cause he jumped out of my arms and startled me. I jumped back and must have hit my head on that low rafter. Damn! I think I bit my tongue off."

Lucy Christopher was alarmed when the men entered the house supporting a blood-covered Craig. She put her youngest baby in his cradle and cried out, "What happened?"

"He'll be alright as soon as the bleeding stops," Watt told her. "At least it will keep him quiet for a while."

Craig shot his brother a spiteful look and sat down hard in the kitchen chair. He was rolling his tongue around in his mouth, trying to ease the pain, while his head dripped blood down his nose.

Lucy filled a basin with warm water and tore some rags to bind his head.

John turned to Watt and said, "I suspect he is in good hands now. Let's go finish unhitching the team."

"Supper will be ready when you men get back," Lucy told her husband.

She set the basin on the edge of the table. Lifting her skirts, she straddled Craig's lap and started to clean his bloody face and forehead.

He closed his eyes and tried not to wince when she wiped near the cut. The warm water felt good and was soothing. Lulled by her ministrations, he started to doze when he felt her breath on his neck.

Scooting up close to his chest, her full round belly pressed against his firm slim waist. She ran her fingers through his hair and down his jaw and neck toward the opening of his shirt.

He opened his eyes, and her face was a fraction of an inch from his. As he looked into her dark brown eyes, he saw what could only be described as lust.

She wiggled in his lap suggestively and placed her hands on either side of his face and whispered, "Let me see your tongue. Ever since you gave me that material, I've wanted to kiss you and say thank you."

Startled by her actions and by the growing warmth in his groin, he lifted her off his lap and held her at arm's length. "Ma'am, John Christopher is like family to me, and I think your stew is burning."

He stood her on her feet. She looked at him with scorn as she picked up the basin and moved to the fireplace just as the door opened.

John and Watt entered. They both had to push the door closed against the wind. By the time they removed their coats and settled at the table, Lucy was dishing up the stew.

Neither man mentioned Craig's red face. Each assumed it was due to the bump on his head. Nor did they question his lack of appetite or conversation, attributing those to his bitten tongue.

The storm lasted three days and three nights. Each morning, Watt and Craig helped John feed the cattle and break ice on the water hole.

On the fourth day, the wind died, and the sun shone brightly. By noon, the ice was beginning to melt, and the river was breaking up.

The brothers decided it was time to return home.

As they saddled to leave, John handed Watt a package wrapped in burlap and said, "Would you please give this to little Queen? I bought it right after the war, and this is the first chance I've had to get it to her."

"I'll see that she gets it, John. Thank you for the hospitality and write us often."

As they crossed the still snowy bridge, Watt looked back over his shoulder, grinned, and told his brother, "At least we won't have to contend with blizzards in Texas. Come on, Bumpy, let's go home."

December 1877

The morning after Watt and Craig returned, Queen went down to the kitchen to find Marthey singing softly.

"When did Watt get back?" Queen asked, chuckling. She knew that was the only thing that would cause her sister-in-law to sing so early in the morning.

"Late last night." Marthey smiled her biggest smile. "Help me get breakfast finished. He's gone to help with the chores and then him and Craig want to talk to everyone about their trip." She continued to pat out biscuits.

"I sent Henry to fetch Lizzie and Jeff. So, you crack some eggs, and let's get breakfast on the table."

After breakfast was finished and the table cleared, everyone met in the parlor. The adults had settled in to hear about the journey to and from Texas while the children played in the corner.

Eli rocked slowly and when everyone quieted, he said, "Craig, do you have something to tell us?"

"Yes, sir," Craig stood, barely able to contain his excitement. "I bought an eight-acre farm in Texas."

Gasps and whispers circulated through the assembled family. "I know it's small, but it was available. And it will give us a base to build from in the area."

"That's all I need to hear," Eli said. "I want to go as soon as possible. But, do tell us about your trip. Was it easy going, and how long should it take with wagons and families?"

"We made pretty good time by going down the trace," Craig continued, "and there's good wagon roads across southern Arkansas. It took us less than thirty days. So with wagons and the family, it should take about three times that long. The weather wasn't bad for winter."

Watt took over and said, "We went the northern route through Indian Territory coming home. We stopped for a few days near Ft. Smith to visit John Christopher."

A loud gasp drew Watt's attention, and he saw Lizzie take Queen's hand and squeeze it hard.

Queen jerked her hand away from her sister and asked, "How is Lieutenant John? Is he happy?"

"He seems to be. He has a really nice place and two little boys and another on the way."

"What about his wife?" she asked. "What's she like?"

Watt didn't seem to know how to answer that question. He was more comfortable describing land quality and horse flesh. He looked at Craig for help and was surprised to see his brother blushing bright red.

Puzzled, Watt looked again at Queen. "She's nice. And pleasant. Seems to be a good mother. Makes a fine stew. John is fond of her."

"What does she look like, Watt?" Queen was getting impatient for answers.

"She's dark skinned with black hair and eyes. I think she has Indian blood. John mentioned she has relatives in the Nation."

"I knew it," Queen burst out. "She's just some squaw he found in a tepee. He felt sorry for her and married her out of pity."

"Queen, that's enough," Lizzie snapped. "If you can't act like a lady, you are excused to the kitchen."

In a huff, Queen rose and exited the room leaving every mouth hanging open in shock.

Craig told Watt, "That reminds me. Where's the present John sent Queen?"

"I'm not sure. It was in one of the packs on the mule. I don't know where it is. I guess we need to look for it."

April 1877

On April 18, the rain started. Marble size hail beat down for ten minutes followed by sheets of water the wind blew horizontal to the ground. Thunder and bright flashes made the animals skittish.

The men were moving the pigsty fences to keep the hogs on high ground. The creek was rising, and for fear of being stranded, all the women were gathered in Eli's house.

The men came for dinner at different times, ate, and went back to move stock or the many other chores in need of attention.

Ed's oldest son, nine-year-old Billy, went to the barn to check the horses, which were his favorite animal.

Billy walked through the stalls patting and soothing the jittery horses. Talking to this one and giving that one a handful of oats.

He was digging in the feed box near the mule's stall when he spotted a piece of burlap behind the box. He pulled it out from between the wall and the box and could tell there was something hard and lumpy inside.

He stuck the parcel under his shirt and ran back to the house through the rain.

He entered the parlor and stopped. The burlap was scratching his chest, so he pulled it from under his shirt. Laying it on a chair in the corner, he went in search of his mother and something to eat.

The next morning, the women had breakfast started well before dawn, and the men were clustered at one end of the table in the parlor, discussing the storm damage and what needed to be done first.

Queen walked to the corner to retrieve a chair and saw the burlap parcel Billy had left there.

"What's this?" she asked.

Watt recognized it and said between a bite of sausage and biscuits, "We've been wondering where that package got off to. John sent you a present, but it . . ."

Before he could finish his sentence, Queen cried out and ran from the room with the parcel clutched to her breast.

". . . got misplaced." Watt finished. He looked at his brothers for an explanation of his sister's behavior.

Mack was eating his breakfast like his belly had rubbed a blister on his backbone.

Henry just shrugged.

Jack and Craig exchanged a look and finally Jack replied, "We knew she was sweet on John when she was a little girl. But I thought she was over it." Then, he turned to Mack, "I'll split those shingles for the hen house first thing after breakfast."

Marthey watched Queen run toward the woods. Confused and concerned, she left the table and went into the kitchen.

"Queen just did the strangest thing," she said to the other women. "John Christopher sent her a present, and she ran out the door crying."

"Oh, my," Maggie gasped.

Marthey frowned and looked confused. She said, "I knew Queen attached herself to the fantasy of Lieutenant John. Obviously, she hasn't outgrown it."

"It was more than a crush for Queen," Maggie said. "Lieutenant John was her hero on a big silver stallion. She would put me to sleep telling stories about how handsome and dashing he was. She convinced herself that one day he would come back for her, and they would ride away on Shadow Dancer like in a fairy tale. To Queen, John Christopher was Robert E. Lee, Sir Galahad, and Jefferson Davis combined."

At noon, Marthey asked Maggie, "Where's Queen? I haven't seen her since she ran out this morning."

"She's just pouting somewhere. She'll be home for supper," Maggie said.

Queen was in her favorite clearing in the woods. She was angry with her brothers for not giving her John's gift when they got home, but she was giddy with anticipation to see what her fantasy lover had sent.

She hugged the parcel one more time and sniffed it to see if she could catch his scent. But it just smelled like dirty leather and horse barn hay. Laughing joyously, she sat on a stump and carefully peeled away the burlap covering.

Inside was a pretty little doll with a painted china face. She had a red wig, big blue eyes, ruby red lips, and was dressed in the fashion of the war years. Pinned to her full hoop skirt was a note penned in ornate script handwriting, "To the little Queen of my heart."

When reality set in, it hit Queen hard. Her heart stopped beating for a second. She sat on the stump, filled her lungs with air, and screamed. It didn't make her feel better. She stood, the doll falling to the ground. She took two steps forward, stopped, and turned around. Picking up the doll, she sat on the stump again, hugged the doll, and cried.

No thoughts were in her head. Only pain and emptiness. She didn't know what to do. Her dreams were shattered.

Oxygen and blood started to flow again, and she said out loud, "Lizzie was right. He sees me as a little girl in short skirts and pigtails."

Gasping again for breath, she murmured, "I'm twenty-one years old, almost an old maid. I don't need a silly doll."

She took the doll by the legs and raised it high over her head, intending to smash the smiling face. Instead, she lowered the doll slowly, clasped it to her, and then cried again.

Deep, agonizing sobs followed by huge gasps for air came from deep in her soul.

October 1877

Eli and Queen settled into their seats on the train. They were going to visit Eli's oldest sister in Carroll County, Tennessee, and he hoped the trip would bring joy back into his daughter's eyes.

Eli dozed off to the clacking of the wheels. When he woke, he looked over at Queen who stared forlornly out the window. His once vibrant and spirited daughter was sad and despondent, and he didn't know why.

"Why are you so sad, Queen?" he finally asked her.

"Do you remember when you started calling me Queen instead of Mattie?" she questioned.

"No, daughter. I'm afraid I don't remember. When was it?"

"Lieutenant John gave me that name. I thought he was so handsome and gallant the first day he came to the farm. And when he came that day with food, he was a bright light in an otherwise dark world. I saw him as a knight on a big gray charger, but all he saw was a silly little girl. I suppose I'm still a silly little girl. A silly little girl with no dreams left."

Eli took her hand in both of his and held it a few minutes, trying to think of something to ease her pain. "Is he the reason you have rejected the young men who have tried to court you?"

"Yes, Pa. I always thought John would come back for me. But he isn't, is he?"

"No, Queen. I don't think he is. John Christopher was a fine example of a Confederate Cavalry officer. His sworn duty to protect the innocent combined with his chivalrous and loving nature drew him to you like a moth to a flame. I could see it when he looked at you." He stopped and thought for a moment.

"You were so young. If you had been a little older or if he had been a little younger, things might have worked out differently. You'll find someone else to share your life, my dear. Just be sure to keep your heart open."

Father and daughter sat, quietly holding hands as the train clicked and clacked its way into the sun. After thirty minutes, Queen broke the comfortable silence.

"Why didn't you marry after Mama died? I know there were widows in the county who would have been happy for your attention. It would have been much easier for Lizzie. She needed a woman to help with the babies."

Eli didn't speak but seemed to be lost in thought. Then, he smiled a wistful smile and said, "I was selfish. Your Mama was the only woman I ever loved, and I didn't want to share you children, who were the proof of that love. Was that a mistake?"

Overcome with emotion for her father, Queen squeezed his hand and said, "No, Pa. We survived, and perhaps we are stronger because of it."

She reached up, adjusted her hat, plumped her curls, and gave her father a sideways look.

Eli turned to look at his daughter and for the first time saw the stunning woman she had become.

August 1882

Watt, Lizzie, Ed and Craig were all settled in North Texas with their families and their father. Queen was waiting to move with Henry, Maggie and their families.

At twenty-seven, Queen was a lovely young woman. The spunky little girl had grown into a mature woman who knew her own mind and had maintained her enthusiasm and sense of fun.

She had met and was being courted by a young man named Tom Moore.

Tom had escorted her to a church social, and as the festivities were winding down on this beautiful summer evening, the stars were shining over the hills. The couple walked around the property. Tom took her hand and stopped her for a moment.

"Queen, your name describes how I feel about you. You are my Queen. Will you marry me?"

"Oh, Tom, I would be happy to. I thought you might never ask," was her, for once, shy reply. Then giggling like a schoolgirl, she started to kiss him on the cheek, but he stopped her and kissed her on the mouth instead.

Flushed and almost embarrassed, she kissed him back with a passion he didn't know she possessed. When they broke apart, she took his hand and led him back toward the house. "Let's go tell Jack. He's the oldest brother left in Tennessee." She giggled like a child. "I know he'll be happy."

The excited couple shared the news with Queen's brothers, sisters, and the Taylors. The next day, Tom came to the farmhouse and the adults stayed up late into the night making plans. It was decided that Queen would move with her family and in a few months, Tom would follow.

Queen wanted her father to give her away so the couple would marry in Texas.

September 1884

Queen settled into life in Texas with ease. She was living with Lizzie and Jeff simply awaiting Tom's arrival.

One fall day Queen was helping Lizzie and Marthey make pear preserves. Lizzie asked her sister, "Have you heard from Tom lately?"

"No, and I don't understand why. I got a letter from him back in January. He planned to come this spring and couldn't wait to see me and get married. I've written him several times since. But here it is October, and there's been no word from him."

Marthey tried to console her sister-in-law. "Well, I'm positive there is an explanation. Perhaps he's busy with harvest and plans to surprise you by coming here after he gets paid. He'll probably show up on the doorstep any day now."

Queen considered that a moment and cheerfully said, "You may be correct, Marthey. It would be just like him not tell me he's coming and just show up with a preacher."

At supper that night, Jeff handed Queen an envelope. "I picked this up in Whitewright. It's from my sister Betsy but it's addressed to Miss Queen Ownby."

Queen took her letter, walked outside, and sat on the porch with her feet dangling off the edge.

She carefully opened the letter and started to read.

Dearest Queen,

We are all good here. Ma and Papa sends everyone their regards, and we wish you would write us more often.

I have some shocking news. Tom Moore ran off with Stella Banks last week. They got married in Murfreesboro.

I know you considered her a friend, but she was a false friend who set her cap for Tom ever since you left. He told my John that Stella said you were living a free and easy life in Texas, and that you were going to parties with different beaus every night. John told him that was hogwash, but it was too late. They were already married.

Tom doesn't look too happy. But Stella looks like the cat that ate the robin. Write soon.
Your dear friend
Betsy Taylor Campbell

September 1918

In September of 1918, Watt joined thousands of Confederate veterans who attended the 28th United Confederate Veterans Reunion in Tulsa, Oklahoma.

The convention officially opened at 8 p.m. on September 24, 1918. Seated with their former regiments and grouped by states, more than 50,000 "boys from '61" bowed their heads for the Invocation after the Call to Order.

Watt found himself seated behind a gray haired, bearded Lieutenant who looked vaguely familiar. After the many speeches, songs, and recognition of local dignitaries, the meeting was closed with the benediction.

When the soldiers all stood, the Lieutenant turned, and Watt saluted smartly. "Sgt. Watt Ownby, at your command, Lt. Christopher, Sir."

The lieutenant's brown eyes twinkled as they locked with Watt's pale gray ones. He returned the salute and clapped Watt on the shoulder. "Well, I'll be damned. How are you, Watt?"

The men walked out of the convention hall together, and Watt told John about the deaths of his wife, father and siblings.

"How is the little Queen of my heart? Married these past forty years with a whole passel of kids, I suspect."

"Queen never married, but she's still the same. Always jolly and nursing all those in need. How's your Lucy?"

John didn't slow a step and said, "She's dead, Watt. I killed her. Caught her in our bed with the neighbor feller. I was holding my shotgun, and without thinking, I raised it and pulled the trigger. Got

74

'em both with one shot. Sheriff called it a 'crime of passion' and didn't even arrest me."

Watt turned and looked at his old friend, "Damnation, John. That would be hard on any man."

"We had eleven babies together, Watt, I thought she was a good wife."

Watt didn't feel like this was the appropriate time to mention Craig's experience with John's wife, so he just nodded and kept walking.

The lieutenant flashed his brilliant smile as he confided, "Right after I buried Lucy, I married me a widow with a young son and daughter. We've been married sixteen years and have two daughters. She's never given me a moment's worry."

They walked in silence for a couple of blocks, then, John asked, "How many children do you have now. Are you a grandpa yet?"

Watt bragged about his grandchildren until they reached their lodgings. They joined a lively party in progress in the main lounge. The singing and storytelling went until the wee hours of the morning.

February 1930

Watterson Knox Polk Ownby, the patriarch of the Ownby family was dying.

Clustered in groups in every room of the house and scattered around the yard, four generations had gathered to pay their last respects.

His surviving brothers and sisters were on the porch watching the children play and reminiscing.

Jack spoke to Craig, "I remember when you came to Texas for the first time. You and Watt were gone for months. We thought you weren't ever coming back, but Pa kept telling us you'd be back any day. Then, one morning, you came riding in: shaggy, dirty, and trail worn. I think you both slept for two days."

Craig laughed. "It was quite a trip. But the blizzard in Arkansas was the worst part of the journey. John Christopher had a nice place there, but it was so cold. The snow blew parallel to the ground at times. But I came back to Tennessee the proud owner of a Texas farm. We lost touch, and I've often wondered what happened to Lt. John."

Jack replied, "Watt ran into him a few years back, in Tulsa. He didn't say much about their visit when he got home."

Craig looked up and noticed Queen watching him with a faraway look in her eyes. Afraid he had inadvertently mentioned a name that brought her pain, he rose and walked over behind her and put his hands on her shoulders.

She reached up and patted his hand. With a sad smile, she said, "I'll go check on Watt."

Queen entered Watt's room and found Lizzie sitting in a chair, watching their brother. She sat on the edge of the bed.

"There's only six of us left out of the 11," Lizzie said despondently.

"I know, sister, but look how big the family has grown. Pa was so proud of his family, and Mama would be too," Queen replied in her normally cheerful manner. "There are 59 grandchildren and 140 great grandchildren. That is a family to be proud of."

Sadly, Lizzie replied, "It didn't seem strange when Ed and Polly died. They were both in their sixties. But when the babies both died, first Maggie and then Henry, it didn't seem right. They were both just barely in their fifties. I can't help but wonder if I could have done something different when they were little to make them stronger?"

Queen stood and patted her sister's hand then put an arm around her shoulder. As she hugged Lizzie she said, "At least we got to see Sam again when he came to visit in '27. And his death, later that year, was the only one. So, it looks like we've broken the curse of two deaths in one year. Watt is ready to go be with Marthey and baby Callie. He's at peace, so let's cheer up and try to make his passing easy."

The End

About Rita Ownby Holcomb

Rita Ownby Holcomb is a fourth generation Texan who has always been fascinated by the question, "Where do we come from?" Her genealogy research led to the birth of the *A Twist of Tobacco* series. She is a proud member of the Daughters of the American Revolution and the United Daughters of the Confederacy.

For thirty years she served on or presided over various civic organizations including, the Community Theater, Historic Museum, Texoma Council of Governments, and Meals-on-Wheels. After serving as an elected City Council member, she retired from civic service to become a buyer and seller of vintage clothing and accessories. Listed in *Who's Who in American Women 2000* and *Who's Who in America 2003*, Rita is now a full-time author. Married since 1972 to Darrell Holcomb, they have one son, Stuart B. Holcomb.

https://www.facebook.com/ATwistofTobacco/
https://www.facebook.com/groups/2013989618829394/
http://rownbyholcomb.blogspot.com/
https://twitter.com/RitaOHolcomb
https://www.instagram.com/ritaoholcomb/
https://www.bookbub.com/authors/rita-ownby-holcomb
https://www.goodreads.com/author/show/14753920.Rita_Ownby_Holcomb
https://www.youtube.com/watch?v=LGQBmayM6-A&t=69s
https://www.youtube.com/watch?v=uFCRMCgnBnk
http://www.fountainspringpublishing.com/
http://www.amazon.com/-/e/B01BMRVENQ
http://www.barnesandnoble.com/s/Rita+ownby+holcomb?_requestid=586209
http://www.booksamillion.com/search?id=6706925861670&query=rita+ownby+holcomb&where=Books
http://www.ebay.com/itm/NEW-A-Twist-of-Tobacco-by-Rita-Ownby-Holcomb-Paperback-Book-English-Free-Shipp-/361681263584?roken=cUgayN
https://books.txauthors.com/category-s/2444.htm

LITERARY FICTION

Focusing on the value of its commentary, literary fiction is used to broaden our viewpoint of the world. Whether it is understanding a person's thoughts or stepping into another's shoes, meaning is emphasized more than entertainment.

And yet, within this defined box, it is performed in an artful way by the depth of the character involved, the rise and fall of tension, and the language drawing the reader in. Literary fiction, then takes on more of a contemporary meaning applying to our present world and the issues around us.

Not everyone agrees with the category of literary fiction. Many simply separate it into good or bad fiction as determined by the reader's perception. We invite you to find out for yourself and make up your own mind.

James William Peercy

LITERARY FICTION: STORY 1

BREAKDOWN

by Kelly Willbanks

Even years later, Marie would never remember what woke her. If she hadn't woke Rob, he'd have slept on through, exhausted from the day.

The strong smell of smoke had them both frantic.

Flames lit the hall.

He was faster and veered for their infant's room. She went the opposite direction, thinking of the other children and screaming for them as she ran.

Their rooms were untouched. Their little faces were startled as she snatched up each. Her feet seared and blistered as she made for the front door, one small, whimpering child under each arm.

Smoke hung in thick clouds. She made it to the door only because she could have done it blindfolded. The heat on her back made her fearful, but she turned to look for Rob. She heard the crash of wood and hoped it was him, escaping through the backdoor.

She balanced her eldest boy, Jay, on her knee and reached to open the door, only to be burned by the knob. The door wouldn't open. She felt Jay reach out his tiny hand to help and stopped him.

She was thoroughly blinded by smoke, but she could make out the flashing of lights outside the window to her right. With strength born of desperation, she shifted both children to one arm and groped for something, anything, to shatter the window with.

As she moved to the window, the door smashed open in a shower of splinters. She lost no time and rushed through the open door before their saviors could enter.

On her heated skin, the air was cold. It gusted in to stoke the flames and chased them out through the doorway.

Outside, the figures of the firemen in their reflective suits swam in her vision as they hurried her to the edge of the street. They shot questions at her, but her coughs came in such great spasms that she was brought to her knees.

She heard nothing. The sirens, the shouts, the engines, the violent roar and crash of the fire, all lost on her. But though her eyes stung from the smoke, they had cleared enough to see.

What she saw was a shock to her system. Everything they had worked long and hard for . . . all the things they had lovingly bought for the kids . . . the wealth of memories . . . a home filled with laughter and love, and the haven they had created together from this crazy world, was being devoured by this enormous, devilish, creature. The creature lit the night with its wild red and orange dance. The EMTs checked the children as she watched everything violently turn to ash.

A big man, wearing a dirty fireman's helmet, finally got her attention as he firmly shook her by the shoulders.

"Was anyone else in there?" he repeated, loud and slow.

He was giving her first aid when his words finally registered. Her gasped cry startled him . . . only then did she remember to look for them.

Her Olympic sprint shot her barefoot past the men spouting geysers of water at uncaring flames. She would have gone straight back into the inferno had she not noticed the soot streaked arm, reaching from the window of the bathroom. Her feet slid on the wet grass as she changed direction toward the window. Had steel arms not pinned hers to her sides, she would have already been there, despite the heat.

She squirmed and kicked with all her might, got an arm loose, and pointed.

"Rob!" She kicked her captor hard in the shin. "Rob!"

She was loose and running, followed by others.

Too high for her to reach, a tiny bundle of soggy towels was handed out the window to the tallest man. The sound the towels made was unnatural and stifled. But once unwrapped, her bright red baby face was perfect.

Marie clutched her daughter as she reached for Rob's arm, an arm which now dangled from the small window. One shoulder was through the window frame. And she could make out a small part of his face through the toxic black that billowed out at them.

She jumped to brush his fingers with hers as the firemen raised their axes to chop at the wall. She thought she saw a smile on his face.

Everything was okay. They had one another, and this was all that mattered.

His limp arm fell back out of view, and her heart fell with it.

The firemen redoubled their efforts on the house siding, the sound of their axes echoed through the neighborhood. But she knew . . . everything was not okay.

After the funeral, days, weeks, a month passed on autopilot while they stayed with her mom. She looked after her children. She healed physically. She made plans which seemed hazy, dreamlike. She bought a used red car. She was numb the entire time, save for a few lucid, broken moments, until she packed what little they had been given into the small trunk of the car.

"That was the last of it, Sweetheart," her mom had whispered, giving her a hug. "Do you have enough money?"

Marie had answered, her voice hollow, robotic, "Yes, Momma.

Don't worry."

She put every penny in the tank and drove.

***

Marie stared at a hole in the old car's dashboard. The car gave a loud protesting sputter and lurched.

Since she began the trip, the firm root in reality, which safe driving required, was taking its toll. She hung on by a thread.

Surely, all of this . . . it couldn't be real. She was in bed about to wake from this nightmare . . . next to Rob in their home. She wasn't running out of gas in the middle of Nowhere, Kansas, with nothing but three crying babies. Another lurch . . . another sputter.

Dear God, please . . . I need help . . .

"Mommy, I miss Daddy," wailed Rachel, age three.

Marie didn't even look over at the little blonde head. She'd cry if she did. She might cry anyway.

Slipping back into her stupor, she let the world fade away. It was too cruel a world to live in. Her eyes glazed; her movements were automatic. At the very least, a nervous breakdown was definitely in her future.

The car choked and the engine struggled.

She burst into tears, although she knew it was dangerous. They were still on their way downhill at a good little clip. Through her wet eyes, the exact speed was a blurred light on the dash.

Unable to see the road she worried she might crash, and then wondered, *Would it really be so bad to . . . but the kids!*

She wailed, her crying drowning out the voices of the two littlest of her children, and thought, *I am a terrible mother to ever think such a thing! Just terrible!*

She furiously wiped her eyes and saw a gas station about half a mile away.

We can make it . . . This stupid, junky little car can make it.

The car sputtered with indignation.

She grimaced and thought, *Sorry, car. Didn't mean it.*

The car slowed down, dead, but still coasting.

No gas can, she told herself. Doesn't matter. We can make it. If we can't, then we push it.

She stared straight at the road, hope and fear having a little war in her head. As it slowed to an excruciating crawl, she steered the car into the parking lot.

It came to rest at the pump. Relief seeping in, she sighed and let her head fall against the headrest.

Wait, she thought. *Money. No money!*

Eyes blurry again, hands frantic, she searched every ashtray and floorboard, but the previous owners had meticulously cleaned the car. She leaned into the back and lifted one car seat, and then the other. She made Jay, her son, unbuckle and checked under his booster and found not a single cent.

She stepped out of the car on rubbery legs and stared at her ragged shoes. They were once just her running shoes, one pair of many. Now they were all she had . . . and she was standing on money.

Right next to her shoe was a quarter. She moved her foot. There were two quarters next to one another.

***

Kassie looked up from sweeping to watch a little red four door pull up at pump two (of two).

All afternoon she'd hoped she wouldn't have to deal with anybody today. She'd just do her time and her dad would pay her and she'd be one step closer to buying her pickup.

The driver of the red car crawled around on the seats, even sticking her head below the dash.

Great, Kassie thought. *A crazy lady.*

She went to stand behind the register.

***

Marie told her oldest in a dull voice, "Watch the babies, Jay,"

"Okay, I will Mom," he told her seriously. He wasn't quite seven.

With the two quarters clutched in her hand, she came out of her stupor long enough to give him a tiny smile.

Fifty cents, Marie thought. *Enough to get us exactly nowhere.*

She wiped her face and went inside.

The girl behind the counter stared.

Marie cleared her throat and made an effort to sound cheerful. "Um, fifty cents on pump two, please."

Kassie wasn't just staring . . . She was gawking. She couldn't help it. She'd only ever seen people on TV who looked that awful. The woman was maybe thirty-something but was badly aged by puffy, bloodshot eyes, black circles and very white skin and lips. She looked dazed and drained, like by a vampire or something.

And seriously, fifty cents? Kassie thought. *That would get her, what, a mile out of that old junker?*

***

Marie started to pump the gas, expecting it to cut off as soon as it began. She poked her head into the car to check on the kids.

The gas did pump unbelievably fast, but it didn't stop. It hit the fifty cent mark, then one dollar, then two, three . . .

By the time she had returned her attention to the pump, she stared in silent, frozen horror. The tank was full, and the amount owed was a lot more than fifty cents.

What do they do to people who can't pay? she wondered. Jail? Or maybe they'd let me work it off? But the little ones . . . tired and hungry already . . . who would take care of them?

***

Kassie watched through the window.

A sad, desperate looking woman had gone to pump gas. A zombie returned. Honestly, the clothes didn't help. They looked borrowed, faded, and limp.

Poor woman, she thought.

Kassie kinda wanted to milk it a little but found she couldn't. She really felt for this lady.

She reached into her back pocket for her dad's old wallet, made over with zebra stripe duct tape, and drew out a hundred dollar bill. For a moment, she held it up between her fingers and then looked at the woman. She put it in the till before she could think too much about it.

She smiled brightly as she counted out the woman's change. She snuck a peek at the lady and witnessed the exact moment when it became clear what she was doing.

"And your change for you, ma'am." Kassie handed her the great wad of bills leftover from the broken hundred.

"Oh, and the things you asked for," Kassie said, holding out a bag bulging with peanuts, crackers, water bottles and other things. "All rung up and double bagged. You have a great day!"

With a little sound somewhere between a sigh and a sob, the woman hesitantly took it, but her smile through the tears was the biggest.

"You, too," Marie managed to say.

***

Marie walked slowly toward the car with the cash and snacks. She wanted so badly to turn, thank the girl, and tell her what it meant to them. But somehow, she knew she wasn't supposed to.

Inside the vehicle, the babies were quiet and happy, their munching sounds a fair substitute for the car's busted radio.

Marie listened, her forehead resting on the steering wheel, eyes closed, and let calm wash over her. Clarity came. She felt fully awake for the first time since the fire.

It wasn't the end, this moment or the one after. Oh, there would be sorrow, but there would be happiness and contentment again, too . . . for both her and the children. She looked down the road at where it curved out of sight over a hill or two. The road was just like their future.

She started the little red car, which also seemed happy after the feeding, and pulled onto the road.

The End

About Kelly Willbanks

Kelly Willbanks is a Texas girl. Her husband and two kids inspire everything she does. Of the dozens of stories she has written, this is the first she has considered worthy to see the light of day. Her goal in writing this story was to remind people that living again is possible, even after something horrible. Her final message, helping others may change their lives for the better, so never be afraid to lend someone a helping hand.

LITERARY FICTION: STORY 2

DIARY OF A MAJIK USER

by James William Peercy

Day 1111

Tearing apart the universe and putting it back together may seem like a simple thing, but it's not. Love makes people do strange things. As once I heard from a pixie as I traveled through an enchanted forest, "Love has the power to change lambs into lions and lions into lambs."

Yea, that's me, sitting with my legs crossed, back against the wall, and out-stretched palms resting on my knees. I breathe, letting the majik flow.

Did you notice how I spelled the word majik? M-a-j-i-k, not m-a-g-i-c. There is a difference, you know. The word magic, with a 'g' and a 'c', refers to supernatural forces or tricks. That's not what I do at all. There is nothing supernatural about the energies which build the universes, no tricks up an illusionist's sleeve, and certainly nothing out of the ordinary...to a majik user, with a 'j' and a 'k', that is.

Lots of things are involved in changing the universe, not the least of which are the opinions of the people involved. You see, people's opinions are powerful. Imagine having control of a nuclear bomb and all you had to do was lean on the switch? That's us, you and me. The very thought of what we can and cannot make happen can change our whole existence.

Breathe, I tell myself.

So many thoughts collide in my mind trying to distract me. I hear their voices from afar though only within my head: people calling out in desperation, people calling out in joy, and people who have entirely given up. It is the curse of a true majik user.

I try to focus. I have to help her, the one I love. Brick by mental brick, I wall out all the voices and become one with the universe. In that instant, my invisible fingers, my astral fingers, touch the Source, the foundation of all creation, which most people ignore.

Yeah, that's the right word, too: ignore. If it doesn't fit our understanding of the cosmos and if it is not what we think we want, we're good at pretending it doesn't exist. If it didn't work for us, no one else can possibly be correct, right?

Slowly, calmly, I sense the connection. It is a knowing I cannot truly explain. I . . . just . . . know.

We think we've come a long way by our scientific perceptions of reality. However, in the practical sense, we are simply regaining what previous generations have forgotten. Some call this knowledge the forbidden fruit.

It's not faith, belief, or religion in the traditional sense. It is simply calmness in the soul, an inner peace which abides within—if we just let go. That, letting go, scares people.

Still trying to focus, in my mind I hear the words, "What do you think?"

A shiver races through me. It is such a powerful question. I am afraid to answer.

I stand on a rope suspended over a canyon, trying to make my way to the light. I can hear the darkness on every side calling me to accept its rules, its limited definition of reality.

The rope wobbles. I hear people laugh, cry, and scream beneath me. One slip and I will become something which is not me, conformed to a world which would use me up and cast away my corpse.

I stretch my foot forward. The wind whips behind me. The voices jeer, but I will not give into the status quo. I refuse to bend to their will.

In that instant, I can feel lightness in my soul, a flutter of wings. No longer does the rope touch my feet. I am lifted into the air by All That Is. I do not struggle to reach the other side. I am already there.

Breathe, I tell myself.

The thudding of my heart prompts me to open my eyes. Instead of a wall at my back, there is a tree. Instead of carpet beneath my body, there is green grass. Instead of air cooled by a machine, the scent of an earthy forest fills my lungs.

I slowly rise. The world is different, vivid, and full of life that loves every moment of its existence.

The sound of water lapping at a shore catches my ear. I turn to see a lake stretching to the horizon. Sparkling blue waters gleam in a sun which shines in bursts of beautiful reds, greens, and yellows. Ducks dive and surface. Sweet singing comes through the trees. As I watch, a path forms to guide me. It creates itself with every step I take.

A white, circular stairway appears through the trees. Made of tall, narrow steps set in swirls of marble, the stairs stretch up to reach the sky.

There is a memory here, something I am supposed to evoke. A connection, which has been lost, teases the edge of my mind.

I place a foot on the first marble step. It slightly sinks, conforming to the sole of my foot: supportive, yet yielding; caressing, yet firm. My heart opens as unimaginable love fills me. Soothing peace flows into me brought on by the wind's tune tickling the leaves on the trees.

A second step completely removes me from the ground. The day's events, those clinging to the edge of my mind, fall away. I feel light and airy, bursting with the sacred knowledge which flows from the very atmosphere of this majikal place.

I must tell someone of what I am experiencing, anyone. I cannot keep it in. Turning, I sweep the green forest with my eyes.

A squirrel scuttles across a branch. A blue jay and a cardinal swoop down in flight. Crickets chirp. In the distance, a bobcat cries. From above, an eagle circles three times before heading toward the mountains. As I feel the wonder around me, I realize no other human walks here.

The voice, a call of pain, the reason for this journey, comes back to me. Love, hope, and peace, they command me and demand I help.

I run up the stairway, two and three steps at a time. It spirals upward, reaching above the green treetops, passing through the leaves until the stairs end, and giving access to a large red marble floor.

There are no supports beneath the floor save where the top of the stairs attach to one side. I step back, staring at the floor. I hear the cry of pain. I want to help, but my mind says this structure cannot hold together.

Fear clouds my vision. The floor begins to fade. A stab of agony twists in my stomach. I do not understand why.

I must help her. I must try. Despite my belief that the structure is unstable, I step out, trusting the marble surface to hold me up.

My foot lands firm. My resolve to help hardens. A single cloud floats into view, morphs, changes, and then forms the softest bed I have ever seen. A thick mist hangs above it. From within the area of the bed, the cry of pain comes.

The voice in my mind asks once more, "What do you think?"

The question makes no sense as it fills my head. It applies to nothing. Yet, in the back of my mind, I know the purpose for the question is clear. I step closer to the bed and wave one hand through the thick mist, unable to understand how this will help.

A translucent female body forms. Pale colors radiate from her shape, auras which are weakened by something from within. I horizontally scoop my hands to brush the faded auras away, feeling the cool mist as it touches my skin.

The auras vanish for a moment. Then the swirls of corrupted majik come back, radiating from within the body lying before me. I feel the faded auras reaching out with barbed claws as the colors reappear. I must find a way to help her.

In my mind, the voice asks the question, again, "What do you think?"

I ponder the words as I watch symbols of protection form, standing like guards on all six sides. They place us in a transparent cube, secured from the outside elements.

The symbols, which hang in the air, vibrate with majik, and become a living organism maintaining the protective walls. These walls keep back the pale colors that have passed beyond the confines of the cube. They bar the way so the auras, which have escaped, cannot return to magnify the issue in her body.

My hands hover over her eyes, then her temples, and then her ears. Shifting her head, I feel the touch of her hair against my palms until I gently cup the back of her head.

On each inhale, I feel the Source, the foundation of all creation, descend. As I slowly let the majik out, it flows around us, compelling additional faded colors to leave her body, creating a spinning vortex that drags that corruption beyond the protective walls.

Lovingly, I shift her head once more as I withdraw my palms. Her head gently floats back into position to be suspended upon a pillow of light. Her eyes are closed, and I wonder if she can feel the majik's touch.

I shift my hands to hover above her throat next. The larynx warms beneath my open palms. She is in pain, but rather than pull away, I embrace her soreness, absorb and release it.

She shifts, but her translucent eyes do not open. They cannot. For her eyes to open would mean an acceptance of what I am doing beyond what she is currently willing to give. I know this. It does not matter. I do all this for her.

There's a stab of discomfort in my head, temporary but real. Even in this very real place, I am not immune to the frailties of the human body.

I hurt for her. I want her to feel better but before that can happen the journey I have begun must be completed.

I remove my hands from above her throat to I shift them to hover over her chest. Her lungs inhale and exhale, slow and steady. The majik shift works. I can see the outline of her beating heart green with the glow of life.

Deep breath, I tell myself. *I must remember to breathe. Let the Source, the foundation of all creation, come through me. Allow the power to wash over her.*

She relaxes in her spirit, though I know she cannot understand why. With a sigh of relief, I pass on: the solar plexus, the stomach, the sacral, the knees, and finally at the insides of the feet.

It is a . . . process, a check on each major area of the body. I align them to what they should be, like a doctor might set a bone. Each has its place. Each has its rhythm. Each is a wavelength all its own.

I step back toward her head and tap her lightly on the shoulder. Her spirit responds turning in the air until she lies upon her stomach.

I wave my scooping hands, once more clearing the residual pale colors. These remnant colors were hiding beneath her in hopes of clinging to her mortal soul.

Touching my palms together, I work them as a plow. As I run them above her spine, head to foot, the colors of the auras divide. This reveals flashes of energy traversing her vertebrae, creating a road map to the divine.

Over her head, I position my palms. Her thoughts and feelings leap into my mind. I must focus to remain detached. I must relax.

My spirit calms my soul, two distinctive parts of what makes me who I am. I continue to rhythmically breathe, which helps to steady my way.

Warmth radiates from my palms. With the gentlest of majik touches, I hover over her shoulders, shift to the lower back, and prepare for what will happen next.

Lifting my hands from above the lower back, I separate them. My left palm is held above where the spine meets the neck. My right lingers where the vertebrae meet the hips.

A barrage of static impulses erupts. I stagger, knocked back, fighting to hold against the onslaught of the distorted wave patterns.

The waves collide, cancel each other out, and interrupt their own function.

My hands shake. A tingling ripples through me. The backlash of energy tries to drive me from her translucent body.

Breathe, I tell myself. *I must breathe.*

The Source, the foundation of all creation flowing through me, slams into the thrashing, dark impulses, which make up the energy backlash. The corrupted auras leaping through her vertebrae dissipate. I hold position against the flood with the knowledge that if I stop, everything completed up to this point can be undone.

The battle passes. The majik steadies. A quiet, peaceful pulse ripples along her vertebrae. The vivid beauty of her natural aura begins to return.

I raise my hands and continue. Sacral, back of knees, and the outside of her feet, each in their turn, follow.

It tickles.

With the loss of the paler colors of her aura, a gateway has opened, and she can begin to heal. Before placing my palms over the heels of her feet, I ground myself by going to my knees.

Like lightning striking a copper wire, majik ripples through me, bearing me down. My focus cannot hold against the memories she shares, unknowing and without warning. The wall I have used to keep control erodes in a torrent of past and future events.

Eyes wide, I stare at nothing, listening and watching. I know this person beyond the now. Without her realizing the truth she has locked away, the many pasts we've shared continue to pour from her, before she was born in her present reality. It explains so much in my life, reactions I could not begin to understand without this knowledge.

I've seen the sparkle in her eyes. I've felt the tug of her heart. I've known her love and hurt beyond what any immortal soul should bear. There is so much truth at one time, I try to look away, but cannot.

Shock sets in even as the wash of majik levels out, and I wonder, *How? How can this be possible? More than one life? How could I prove it? Intertwining souls? No, it cannot be.*

Yet, it is true. A millennium of memories from the foundation of all creation, the Source, is hidden at the birth of every single child. A wall created to block those memories from changing what we accept in this life as our reality.

The deluge of memories trickles to a halt. Struggling to rise, I stumble to stand beside her.

She can never know the truth of our reality . . . or at least not yet. The promise is there. It can happen. Will the situation ever be right? Only time will tell.

I rise to my feet and then place both palms together in a prayer-like formation. From foot to head, I use my touching palms to trace along the vertical center of her body, closing the auras I have opened and sealing them shut.

She's resting now. I can hear her light breathing. She sleeps and will heal. She needs the rest.

In my mind, the voice asks for the last time, "What do you think?"

The end or the beginning, depending on your point of view.

Inspiration for Diary of a Majik User

With great mental debate, I thought over what genre to place this story. Is it fantasy? Some may agree. Is it reality? Others would concur. Is it historical fiction? Yes, it has basis in real events. Is the author crazy? That is entirely possible, for those who think they are wholly sane must either rationalize away or cutout the unexplained from their life.

A few years back, I was curious about a technique of healing called Reiki. It is based upon the idea that the therapist can be used as a channel to heal the physical and emotional well-being of a person, both for self-healing and others.

Under the training of Reiki Master Terri Malek, I explored this topic in-depth, and it explained many things throughout my life.

As a child, I could always see auras, colors that would appear around people, places, and things. I also discovered the source of the auras and what meaning they could hold. I learned to be sensitive the energy of life, which so many ignore and thus dismiss with many explanations. Like tuning a musical instrument, the notes only play true when you know what the sound is supposed to be.

About James William Peercy

James William Peercy fell through a portal into the publishing biosphere in 2012. Previously, he had been observing his own world and recording it since the age of 10. James continued writing while attaining a degree in Computer Science, getting married, raising dogs, and starting a business.

Since all worlds exist simultaneously, he has added four book series, the Cliff Fulton mystery series, the Xun Ove fantasy series, the Clan Ravensmith series, and the Ivan, Universal Space Tech series. With a mind constantly moving, he devotes his downtime to writing, enjoying a bit of travel, and adoring his wife, Claudette.

If you like poetry, fantasy, sci-fi, and mystery check out his website!

https://www.JamesWilliamPeercy.com
https://www.WithinTheHeartOfSilence.com
https://linkedin.com/in/james-peercy-26252477
https://www.StoriesToTell.com
https://www.facebook.com/jameswilliampeercy
https://www.instagram.com/jameswilliampeercy
https://twitter.com/JamesWPeercy

LITERARY FICTION: STORY 3

LIGHT OF LOVE

by B. Ellen Gardner

Lovey Spencer's life could be compared to a game of baseball. It was thrilling and exciting, filled with challenges, vigor, and disappointments.

There was nothing soft about it. There were times when Lovey had found herself on the winning side of the game. As she grew older, more times than not, she was on the losing side.

A younger Lovey had always been an active participant in the game, eager and enthusiastic. She would anxiously await her turn to play so she could prove her worth.

Lately though, she seemed contented to sit on the bench and cheer on her teammates. After all, she had worked a lifetime to get where she was. Rest was a welcomed relief.

Today's game was different. Her teammates were struggling as much as she was. The opponent seemed to have the momentum.

Lovey looked at the scoreboard. At the end of eight and a half innings, her team was behind by one run. It was a nail biter for the crowd. Lovey wondered why she couldn't muster up the motivation to defeat this rival team, an opponent she had faced before.

As the home team, she knew they had one more chance to win. She also knew it wasn't fair to expect her teammates to carry the full load. She should play her part but lacked the faith to trust in her abilities this go-around. How many times must she face this same adversary?

Before she could ponder the outcome of the game any further, Ben, her husband and coach, approached her. At 65, Ben was handsome with broad shoulders and a full-head of dark, heavily salted hair. He positioned his frame in such a way as to hover over Lovey.

She felt so proud of this man with whom she had shared a lifetime. She had a desire to brush a hand through his mass of hair, and maybe take him to a secret place where she might show him what he meant to her. Lovey laughed to herself. She was a woman in her sixties. She had no business entertaining such thoughts.

The idea was especially absurd at this juncture in her life, since the breast cancer she had fought so hard to conquer had made its fateful comeback. Still, with her husband of forty plus years standing so near and looking so dashing, she felt a latent stirring. It was as if her youth had somehow returned and the disease, which was once again robbing her of life, had vanished.

When Ben reached for her hand, she blushed. To cover up her flushed state, she said something foolish about the heat of the day.

Ben held her hand. "I'm playing you, Lovey."

Lovey was stunned, as if she didn't correctly hear him. "No, Ben. Another player would be better for the team. I'm very tired today and I'm sick. You know that. I don't have it in me anymore."

"Nonsense," he stated. "You're playing. So get ready. It's your turn to bat."

Before she could continue her argument, Ben walked onto the field and stood by third base. Lovey reluctantly looked at him, but he only gave her the thumbs up sign. She tried to smile but couldn't. The return of her cancer had shattered her confidence.

She looked in the direction of the stands and saw her two daughters cheering for their mom. Her daughters were the physical embodiment of the love Ben and she shared. Next to them were their husbands and children – Lovey's grandchildren. They called out to her.

"Go, Grandma! You can do this!"

Less assured than her family, Lovey made her way to the batter's box. Her legs were like rubber as she bent them into the familiar batting stance. Once more, Lovey was facing the possibility of dying from cancer. As she gripped the bat firmly in her hands, she was overcome with a renewed hunger to win this last battle and defeat, once and for all, this heartless monster called cancer. The pitcher threw his first pitch.

Strike one.

Lovey let out a whimper and once again looked toward Ben. He urged her to continue. She looked at her family watching from the stands. They were encouraging her, as well. The pitcher threw the second pitch.

Strike two.

Her heart felt defeated, and tears filled her eyes. Maybe this was a game she couldn't win anymore. Then, she saw an apparition from her past standing next to first base. She rubbed her eyes and blinked to make certain she wasn't seeing something that wasn't there. She knew he was an apparition. He was Thomas Jackson, her father, standing in front of her. She was elated. Though she knew him to be dead, he stood before her today as if real.

"Daddy," she whispered.

Dead almost twenty years, Lovey could scarcely believe he was standing before her. He held out his arms to her, just as he had done when she was a child.

Lovey, by chance, saw an opening between center and left field. She knew if she could manage a clean hit there, she could make it to first.

The pitcher threw his third pitch. Lovey never took her eyes off the ball. With all her might, she swung her bat and made contact. Just as she had planned, she hit the ball on the ground where it sped past the shortstop and through the opening between center and left field.

Lovey ran to first base and into the arms of her precious father. Her heart was filled with joy and love as she beheld him. They held each other tightly for some time before they broke their embrace. Certainly, he didn't look the way he had the last time she had seen him after his fatal heart attack. She noted that her father was once again agile and strong, the way he was when she was a child.

"Daddy," she said. "Is it really you?"

"It's me, honey."

"You came back to me." She wept, completely overcome.

"I had to be here for my Lovey. That was a strong hit. I knew you could do it. Now listen to me carefully, and I'll get you to second," said her father.

"Will I make it, Daddy? Will I get home?"

"I can't say, but I'm going to help you try."

"Promise you won't leave me again, Daddy."

Thomas Jackson stood solemn. "Know the game, Lovey. Do whatever it takes to win it."

Lovey heard the crack of the bat and her mind was brought back to the game.

She heard her father's strong voice directing her to second. "Run now, Lovey. Run as fast as you can."

Lovey ran without hesitation, never looking back. When her shoe touched the surface of second base, she felt as though she had once again thwarted fate.

She turned to face her father at first base, but he wasn't there. She looked for him on the field and in the stands. He was gone.

She was overcome by sadness and was inclined to give up on the game. Then, a gentle hand touched her shoulder. With tears streaming down her face, she barely had the presence of mind to turn around. Yet when she did, she saw her mother's warm smile. Exhausted, Lovey could do nothing but fall into her mother's arms.

"First Daddy and now you. Is this a dream or have I gone completely mad? Have I died and you and Daddy are here to direct me? Tell me, Mother, tell me what's going on?"

Rebecca Jackson held her baby girl. "I'm here to help you make the choice."

"Choice?" Lovey asked confused.

"To stay or leave."

"I want to live. I want to stay. Ben needs me. My children need me. My grandchildren need me."

"Sometimes," Rebecca said, "your love is proved more by leaving than by staying."

"How can that be? You left me, Mother. I never got over it. Was that love?"

"Had I stayed with you, my darling, I would have only given you more sorrow, more burden. It was best I left when I did. You grew to be strong, Lovey. You became a fighter. You must continue to be strong. You must continue to fight."

Lovey looked at her own battered body, a body which had once been something to behold. Now it was disfigured, mangled by a surgeon's knife. For nearly five years, the surgery had been a success. Yet, the invasive cancer made its return.

Lovey thought of her war with cancer. She had given everything to combat the disease.

What am I to give now? she thought.

Then, Lovey looked at her Mother, really looked at her. Her mother's body was whole once again, beautiful. She was restored, transformed.

"Mother?" Lovey speculated, more than asked. "The same illness that now grows inside me, once flowed through you. Yet, what I'm seeing is a whole woman, a woman unaffected by a heinous disease. How can this be? You were like me, butchered and marred."

"My darling, do not focus on me, but on the game. So long as you can still play, you must do everything you can to win. When the time is right, your body will be restored, but for now, the only thing to think about is reaching home."

"I want to be like you, Mother. I want to be whole again."

"Your spirit is whole, Lovey. Your heart is full. Please try. Please don't hesitate."

Just then, a ground ball was hit toward right field. Lovey saw the runner on first quickly move toward her at second base. She felt her mother's hands push her toward third base.

Without a moment's thought, Lovey raced ahead as if they weren't really her legs doing the running, but she was being controlled by something she didn't understand. As she neared third base, she saw

Ben motioning her forward. When she was almost there, she slid on the ground and felt the tip of her shoe touch the base. Then, she felt Ben's arms around her. Her shaky voice expressed her fear.

"You weren't paying attention to the game, Lovey. Your hesitation caused the runner behind you to be tagged out. Be alert, Lovey. This a game we can't afford to lose. There's no room for errors."

Lovey broke down in tears.

Ben's temperament faded. He gave her a warm smile of encouragement. "You're almost home, Lovey, but we must be smart. We must always be on guard."

When the next batter came on the mound, Ben signaled for him to bunt. He was the best bunter in the game. If anyone could get Lovey home, he could.

True to form, on the first pitch, the experienced batter bunted the ball toward first base. It was beautifully executed. Still, he couldn't beat the throw to first base, where he was called out. The inning now had two outs. When the batter was called out, Lovey was already halfway between third and home.

Should I return to third, the safer bet, or try for home? she thought.

There might not be another opportunity. Home was so near. Victory was so close she could taste it. With determination so characteristic of Lovey, she decided to continue toward home.

As she ran, her worn body betrayed her. She fell just feet before she reached home plate. She heard Ben and the crowd calling for her to get up and run. She heard the voices of her children and grandchildren from the stands. With all of her might she tried to get up, but she was too weak. By a stroke of luck, the first baseman's throw to home was inaccurate. The ball sailed behind the catcher. Lovey saw a glimmer of hope.

An inner voice screamed out to her, *"This is your last chance, Lovey. Get up. Get up."*

With every ounce of strength she possessed, she willed her broken body to stand. Ahead was home. Ahead was her cure. Behind her was her affliction, a world filled with sickness and despair. She had no choice but to fight. With a relentless driving spirit, she stood tall in the face of adversity and willed her body to move forward.

Each step was a struggle, weighted by her need to win this last war. Her breath caught in her chest. Images of those she loved and had loved filtered in and out of her consciousness. Ben. Her children. Her grandbabies. Her parents. Her brother and sister. And little Faith, her precious firstborn, her freckled-faced, red-haired beauty, who was only eight years old when a car struck her while she was riding her new bike. She had died in Lovey's arms.

Faith, Lovey's heart cried out. *My darling.*

Lovey was sure she heard Faith's faint voice calling out, *"Mommy, Mommy, I'm here. I'm here for you. Mommy, your Faith will carry you home."*

Lovely knew her voice so well. She had heard it a million times since her child's death, in her dreams and in her heart. *Faith.* Just as she was about to respond to her sweet daughter's beckoning call, Ben's strong arms were thrust around her waist, directing her toward home plate.

As absurd as it seemed at such a pivotal moment in the game, all Lovey could think of was to share with Ben she had heard Faith's voice. Faith was calling for her. Yet, she looked into his eyes and saw no joy in them. As they lumbered the final steps toward home base together, she could see he was fighting for both of them.

Her hand touched the base. She had made it home. She was safe.

As she was about to celebrate her defeat over the dreaded disease which possessed her day in and day out, she felt the catcher thrust the ball across her back. With all the dust flying and the excitement of the crowd, the umpire had difficulty making the call. Lovey's heart pounded with life as she waited, certain the umpire would declare, "Safe!"

It would all be official.

She heard a thunderous shout seal her fate as the official called out his decision.

"Out!" he roared. "You're out of the game, Lovey Spencer!"

Lovey argued in disbelief, "I was home! I was safe!"

Her words fell on deaf ears. Lovey turned to Ben, who was brushing the dust from his uniform. He was looking beyond her, not directly at her.

"Tell him I was safe, Ben."

There was sadness in Ben's eyes as he looked toward the stands where his children were. He quickly moved toward them. They had the same look of defeat on their faces. Lovey had lost the game.

She watched as they held onto each other for comfort. Lovey heard their mournful cries and ran toward them to assure them she was fine. She hadn't gone anywhere.

When she touched their shoulders, it was as if she didn't exist. She kept calling out their names, but they didn't hear her. They started to leave the ballpark and she ran after them but was stopped by a fence that hadn't been there earlier.

She fought hard to open the gate of the fence, but her efforts were in vain. When she tried to climb it, the barrier seemed to grow, spanning as far and high as she could see. There was no hope of reaching her family through the gate. She desperately looked around for another way out.

As if she were watching a movie, she saw her family fade away, to disappear in the horizon. Each member of her family was now broken, she knew. They thought her dead. She saw a groundskeeper clearing off the field to prepare it for another game and ran to him for assistance.

"I need to get to my family, but I can't find the way out of the ballpark," she said.

The groundskeeper kept on working.

Again, she beseeched him, "How can I get out of this field to get to my family?"

He stared at her confused. He was sure she knew the truth.

"I'm sorry. The only way off the field is to play your way out," said the groundskeeper.

"I did play the game. I was safe. I was home. The official made a bad call."

He grunted. "The official's call stands."

"But, where am I to go?"

He shrugged. "Couldn't say. My job is to prepare the field."

"Let me play the next game. Let me play once more. I know I can win this time."

The groundskeeper looked at Lovey with compassion. "I'm sorry, Lovey. This was your last game, your last chance."

Frustrated, Lovey kicked up red dirt. *Am I in some sort of dream-limbo I can't explain?*

That was when she witnessed the transfiguration of her body. She looked down to see her maimed form had been restored. She was a whole woman. She was new, just as her mother had become new. For a moment, she searched the field for her mother to share her glory with her. Her mother of all people would understand her elation.

Lovey felt free. She felt so alive. She fairly leaped. Impulsively, she began running the bases the way she had done in her youth. She never tired. She was turning summersaults and giggling like a sprout girl. She was a complete person. She was whole, not only physically, but spiritually, as well.

She shouted to no one in particular, "I won! I won!"

On the other side of the fence, a small child gleefully clapped her hands. Lovey stopped her antics to face the child. The child was dressed in white, and her sleeves had gold tips on them which glistened in the sun. Her long red curls shimmered in a golden light.

Lovey was mesmerized by the sight of her. She thought she should know this enchantment glowing before her. The girl's light was so intoxicating that Lovey could do nothing but stare.

The child called for Lovey to come to her. Her voice was sweet and angelic. Lovey remembered the gate and was suddenly saddened she couldn't get to the child.

Lovey called out, "I cannot come to you. The gate is locked."

"Try it again," the child instructed.

Lovey tried the gate one more time to find it was no longer an obstruction. She opened the gate and moved toward the child. She thought the child to be some kind of angel sent to help her.

As Lovely moved closer to the mirage, reality took over her spirit. Her heart was filled with complete love. She understood the truth of the moment. It was the truth of knowing life never ends, not for her, not for this precious gift standing before her.

When Lovey was close enough to touch the child, she took her hand. How well she recognized this angel had lived in her heart and dreams for so many years. It was her angel, her precious Faith.

Lovey fell to her knees. "Oh, my precious, darling. It's been so long. I've missed you so much."

Faith stroked Lovey's hair. "I really haven't been gone, Mommy. I've always been with you."

Lovey stood up slowly and caressed her daughter's beautiful face, her fiery red curls. "Faith, am I dead? Or, are you a dream, some sort of hallucination?"

"I am real, Mommy, but you are not dead. There is no death. There is only life. You are now in a new phase of your spirit's journey. Where we are going is the most wonderful place you could ever imagine. It's a place where sorrow and pain and disease do not exist."

"But what about those we love? What about those we leave behind?"

"Love goes where we go. Their love never leaves us, nor does ours leave them. Soon we will be with those we love, almost before we can miss them."

"I know how much I hurt when I lost you," Lovey expressed. "I almost didn't make it. How can I be sure those I leave behind will be all right?"

Faith smiled. "We have our little tricks to make sure those we love are all right. We will love them enough to make sure they will be okay, until it's their turn to join us."

Lovey took Faith's small hand and once again the joy of touching her firstborn after so many years overwhelmed her.

Lovey wept.

Faith fell into her mother's arms.

Lovey held her as if she would never let her go. Faith pulled slightly away and kissed her on the cheek. She brushed away her mother's tears.

"No more tears, Mommy. Come walk with me into the Light of Love. Love will give you understanding. Love will give your spirit peace."

Lovey nodded, already feeling the excitement of journeying to her new home. For a moment, she looked back at the ballfield. Without speaking, Faith understood her hesitation.

"Trust me, Mommy."

Lovey looked into her daughter's eyes. She was no longer a child, but a beautiful woman. She was a glorious vision. Lovey understood that time was a design symbolic of her past world. Here, in the Light of Love, time was unnecessary because there was no beginning or end.

Faith stood before her, an entrancing spirit, unlike anything Lovey had witnessed. Her daughter was love personified.

She saw in her daughter's face her own face, as well her father's face. There was someone else's face, as well. Lovey guessed it was the face of the One known as Love. It was the face of God.

When Faith smiled, she shone like beams from the sun, and her love for her mother radiated in her smile. She was confident and luminous.

Lovey had never seen anyone so breathtaking. It was difficult to discern where her image began or where it ended. Her light glowed intensely. Lovey marveled at colors she had never before beheld, which surrounded her child. The blues of her eyes shone like sapphires, but far more brilliant. The hues of her hair glowed *like* an inferno, a mixture of vivid reds, oranges, and golds.

Lovey was incapacitated by the wonder of what she was experiencing. There were no words to capture either her child's beauty or the beauty of the place which surrounded her. There were no feelings which could define her soul's wide field of emotions. Everything was so intense, so real. Lovey could not contain, nor did she have the desire to contain, the love which swept through her being.

As her daughter led her to her new home, Lovey was uncertain as to why she hesitated. She had no wish to ever return. Yet still, she was compelled to look back one last time. It was to let go of her last bit of doubt before she could leave this previous world behind.

There was one thing she had to know.

"Faith, my love, you are my beautiful angel. I do trust you," Lovey assured. "I do. It's just that I know I was safe. I know I made it home."

Faith's smile widened. "Yes, Mommy, you were safe. You did make it home."

The End

About B. Ellen Gardner

Ellen Gardner is a best-selling author of romance novels. Her novels reflect a variety of genres such as historical, contemporary, and mystery, all possessing a common thread - romance. A graduate of Texas Woman's University, Ellen has taught school for over twenty years and has been writing for as long as she can remember. Her novels include *Guardian Spirit*, *A Trail of Twenty Winters*, *The Lamplighter*, *Shae's Song*, and *When Warriors Cried*. When Ellen isn't writing or teaching, she enjoys the love of her husband, children, and grandchildren.

Website: www.bellengardner.net
Amazon Author Page: https://www.amazon.com/B Ellen-Gardner/e/B0083HROI8
Twitter: B Ellen Gardner/Author@BewGardner
Facebook: B. Ellen Gardner – Author

LITERARY FICTION: STORY 4

REPLACED

by Elizabeth Silver

It is on a bright afternoon in spring that Byron Monroe finds out he has been replaced. The day seems like any other. Byron returns to his shared dwelling after training all morning and afternoon. Upon arrival, he finds the house oddly quiet: no music playing, no discussions between the two beings with whom he lives. The energy leaves his step as he senses the change, his bag hanging lower on his shoulder as he enters the common room.

Mo and Dee, his two roommates, sit on the floor close to a small enclosure Byron has never seen. They greet him, but he scarcely hears, his attention fully on the unfamiliar object.

Mo speaks in a gentle tone saying things Byron doesn't understand. He often has difficulty understanding the language of these beings if there is something new involved or if he's distracted as he is now. Frowning, he moves closer, peering over the edge of the enclosure.

The creature looks back at him with small black eyes, wrinkled red skin, and a slightly elongated skull. Byron looks at Mo and Dee, who stare at it completely mesmerized. Byron then looks back to the creature, who regards him with disinterest. It makes an indistinct sound, claiming the immediate attention of Mo and Dee as if they are under a spell. Even the creature's nondescript scent seems to draw them in deeper.

Byron has lived with these beings for years. He has never seen the two of them so intensely focused on something that is so unaware of his presence. Feeling crowded and overwhelmed, Byron moves to his room, shutting the door behind him a bit too firmly.

Some hours later, it is Mo who brings a meal to him, a bribe to ensure his approval of the new creature. Byron eyes the tempting dish but turns back to the prototype building he is designing, refusing to concede. Dee enters the room after Mo retreats and tells him the creature will be with them from now on, and he should try to accept it into their dwelling.

Byron listens angrily. Mo and Dee hadn't even asked his opinion on bringing such a thing into the home they share. Even if the two beings are the ones who pay for the expenses, it is discourteous.

That night, Byron is awakened several times by the demanding shouts of the creature. He clasps his hands over his ears, gritting his teeth at the unbearable noise. It speaks in a language he doesn't know, but Mo and Dee seem to understand it and cater to its demands. Byron watches their movements through his cracked open door, frowning at the power the small creature holds over his roommates.

In the morning, Byron is tired and irritable. Mo and Dee don't seem to notice as he struggles to open a container, which is not meant for his hands, but for those of his roommates, who, though similarly built, are easily three times his size. He manages to finally open it, throwing a triumphant look in their direction, but it is lost on them. All they speak about is the new creature, chattering back and forth, discussing things Byron doesn't understand and using words he doesn't know.

Successfully excluding him from their conversation, they next try to convince him to carry the creature, explaining it is completely dependent upon them.

As suspected, it is a parasite. From what he gathers, the world the creature comes from has gravity so different from here it is unable to move by itself until it adjusts. It can't even lift its own head.

Byron, not wanting to risk being thrown into the creature's manipulative powers, repeatedly refuses any contact with it.

Had Byron been a more ruthless person, he might have reflected on ways to purge the dwelling of this parasite, considering how weak and dependent it is. He could never harm a living thing, though. He wonders if another in his situation might ridicule his passivism, but the thought doesn't alter his resolve. He will find another way.

His morning's frustrations are furthered when he has difficulty donning the uniform he must wear for daily training. Normally, either Mo or Dee assists him with the complex garment, but it takes them several minutes to recognize his plight today.

Dee moves to assist him, but Byron angrily pulls back, determined to demonstrate he doesn't need assistance from either of these two beings. He can accomplish this daunting task himself.

He relents, several moments later, as Dee reaches to help, again, more insistently. Byron doesn't respond to their farewells as he boards the transport, still frustrated.

The day is long and practicing the spoken and written language of these beings proves especially difficult. By the end of the day, he's done poorly in his training. His heart was not in it.

These past years, his two roommates had always made him their priority. They made sure he'd eaten and had his uniform on, ready for the long days of training which would prepare him for this world - a world which isn't made for him, but beings more like Mo and Dee. Now, this small red creature has taken his place and has complete control over them.

For the rest of the week, Byron tries to draw Mo and Dee's attention away from the parasite but to no avail. Trying to describe his concerns to the large beings is also fruitless, the language barrier proving too great. Byron attempts to get a sense of their thoughts on the creature, but he has great difficulty reading their expressions and voice tones, as usual.

By the weekend, Byron feels his resolve starting to slip as the sounds the small red parasite makes and its scent, become more familiar, enticing him to serve and protect it.

He knows he must leave before he is completely under its control, as Dee and Mo are. Perhaps he can come up with a strategy to open their eyes, but for that he needs a clear head. Knowing the two will try to stop him if they find out, he waits until well into the night before taking his bag and exiting the dwelling, leaving the home he'd happily shared with the two beings these past years. He wonders if they will even notice his absence.

Uncertain where he should go first, he decides on somewhere familiar: an inactive spacecraft. On training days during lunch, he has explored the scrapped ship many times.

Relieved the weather is mild, he climbs into the spacecraft's open cockpit. He sits for a long while, pondering his next steps, distractedly pressing the inoperative controls of the ship. He will have to find another dwelling and continue training if he is to learn the ways of this world and become independent. Once he no longer needs assistance from any being, he can never be replaced.

His thoughts eventually go back to his former companions. He wonders if perhaps he should simply return and continue with them, even though he's been replaced by the red parasite, which now draws all attention, energy, and affection Dee and Mo have.

He is still ensured food and shelter. Perhaps he can convince them, once and for all, the wrinkly red creature is using them. Or perhaps, he will fall under the parasite's spell too and be unable to resist servitude.

He considers the latter. If he is unsuccessful in convincing Mo and Dee and falls for the creature's manipulations, will he have enough free will to escape, again?

It is nearly dawn when Byron finally reaches a decision, descends from the spacecraft, and heads back to his dwelling. He must try, at least once more, to open Dee and Mo's eyes to the obvious truth about the creature; it is controlling and using them for its own ends. He owes it to them. They had been there for him these past years, and now he must risk the creature's brainwashing to save them.

The sun peeks over the horizon and the air is heavy with mist as Byron approaches his home. An unfamiliar transport is parked in front of the dwelling, and Byron pauses a moment to stare at the colored lights flashing from it, something he hadn't seen up close before. Most transports have lights with no color to them.

Entering the dwelling, he scarcely sets his bag down when Mo lifts him completely off the floor, tightly gripping him, speaking fast in high pitch tones. Dee is only an instant behind her, wrapping his long arms around them both.

Byron can sense their exuberance, and he knows, despite his doubts, they have noticed his absence even though it has only been hours.

He doesn't have the heart to leave these beings. Even if he has been replaced, there's still something for him here. He will either succeed in freeing them from the wrinkled red parasite or be brainwashed with them. Either way, he cannot abandon them again.

The being whose transport is parked outside leaves shortly after Mo apologizes to it. Mo and Dee animatedly pace back and forth, speaking in loud tones for the better part of an hour.

Byron knows he's being scolded and admits he should have at least attempted to write a farewell letter or record an audio message. His companions finally calm down and things return to the new normal: the red parasite ruling the house.

Byron Monroe holds up for another week before succumbing to the manipulations of the wrinkly red parasite, after which he, too, with Mo and Dee, unquestioningly serves the creature.

***

"How is Byron adjusting Mrs. Monroe?" The occupational therapist asks, watching as the little boy works on an impressive Lego building, one she is told he has been building for weeks.

Byron's mother smiles, shifting baby Maria in her arms. "When he came in and saw her in the bassinet, he wasn't very happy. The first couple of weeks were tough, but he's finally accepted her.

He was acting out initially because his father and I were not giving him as much attention. He even went outside, alone, in the middle of the night, which he's never done before. We've started locking the doors at night as a precaution, but he hasn't done it since."

The therapist nods. "Some abnormal behaviors are to be expected. He has always been the center of attention. Then, all of a sudden, he feels as if he's being replaced. Any child would feel that way, but with Byron's level of autism, it is much more difficult to accept change."

Mrs. Monroe nods. "He is such a sweet big brother now, helping me give Maria her bottles, and he loves holding her. He is also learning to be more patient when he needs help with his school clothes."

The therapist breaks in, "Is he still having trouble with the buttons?"

Byron's mother nods. "He's getting the hang of zippers, but the buttons are still too much for him. His teacher has done amazingly with his speech practice. He understands more and is talking better, but still has some difficulty when he gets excited."

Mrs. Monroe grins. "I am still Mo, and his daddy is still Dee. He is too used to calling us those names to change now. Byron isn't sure what to call Maria yet."

The therapist nods, scribbling notes on her clipboard. "Is he doing any better making friends at the playground or does he still just sit in the rocket ship?"

Mrs. Monroe sighs. "He still plays by himself, though last week the school bus driver told me he intentionally sat next to another little boy, one from his inclusion class."

The therapist nods, smiling and scribbling another note. "It sounds like he's doing really well. It isn't uncommon for autistic children like Byron to feel out of place, like they just don't fit in with the world. It's important to let Byron know, even though he's been replaced as the baby of the family, that he has a new role as a big brother, which is just as important..."

The End

About Elizabeth Silver

Elizabeth Silver was raised on her family's small farm in North Texas where she was homeschooled with her four siblings. As a child she loved books and began writing when her thirst for adventure could no longer be quenched through reading alone.

"I love to read. When you read you create a world in your mind no one else has ever seen or will ever see because you interpret words and descriptions like no one else can . . . I realized I want to write the stories that inspire worlds."

Expanding over several genres by her teen years–including Westerns, children's, non-fiction, science fiction, and others–it wasn't until after college that she began publishing her work.

Facebook	https://www.facebook.com/elizabeth.silver.37853
Instagram	https://www.instagram.com/author.elizabeth.silver/
Twitter	https://twitter.com/Elizabe64824553
Pinterest	https://in.pinterest.com/elizabethsilverbooks/
Domain	http://www.elizabethsilverbooks.com

PARANORMAL

Beyond the normal, paranormal directs us to observe and record phenomena and events, which are not part of our customary scientific understanding. Also referred to as supernatural, many subjects fall into this category of unexplained science.

In times past, it has been associated with the occult, demeaned by churches, and treated as something demonic by those who fear what they do not comprehend.

Many times it is explained away as something normal, simply because those that observe it are not willing to accept anything else. If they did, their world would crumble.

It is human nature to explain our surroundings, to seek to understand how the universe works. It is also in our nature to make our surroundings fit in our own universal box. Which do you choose?

James William Peercy

PARANORMAL: STORY 1

OLD SOULS AT THE ANTIQUE MALL

by Natalie Clountz Bauman

What do you expect to find in an antique store? Most likely, you would encounter many antique collectibles and old furniture items with the associated patina and dust. Often these stores are filled with nostalgic charm and an atmosphere, which brings back memories of happy times with family members long passed. What we do not expect to find are unsettling feelings and the appearance of the spirits of the departed.

When one approaches the Main Street Antique Mall in Denison, it seems quite inviting. It is a pleasant red brick building with a nice, dark red sign. There are many antique treasures to be discovered each day on two floors filled with booths. The employees are always friendly and helpful. Upon entering, there are two beautiful, round, mid-century light fixtures of yellow, red, blue and green left over from the old Jennings Furniture days.

It seems this cheery building may house more than just the antiques. Customers and employees at the Main Street Antique Mall in Denison have reported they have seen and/or heard at least one of the former owners of the building—owners who are no longer in the land of the living. There are also some encounters in the building with spirits, which engender very negative emotions.

According to the *Denison Press* in 1941, the original structure where the antique mall now sits was built in the late 1800s as a business college. It stood at Main and Fannin Streets where the Walter Jennings Furniture Store was later built. and was later converted into a hotel called "The Denison."

"The Denison" hotel had a fire in the early 1900s. (Do not confuse this early Denison hotel with the Denison Hotel which still exists today one street to the south.)

The main ghostly presence in this store is said to be Mrs. Mary Jennings Shirley. She was the daughter of a prominent merchant, Mr. Jennings. In the 1940s, this building was Jennings Furniture Store, at one time, owned and operated by Neil and Mary Jennings Shirley, who were themselves a prominent Denison couple. It was later sold, but many believe the affinity Mary felt for the place never left, even after her death. Unlike Elvis, it seems she never left the building.

To add further to the background of the story, she married Neil Shirley, a well-known band director for Denison Schools. Neil met his future wife, Mary Marie Jennings, when she was one of his band students. They did not start dating until she was in college. They were married June 29, 1941 in Denison.

Neil graduated from the University of Oklahoma in 1938 and was the first paid band director for the Denison School System. After Pearl Harbor, Neil joined the Army Air Corps, and was stationed in Independence, Kansas where his job was an Army Supply Sargent and the director of three dance bands for the military.

After World War II, he and Mary came back to Denison and joined Mary's father, Walter Jennings, in his furniture store until Mr. Jennings' retirement in 1984. In addition to the furniture store, Neil co-owned Better Television, which was the first cable TV system for the Denison area, and the second in the state of Texas. Mary died July 3, 2006, and her husband Neil died at the age of 100 years on April 19, 2016.

People shopping at the antique mall have reported feeling a rush of cold air and feeling the hair raising up on their neck right before they see Mrs. Shirley's image floating in front of them. People have heard footsteps walking when no one else was present.

Employees say this happens most on the secluded top floor. Many believe Mrs. Shirley's presence is most strongly felt on the third floor because many of her possessions still "rest in peace" there on the third floor.

It is also said Mrs. Shirley's spirit isn't the only one at the antique mall. Some people have seen a male presence wearing a top hat so clearly, they asked him a question, but received no answer. Others have seen a figure in gray and white with a little coat or frock who looked like a young, petite, Victorian woman, who then disappeared into the back wall where there were no doors.

None of the apparitions who have appeared in human form seem harmful, just old souls hanging out with the other antiques.

Mrs. Shirley has been seen in the company of a gentleman of late, where before she was seen alone. Since Mr. and Mrs. Shirley have now both passed on, perhaps they are both together in a place where they were happy.

The store manager of the Main Street Antique Mall is used to encountering strange things at work. Doors sometimes close on their own. On a regular basis, customers report feeling "a presence" in the store, especially in the corners of the building.

The store manager regularly goes to the third floor to move store stock, and in one large room, he experiences a presence, which he feels is male, watching him with disapproval. One day he accidentally entered a supply room which branches off this room. He will never enter it again (more about that later). Up on the third floor, people outside on the street have seen a woman standing in a window when no one is up there.

Every morning, the manager comes into the store early to turn the lights on and get everything ready for customers. However, this day in July 2017 was different. There was extraordinary activity before the store even opened. He was cleaning the outside of the windows with paper towels and just tossed the roll inside the door while he remained outside. The roll of towels, as they often do, took a notion to unroll themselves all the way down the aisle.

"Well fine," he thought.

He figured he would roll up the towels when he went back into the store. When he returned, the towels had mysteriously completely rolled up onto the roll, even though no one else was in the store, no one except Mrs. Shirley, of course.

There was no slope in the floor and no big fan running which could have rolled up the towels. She must have been a very tidy lady, impatient with the messy roll of towels lying on the floor!

After picking up the towel roll and returning it behind the counter, the manager saw an inexplicable flash of light in the mirror at the top of the nearby stairs. Even though there were no cars on the road with headlights to account for any possible reflection in the mirror, it was there.

When this happened, he felt an extreme chill as if all his hair was standing on end, complete with goosebumps.

If this wasn't enough, the manager proceeded to the back of the store, and a door closed on its own right in front of him and locked itself. After this happened, he proceeded directly outside to wait on the sidewalk for someone else to arrive, so he wouldn't be alone with Mrs. Shirley or whoever was doing this.

Most people who open and close the store give a friendly greeting to Mrs. Shirley. This engenders a good, friendly atmosphere and acknowledges her "ownership" of her space.

Mrs. Shirley is often encountered by customers, usually in corners, for some reason. Just come in and say "Hi, Mrs. Shirley."

However, it seems Mrs. Shirley is not always confined to the indoors. There may have been a sighting outside the building she usually inhabits, the Main Street Antique Mall (once Jennings Furniture Store.)

During the Denison Fall Fest event in October 2017, a ghostly woman and man, who appeared like living people, were seen outside. This author had a booth in front of the Book Rack bookstore on Main Street in Denison, and I spoke to a girl who is "sensitive."

Speaking to her was a very nice experience. She seemed completely sincere and had a complete lack of guile a young child possesses, which makes you trust them. After she told what she saw, I mentioned Mrs. Shirley. She had never heard the story about her and had never known ghosts were reputed to inhabit the Main Street Antique Mall. She merely related what she saw.

She and her family and friends said they were at CJ's Coffee shop next to the Antique Mall. At that time, the girl pointed out there was a white woman, in older period clothes with a flowery blouse, standing next to a darker looking man wearing a white shirt, watching the activities at Fall Fest. It seemed no one else could see them except for the girl.

Though they looked like real, solid people, she knew they were ghosts.

The two people seemed to realize she saw them. The man looked at the ghostly woman, pointed with his hand, and they both disappeared. They were at the northwestern corner of the Main Street Antique Mall, which had once been a college, a hotel, a mortuary and Jennings Furniture. (Did I not mention the mortuary before? More later.)

Just before Halloween, on October 26, 2017, a local TV news station sent a crew to the Main Street Antique Mall to record and investigate a story about ghosts appearing there. I was present, as well as the store manager, and we all climbed up to the third floor. We first came to the large room where the manager experienced the watchful, male presence. Off this room is the supply room. We know this because there is a very old sign on one of the doors labeled "Supply Room."

The manager said he would not enter this room. He said the one time he accidentally entered, he felt paralyzed for a while, and it was difficult to leave.

I looked and was unimpressed with the dilapidated room, which was full of old, dirty mattresses. It didn't seem spooky to me, or so I thought, until I entered it. I decided, why not? So, I went in and expected nothing.

Boy, was I wrong!

Two news reporters and I went into this room. Once we were

about ten feet inside, we slowly began to walk and to ask each other - "Do you feel dizzy?"

The whole time we were in this room, we felt dizzy and faint from lack of oxygen, like one does when on a high mountain. Once we left the room, we were fine. I did not expect to feel anything before I entered that room, but I did, and the others all said the same thing afterward.

We then went westward on the third floor to another room. This room was long and narrow with a beautiful, old, huge, angled, glass skylight in the roof, making the room very bright.

Once again, looking in, the room seemed fine, and we were not warned ahead of time or told anything about this room. We expected nothing. Despite the cheerful paint on the walls and the bright sunshine, the further we proceeded into the room, the heavier the atmosphere became.

It was as though something heavy was pressing on us from all sides, or we were entering a high-pressure chamber. It seemed very somber and very sad in this room. It seemed wrong to even speak in this room. It became worse as we approached the center of the room directly underneath the skylight, where the pressure and sadness became oppressive.

There is a large room beyond this one with many windows facing Main Street. Once we entered this room, we felt normal again. We stood and talked in this room for a long time, not wanting to enter the other room again, but we had to in order to leave. We all discussed how we had the same feelings.

The store manager filled us in on the history of the room and our feelings made sense. The two rooms had once served as a funeral home, and the room where the skylight is, was where the family would view the body, probably underneath the skylight in earlier years for better viewing. That explains the overwhelming sadness of the place.

It was unusual because everyone experienced it, whether they were "sensitive" to such things or not. The large room past the former "viewing room" is the room where the woman has been seen looking out the windows down onto the street. As we left, we once again had to pass through the "viewing room" and had the same sad, oppressive feeling. We had trouble drawing a breath and all sounds seemed muted.

The third floor is a strange place, and I experienced it myself with four others, having had the same experience. We stood around for a long time afterward, feeling the need to discuss our experiences like people do when they have been through a traumatic occurrence.

We didn't though, did we? Are there truly old souls inhabiting the antique mall on Main Street in Denison?

The End

About Natalie Clountz Bauman

Just a few years ago, Natalie Clountz Bauman was laid off from a job of 11 years due to failing health. As a middle-aged woman with multiple, incurable autoimmune diseases, they only get worse and more disabling. Some might have just given up, but she put her trust in God to work things out.

The doctor "prescribed" a hobby to help her with depression. It would also help her stay physically fit. She got busy doing something she loves, writing about history.

So far, she has written twenty-one Grayson County history books including *The Many Faces of Texoma's Red River* and *Quantrill's Raiders in North Texas Including the James Gang*. Her books are available on Amazon and Etsy, local venues, and on the author's Facebook page *Pottsboro Texas Genealogy - Old Times Remembered*. Natalie does historical speeches for groups, living history demonstrations, and is also an historical columnist for the *Pottsboro Sun* newspaper.

Her story is, never give up, and don't get discouraged whatever your challenges. If you keep swinging, you at least have a chance of hitting the ball out of the park!

https://www.amazon.com/Natalie-Bauman/e/B00O5JLWCC/ref=ntt_dp_epwbk_0
https://www.etsy.com/shop/PottsboroTexasBooks
https://www.facebook.com/PottsboroTexasBooks/
https://www.facebook.com/PottsboroTexasGenealogy/

PARANORMAL: STORY 2

LADY SCARLET

by Susie Clevenger

Two silhouettes stir the water as they slowly and erratically row, determined to keep pressing toward their destination. Six feet from the oars, an alligator watches the boat struggle through clinging water hyacinth, a bulbous water lily. Thankfully for the pair, the alligator, because of its full stomach, allows them safe passage.

"Granny Nell, I'm hungry."

The young girl knew she was in trouble when she saw Granny's face. Granny was soft and fluffy when she wanted to draw her in for a hug, but when Granny Nell was impatient, she could stone-eye her into a whimper.

"Oh hush, Winnie! You're a big girl. You've been braggin' to everyone about bein' ten years old! Besides, I fed you cornbread and honey two hours ago at my kitchen table," barked Granny.

Hearing a rumble in her stomach, Winnie whipped back, "But you told me when my tummy growls it's telling me it's time to eat."

"Well, it's gonna have to chatter a while longer. I haven't rowed my arms into knots to just turn around because your belly has a hunger twitch."

The fact Winnie had already put a burr in Granny's patience didn't stop her from testing it further, "Why are we out here in this old pirogue? You didn't tell me anything except we were borrowing Uncle Bo's boat for some night rowing, Mama told me anybody who goes out after midnight is just trouble-walking. I can't see much farther than the tip of this boat. I want to go back home."

"Stop it, Winnie! You're actin' like your Mama, scared of her own shadow. She sleeps with a night light on so bright she can read by it."

Getting as agitated as Granny, Winnie snaps back, "Mama doesn't like the swamp. I'm not supposed to be near it in daylight. She'll pitch a fit when she finds out you took me out here in the middle of the night!"

"Well, we won't tell her. It'll be our secret. I'm on a mission to find what the ghost people call the Lady Scarlet. Uncle Bo says there are rumors she shows up every new moon near Blue Tail Point. Ret Jenkins told me he was fishin' there last month and saw her standin' next to a cypress tree about six feet from the bank."

Winnie was already uneasy about what she couldn't see in the dark water, and now Granny was talking about a ghost.

"Who is she? Mama never talks about ghosts or anyone named Lady Scarlet."

"Winnie, your mama doesn't talk about a lot of things. No one knows who the swamp woman is. The locals here in St. Belviu call her Lady Scarlet because of the faded red dress she wears. It's rumored pieces of it are found in the ferns just above the water line. Tom Wilson, the stingy old gator man, claims he has a cigar box full of satin scraps he's collected over the years. He won't let anyone get a peek inside to see if he's tellin' the truth."

Winnie didn't want to hear any more about a red dress or a lady named Scarlet. Mama had ordered her to not go near the swamp, and she was sitting right in the middle of it listening to Granny Nell go on about a ghost.

"Granny, why do you care? She might be a witch or a swamp fairy. She might not like little girls. Let's go home! Besides, I don't even see the moon."

"Shush Winnie! Just because there are clouds in the sky doesn't mean the moon hasn't shown up. Wait, look over there in the cypress! I see red peekin' through the mist."

***

I haven't been in St. Belviu, Louisiana since I was a child, to be here in 2008 saying goodbye to my mother is surreal. I'm trying to bridge the gap between Granny Nell and Mama. Even in death they are pulling me apart. Granny's been gone for years, but I can hear her fussing about the dress Mama chose to be buried in.

Granny never liked to wear any shade of blue. She said no one had any business trying to compete with the color of the sky, how fitting to see my mother lying in a pale blue casket wearing an expensive navy linen dress.

Mama was too young to die. She was dogmatic when it came to her health checkups. But with no family history of breast cancer, she hadn't done a mammogram until she felt a lump in her breast.

She fought hard for two years, but cancer won. Tears mixed with anger pool on my cheeks. And as if prompted, I see a tissue placed in my hand by a woman who evidently had been patiently waiting to speak.

"Winnie, I'm so sorry for your loss. Your mother was always kind to me. When my son, David, broke his leg, she stopped by my house every day to see if she could help with anything. She was such a blessing."

Not sure if she had the right name, Winnie wipes tears as she says, "Mrs. Tompkins? I'm sorry. It's been a few years since I've been in St. Belviu and names and faces are hard to connect."

"Yes, I'm Ginny Tompkins. That's alright, hun. You are going through a lot right now. It will all come back to you in a bit. Perhaps later, we'll have a chance to chat."

My mother was a blessing? I thought.

That's at odds with the description of the woman who took me away from St. Belviu thirty years ago. Mama had found out Granny Nell had taken me out on the swamp to search for the Lady Scarlet.

When she discovered we were missing, she knew who to ask to find out where we had gone. She drove to Delta Bait to confront the owner of the boat, Uncle Bo. As soon as she stepped inside his shop and demanded to know where we were, he knew the only choice he had was to tell her the truth. Granny Nell had borrowed his pirogue for a trip to Blue Tail Point. Her second demand was for him to take her to find us.

Granny Nell didn't argue with Mama when she found us on the water. It was an eerily quiet exchange. With a promise from Uncle Bo to return to help Granny get back to the shore he helped me into his fishing boat and delivered Mama and I to the dock.

The entire ride home, Mama stewed about Granny defying her wishes. I heard her mumble about how red satin held too many secrets.

As soon as we got home, she told me to pack. She had connections in Houston, and we were going where people didn't breed tales from swamp legends. I knew from the tone of her voice I couldn't ask questions. I thought we'd head to Texas, Mama would get bored, and we'd move back to St. Belviu in a couple of months. Sadly, I hadn't figured in the depth of Mama's anger.

***

I can't believe Mama never dealt with Granny Nell's house. It's been thirteen years since Mama had her cremated in Houston and returned to St. Belviu for burial. Granny's will was simple. She left everything she owned and her small bank account to Mama. She stipulated if land and home were sold, I would get to choose any items I wanted from the contents of the house.

Mama made an overabundance of decisions with her own assets, as I found out through her will. She gave details for her funeral. The Lexus would be auctioned to raise money for a local cat rescue. Her stocks would be released to me two years after her death. The money in her bank account would be mine, but I was charged with managing a second account she had created to fund tutoring for at risk youth. And, I would own her luxury loft condo with the condition it could never be leased, only sold in the event I didn't want to keep it.

She didn't do anything with Granny's house or possessions except hire someone to oversee the upkeep of the property. I am so thankful Dennis Boyd called me yesterday to inform me he had been the caretaker and would meet me at the house today at 10:00 a.m.

I'm almost to Granny's driveway. Everything looks familiar, yet I feel like a stranger. Mama and I never came back here. She told me nothing ever changed, so there wasn't any reason to go back. She bought tickets to fly Granny to Houston for the holidays and two weeks in the summer.

Oh my, there it is! I thought. It is exactly as I remember.

I feel the disconnection dissolve. The porch swing still needs painting. The shutters are an odd, yellow-green color with a stenciled, pink rose border. Clay flowerpots filled with red geraniums line the sidewalk where Granny always hid a spare key, beneath the brick closest to the house.

Another car, a bright green '63 Chevy, pulls into the driveway. When the engine stops, an elderly man pushes open his door with a cane and steps out. He introduces himself as Dennis Boyd.

"Good mornin', Winnie Jane! I'd recognize you anywhere. You look just like your grandmother. Did you know she and I were best friends? Oh, she was a looker. She could dance an atheist right into her parlor, serve him chocolate cake, and get a promise he'd attend prayer meetin' before a fork reached his mouth. Well, I'm sure you don't want to listen to this old man chatter on. Let me unlock that front door so you can get inside."

I didn't want to forget anything. In my childish imagination, I believed it would be like I never left. This house and Granny had always been my anchor. After Mama took me from here, I felt lost. For days I wrote down every memory I had of Granny and the time spent with her.

I don't want to cry as Dennis finishes. If I start, I won't stop. The outside of the house looks just as I remember it, but what will it feel like once I cross the threshold, knowing Granny Nell isn't there to greet me? I hesitate.

"Winnie, are you comin' inside?" asked Mr. Boyd.

"Mr. Boyd, it is a bit overwhelming."

"That's understandable, Winnie. Comin' home isn't always easy."

I step through the open door into the scent of cinnamon. Granny always baked cinnamon cake when she knew I was spending the night with her. She would cut a huge slice, top it with vanilla ice cream, and then sit me at the kitchen table where she'd quietly answer questions about everything that occurred since my last visit.

Is it my imagination, I wonder, or is there really a cinnamon cake in the oven?

Before I can look, Mr. Boyd, walks to the stove.

"Yes, it is here as I requested. I had instructed a woman I'd hired to keep the house clean, Miss Jenkins, to use Nell's recipe for cinnamon cake and leave it in the oven on warm so it would be ready when you arrived. You can't believe the list of things your mother left to have ready when you made your first visit home."

"What? I thought. Mama didn't want to ever return to St. Belviu, or even talk about it. Why would she leave instructions to bake a cake?

"Winnie, your mother knew this would be difficult for you. She wanted to make it as easy as possible, under the circumstances. She wanted you to feel a bit of the love Nell always put into your time together."

Everything I've seen and heard since my return to St. Belviu doesn't add up to what I knew about my mother. She was a strong, opinionated woman who didn't care for what she called "fluffy" sentiments. Twice in one day, I've had someone share about my mother's kind-hearted gestures. I'm so confused.

I wonder, Did I ever really know my mother?

"Winnie Jane, I have another appointment, so I'll be leavin' you for now. If you have any questions, just call me. I'm so happy to see someone stayin' in this house for at least a little while. Nell may be gone, but she left a little heaven here."

***

I can't put it off any longer. There's a lot to do to get Granny's house ready for sale. I'll start in the living room with the china cabinet. It was the only place in the house I wasn't given free rein to investigate. Granny was afraid I might break one of her prized Dresden china pieces.

Goodness, the bottom right door doesn't want to budge. With another pull, I realize it is locked. That's strange. Granny never locked anything in the house. I have no idea where the key is unless it's on the key ring I saw hanging in the kitchen. I'll go get it to see if it works.

The key fits perfectly, and with a single turn, the door falls open. Inside are shelves filled with photo albums. I choose one and discover a black and white photo on the front with my mother smiling at me. I've never seen this picture before. She appears to be around sixteen years old. Her hair is long, straight, and pulled up in a ponytail.

Opening the photo album, I find a photo of my mother with another girl who looks the same age. The girl has a short, curly bob and the most engaging eyes. With each page, I turn I find more smiling images of them.

When I reach the end of the album, I discover a page less pristine than the rest. It holds one, terribly wrinkled photo of Mama and her friend in matching dresses. They are long and sleeveless with lace around the neck.

The water stains on the image make it hard to pick out details, but I can see part of the china cabinet over Mama's left shoulder, so I know it was taken in this room. An uneasy feeling settles over me. Why, after being comforted by Mama and her friend's obvious friendship in every other photograph, would this one put me on edge?

I slam the album shut. I have no reason to be freaked out by a photo. It's only paper and ink. There are plenty of other things to do around here. I'll work on cataloguing the china in the top of the cabinet for now.

***

After four hours, I've managed to get everything in the living room ready for auction. Per my mother's instructions, I've made a record of items to sell and to set aside. I'd like to keep everything, but my apartment isn't big enough. I have some tough choices to make.

The next room to inventory is my mother's old bedroom. I didn't spend much time in her room when I visited Granny. Mama's constant warning to stay out of her things carried over to her childhood bedroom also. Other than being sent on the occasional errand to open the shades in the room, I stayed away from it. Even now, I can't shake the impulse to leave it unopened.

I walk into the room to find myself pleasantly surprised. Even with the shade pulled, it was bathed in light. Across pale green walls, shadows from an oak tree outside the window place patterns with leaf silhouettes.

A poster of the Beatles hangs above the bed along with pinned watercolor paintings of butterflies. On a nightstand is a pile of books, and a silver ring engraved with the letter C. I pick it up, knowing it was my mother's. It always caused a stir when people asked about her name.

My mother was born Charlie Anne McCleary. My grandfather had named her. He loved Charlie Chaplin and was insistent his child would be given that name whether it was a boy or a girl. Secretly, I think my mother loved the attention.

I place the ring in my pocket, knowing I couldn't part with it. I continue around the room writing down items until I reach the closet. Making a mental note to donate the clothing, I casually push aside hangers until I reach the back of the closet. A final hanger holds a long, red satin dress.

It is exactly like the one in Mama's photo album. She and her friend had been wearing matching dresses. Reaching for the dress, I feel goosebumps form along my arms as I watch the fabric move before I even touch it.

I pull back my hand and step away from the closet. Turning around, I look to see what could have caused it to move. There's no breeze because all the windows are closed. Unnerved, I decide I've spent enough time in the room for the day. I return to the living room with my list.

I walk to the china cabinet to take another look at the tattered photo. I'm sure it was in the plastic sleeve when I looked at it before. But now, it is loose and lying on top of the covering.

My mother and her friend look so happy. I hadn't noticed the wrist corsages. Tiny bud roses curl around both girls' left wrists. My mother, as far as I knew, never wore anything on her left wrist. She said it was uncomfortable, restraining.

I am certain Granny didn't take the picture. Every time she tried to snap a photo of two people, she managed to take it off center leaving someone partially cut out of the image. I wonder if Mr. Boyd would know anything about the photo, and who the girl might be. He said to call him if I had any questions. It's still early. I'll call.

"Hi, Mr. Boyd, I was looking through a photo album with pictures of my mother and another girl. She has short curly hair, the most intriguing eyes, and is the exact same height as my mother. Do you know who she is?"

"Her name is Idona Winston. She and your mother were best friends. They spent every moment together. It was so sad when Idona disappeared the night of the high school spring formal in 1968. Charlie was never the same after that."

What? I wonder. *Mama had a best friend who disappeared? Neither Mama nor Granny ever talked about anyone named Idona*, I think to myself.

I know Mr. Boyd was Granny's best friend, but he wasn't the only one who knew about the girl's disappearance. The whole town would have known. Again, why didn't anyone tell me?

Mr. Boyd continues, "Hun, it was so tragic. They were a sight in those red dresses. It was their sophomore year of high school. Charlie and Idona were a bit mischievous. There'd been so much fuss about proper formalwear for the event. A letter was mailed home from the school to parents statin' girls' dresses should be modest and can't go above the knee.

Since it didn't mention color, your mother suggested red. Nell talked to Idona's mother and between them they decided to let the girls make their dresses out of red satin. They were all giggles when

Nell and I watched Tim Carson take their picture before the three of them left.

It was two hours later when your mother called Nell from the principal's office cryin' she couldn't find Idona. Charlie told Nell shortly after they arrived at the school Idona had to go to the restroom. Your mom lost track of time while talking to some of her classmates. When she looked at her watch, she realized it had been almost an hour since she last saw Idona.

She searched the restroom and as much of the school as she could. She finally approached Tod Strum, the principal at the time, and he and the staff did a search of the school and parking lot. After an hour, they determined Idona wasn't anywhere on the property."

Feeling angry and numb, Winnie asked Mr. Boyd, "Why didn't Mama or Granny tell me about this? I thought Granny Nell told me everything. She always emphasized the importance of family history. I can't fathom why she would leave something this tragic out of our conversations."

He quietly answered, "You were so young when you left St. Belviu. I suppose Nell thought it should come from your mother when the time was right."

"My mother didn't talk a lot about her high school years. She simply passed over it saying it was boringly normal. I don't find anything normal about the story you shared with me."

"I don't know her reasons, Winnie Jane. When Idona couldn't be located at the school, the principal called the sheriff. He and his officers searched the school and grounds again but couldn't find a clue as to her disappearance. For weeks, they combed the area, followed a few leads in attempts to find her, and finally gave up.

Some in the community felt Idona ran away. Charlie was sure that wasn't true. She carried a lot of guilt about lettin' her out of her sight so early at the dance that night. Everyone tried to comfort her. There was no way she could have known anything would happen to Idona. After about a year, Charlie quit talkin' about Idona altogether.

Personally, I think she never stopped blamin' herself for Idona's disappearance, especially since someone saw a girl in a red dress near the backroad gator hunters use. The hunters launch their boats at Blue Tail Point, and Idona was scared of the swamp."

Still trying to process what I learned, I ask one last question, "You mentioned Tim Carson. Is he still in the area? Is there a way to reach him?"

"Tim's still around. He owns a tourist business called, Swamp Flight. It is located on Jefferson street next to Tinner's Bait Shop.

***

Awakened by loud crowing, I look at the clock to find it is only 5:00 a.m. I had forgotten Granny always had at least one rooster on the place. Feeding the chickens and gathering eggs was my responsibility, whenever I stayed overnight. If it is truly like Granny ran the place, it is up to me to get dressed and head for the barn. When Mama said she wanted me to feel at home, she didn't have to include chickens!

Grouchy, I stumble to the back porch to discover a wicker basket hanging from a nail beside the door. Grabbing it, I step out into a beautiful sunrise. I should have known I wouldn't need to search for it. Granny had a place for everything. Once she determined what went where, it never changed. In Houston, I had few opportunities to see mornings like this. Pesky rooster, be thankful you get amnesty this morning!

With this chore done, I walk to the barn to fill a bucket with feed. As expected, the feed, scoop, and bucket are sitting on an oak barrel next to a horse stall.

Reaching for the scoop, I notice a calendar on the wall. Below an image of sun-bleached moon cycles is a page from the month of April 1978. Written in my grandmother's handwriting, I read the words, full moon, on the 23rd.

Tiny, electric sensations pulse through my body. I look again to make sure it was a calendar page from 1978. My eyes hadn't deceived me. I am staring at the exact date, exact year my childhood was turned inside out.

Anxious, I look at the date on my phone, April 18. Tomorrow, April 19, will bring a full moon! Almost thirty years to the day, I am standing where Granny Nell marked the date to search the swamp for Lady Scarlet. And, she is telling me it is my turn to travel to Blue Tail Point to search for the illusive woman in red.

I must find someone to take me to the swamp tomorrow night. Mr. Boyd told me Tim Carson owned a tour business called Swamp Flight. I return to the house to get my purse and keys.

I pray he says, "Yes."

***

Driving down Jefferson Street, Swamp Flight was easy to find. I park the car and try to calm myself. I don't know how to ask a total stranger about a night in 1968 or plead with him to take me out beneath a full moon to search for someone, or something, I'm not sure even exists. The worst he can think is I've lost my mind.

With that bit of non-encouragement, I open my car door, take a deep breath, and walk toward the door of the business. Once inside, I approach the counter and ask, "May I speak to Mr. Carson."

"Well, Miss, you are talking to him. What can I help you with?"

"My name is Winnie McCleary. My mother was Charlie McCleary."

Before I can say anything else his demeanor changes, the pleasant smile fades into a somber expression. He steps back from the counter and looks toward the street.

"I know you don't know me, but I've been informed you knew my mother and her friend Idona Winston. Do you mind if I ask you a few questions about them?"

He stands there silently staring at me. I anticipate an emphatic 'no' when his shoulders slump, and he begins to speak.

"I don't want to discuss it here at the counter. Let me speak to Don, and I will take you to my office."

Now that I'm here, I feel nervous about bringing up a tragedy he is reluctant to relive. I hope he can give me more information. Tomorrow is a full moon and finding Granny's note can't be a coincidence. She or someone is telling me to search for Lady Scarlet tomorrow night.

He offers me a chair and takes a seat at his desk, "Now, Miss McCleary, what questions do you wish to ask?"

"I hate to be so blunt, but do you know anything about the night Idona disappeared. I was only recently informed about the tragedy, and I don't know much, other than she disappeared from the spring formal in 1968."

He shuffles the papers on his desk and turns away from me to look out the window. I am certain he doesn't want to answer me. Just as I begin to believe this is a dead end, he begins to speak.

"There are so many things about that night I wish I could forget, I wish I could change. Your mother, Idona, and I were good friends. For a long time, I thought of the three of us as simply buddies who enjoyed being together. Then all of it changed.

I came to realize I was in love with Idona. I knew she was warming up to a relationship with me. We started spending time together, alone. It felt so right, I decided to ask her to be my date for the spring formal.

She told me, she and Charlie had a plan to put a shock factor in the event by wearing matching, red, satin dresses. They thought the school administration had been too prudish in their demands about dress length and style.

She laughed when she told me she couldn't go with me because they wanted to see the sponsors' faces when they walked into the auditorium together in identical dresses. Idona equated it to their contemporary version of Hawthorne's *Scarlet Letter*.

I was hurt she brushed aside my invitation so easily. At that point, I made the decision not to attend the dance."

"But Mr. Boyd told me it was you who took the picture of them and the three of you left Granny's house together to attend the dance."

"You're right. I did take the picture. Even though I was hurt, I wanted to see them in their red dresses. I promised to drive them to the school. I dropped Idona and your mother at the front entrance and drove away.

I had another reason not to attend. I had bragged to my friends I was going to take Idona Winston to the spring formal. After she turned me down, I didn't want to face the ribbing I would receive when it became obvious she wasn't my date.

It was later in the evening I found out she had disappeared. I volunteered to help search for her, but the police turned me down. I was placed on a list of those who had seen her last."

Tim Carson was a suspect? I thought.

I wasn't prepared for that. I became aware I was alone in a room with a stranger who was and may still be a suspect in Idona's disappearance.

I look up to see Tim standing at his desk. I knew at that point I didn't want him to take me to Blue Tail Point. From the looks of what I saw in the short time I was in the shop, he had a large touring business. There were posters everywhere about various tours provided.

I continued in my thoughts, Surely there are other guides who could escort me tomorrow night.

"Mr. Carson, do you have someone who can take me to Blue Tail Point tomorrow night."

He fires back at me, "No, Miss McCleary I don't have anyone. Neither I nor my employees take tours to that location. I suggest you stop by Swamp Haunt to book an excursion. You can find it on Riley Road at the north end of town. I believe you can find your way out."

I've never been one to hide my emotions. From the twitch of his cheek, I know he can see my opinion of his rude dismissal when I glare at him as I leave. Taught by my mother and Granny to be polite, I swallow the words I want to say, and leave him with my gratitude for answering my questions.

Not ten steps beyond the office door, the employee I had seen Tim talking to earlier steps out from behind the sales counter and reaches for my arm. Before I can react, he drops his hand and quietly speaks.

"I'm sorry. I didn't mean to startle you. My name is Don Trent. I am Tim's business partner. I wasn't eavesdropping, but the walls are thin here, and I heard you say something about Blue Tail Point.

I really don't think you should go there. No one locally will go there anymore, except Bob Dupre over at Swamp Haunt. It was once a prime spot for alligator hunters because it was so secluded. It was common for them to come back with at least one huge alligator each hunting season.

The old gator hunters kept feeding the legend about seeing a woman in red walking along a cove at Blue Tail whenever there was a full moon. I laughed myself when they would come in at Duff's to sell their catch with a new story about the woman they called, Lady Scarlet. I thought it was just another part of their fish bragging.

All the humor ended fifteen years ago when Tom Wilson's son found Tom in his boat with knife in his heart. When the coroner began his investigation of the body, he found a small piece of red satin on the tip of the knife.

The authorities spent months trying to find a motive and the killer. The murder was never solved. With Tom's murder, any interest in hunting Blue Tail Point dwindled. Rumors spread hunting at the Point wasn't worth the trip because no one could catch even a small alligator there anymore. Frankly, I think it is fear that keeps them away."

"Thank you for sharing your concerns. I admit it does sound ominous. As I'm sure you heard, I have questions about Idona Winston's disappearance," said Winnie.

"Tim has been my best friend since grade school," Don Trent continued. "I will do all I can to not have him torn to bits about that night again. Good day, Miss McCleary. I won't wish you luck. There is nothing lucky where Idona Winston is concerned."

***

Swamp Haunt certainly looks the part from the outside. Torn window screens droop from tattered window frames across the front of the building. A neon sign sporadically flashes 'Open' above a small porch wrapped in dying ivy. While debating whether to enter the business, a man opens the door who looks exactly like Granny Nell's friend, Uncle Bo!

"Hello! Good thing you caught me before I left. I was taking off a little early to get some work done at home before tomorrow. A full moon is always busy around here. Step inside pretty lady, and I'll see what I can do for you."

This jovial man looks and sounds so much like Uncle Bo I can't move, let alone speak. Unaware of my dilemma or perhaps because I wasn't moving, he steps aside to hold the door open for me to enter.

"So, what brings you to my business?" he asks.

"Um, I'm sorry. You look just like Uncle Bo who ran a bait shop called Delta Bait years ago. I know you can't be because he's dead. I'm a little shocked."

"I have good reason to look like him. I am his son, Bob. When I was younger, I didn't favor him at all, but when I turned thirty-five, I began to age right into his spitting image"

"I really thought I was going mad," Winnie continues. "I didn't know Uncle Bo had a son."

Bob grins and teases, "No, you aren't crazy. In my business it's a plus. I've got you seein' a ghost before we're even on the swamp. It makes me the walkin' dead.

Dad and I didn't get along very well. When I was thirteen, I moved in with my aunt Bertie. I never spent much time at the shop even when I was younger."

His infectious laugh is calming. The initial shock subsides, and I regain my composure.

Cautious after my encounter with Tim Carson, I state the reason for stopping at his business. "I want to go to Blue Tail Point tomorrow night. I've heard stories about the lady in red. I've never been one to believe in ghosts, but my curiosity is getting the best of me. Can you take me?"

"Hun, I'm familiar with the story. It's been stirrin' people up for a long time. I have a buddy who can handle this month's ghost tour. I'll send him to Bayou Bend and take you personally to Blue Tail. I know more about the place these days than anyone else since I am the only one who goes there now. Meet me here tomorrow night at 10:00 p.m."

Anxious, relieved, elated, I drive away knowing I have a plan to bring some closure. I don't know if I will see a ghost or solve a mystery. What I do know is I have to try. There will be no 'what if' when I go back to Houston.

***

M̲y mother's red dress and photo album are in the bag under my arm. I'm hoping, if the woman is Idona, she'll respond.

"There you are! You're early. That's great. The sooner we get out on the swamp beneath this full moon, the better we can take advantage of its light," Bob said as he opened his truck door.

The drive to the boat launch is beautiful. Nights like this, Granny would take me for a moon walk. She'd tell me it was time to drink from the big dipper, count stars, and watch the moon play hide and seek within the Spanish moss hanging from the live oak trees. Confident I'm doing the right thing, I say a quick thank you to the universe when we pull up to the dock to unload Bob's boat.

"Watch your step. The moon is a great night light, but it can play tricks with your eyes." Bob pointed. "Put your bag in the wooden box to the right."

"Thank you for doing this," I said. "If the lady in red is real, I hope to see her tonight."

"I hope you do too." said Bob.

On the way to Blue Tail Point, Bob shares, "In this spot in 1946, Jim Thibodaux went out alone to gator hunt. He reached in the water to bring in a 13-foot alligator, slipped overboard and the beast killed him. Some boys out giggin' frogs discovered him wrapped in his own gator line with a single, large bite in his chest. They know it was a 13-foot gator because when the police came out to retrieve the body, the beast was swimmin' next to Jim carryin' the yellow ribbon Jim used to locate the bait pole. Gossip around town is you can hear Jim moan on windless nights when you pass by here."

Winnie responds with, "Bob, that sounds like a tall tale to me."

"It does? It's all about what you want to believe. I am in the ghost business."

We both laugh at his comment. The slight breeze, which accompanied us on the ride, stopped. Instead of feeling warmer without the wind, I rub my arms trying to dispel the chill.

"Blue Tail Point is around the bend. I will pull up as close to the tree line as I can. Debris along the bank can be treacherous to a boat rotor," said Bob.

Winnie speaks to herself, "This could be my chance to find answers or be content with my efforts."

"We're here," said Bob. "Take a deep breath and prepare to wait. Ghosts don't appear on command."

I adjust to the slight rock of the boat as I reach for my bag. Untying the knotted closure, I take out my mother's photo album as well as her dress. If Lady Scarlet is Idona Winston, these items will have meaning to her. I am about to explain them to Bob when I find the congenial boat captain is gone. Bob is now a sinister, angry man.

"I've seen that dress before. Idona Winston was wearin' one just like it when she disappeared. Unless a dress can reincarnate itself, where did you get that one?" asked Bob.

Afraid, I force myself to respond, "It's my mother, Charlie McCleary's dress. She and Idona were wearing matching dresses the night Idona disappeared."

"Really? I only saw Idona in one. She was a looker. When I saw her through the front door of the high school, I felt it was my chance to get to know her. The tart snubbed me when I approached her so I thought a ride in my truck might warm her up. She was a hell cat when I drug her across the seat. She fought harder when I brought her here."

Terrified, I know I must put distance between myself and Bob! Without thinking I dive into water a few feet from where the boat is anchored. Winded, I swim to the shore and claw my way up the edge of the bank.

Bob is in the water making his way toward me shouting, "I couldn't even wrestle a kiss out of Idona. We both fell into the water, and she went straight down with the weight of her red dress. I pulled her out by her hair and drug her to the shore. I thought she'd be grateful enough to give me a reward, but she had some scratch left in her.

I slapped her, and she fell against a cypress root. I didn't stay to see if she was dead or alive. I swam back to my boat with plans to check on her the next day, but a storm blew in. After it cleared, I didn't bother to come back to check on her.

You can join her in hell Winnie! I'll pass around the story I didn't want anythin' to do with your crazy ghost hunt. No one will connect me to you. You'll be another ghost added to my tour."

I struggle to climb the bank's slight incline. I reach for a cypress root and look over my shoulder to find Bob's no longer following me. My heart pounds in my chest when I seem him watching me from the boat deck. He doesn't say a word when he walks to the stern to start the motor. In a hideous cat and mouse, he revs the motor, then lets it idle for what seems like an hour but is only a few minutes. Without a glance in my direction, he rises to free the anchor, returns to his seat and leaves.

Exhausted, I fall on the ground. There's no time to rest. Bob could come back at any moment, so it's vital I find a place to hide. I need shelter. The only thing I have is Mama's red dress I somehow managed to drag to the shore with me. I rise to a seated position to see a red glow moving toward me. Alarmed, I prepare to stand when a soft warmth gently presses me back to the ground.

I hear a voice coming from the red mist telling me her name is Idona. Tears begin to pour down my cheeks. I don't know if I'm hallucinating.

Quietly, she speaks to me again, "I've been waiting for someone one to find me. You look like Charlie, but you're much older."

Still unsure of my grip on reality, I answer, "My name is Winnie McCleary. Charlie was my mother."

Mama's dress begins to rise from the ground beside me. Before I can pull it back to me it joins the red mist. Both rise and fall in a rhythmic motion. When they stop, lace is the only thing left of my mother's dress.

A slight breeze from the mist ruffles my hair. I'm certain it's Mama. In her few tender moments when I was young, she would run her hands through my hair and tell me I was her blessing, her strong little girl.

Realization floods me, Mama brought me back to St. Belviu to find Idona. She'd have no peace in death without it. Mama knew if there were any clues in Granny's house, I would find them. Also, I know I wouldn't have found the lady in red if Granny hadn't left a message through her calendar.

I don't want to let Mama go, but I must. She and Idona have suffered too much in life and death not to be given freedom. Bawling, I place my hands into the mist and speak, "Mama, Idona, you are no longer bound to pain. You are free to rest in peace."

Like smoke from a snuffed candle wick, the red mist slowly rises toward the tree canopy above me. Feeling weightless, I turn my eyes to watch the swamp water sparkle in the moonlight.

The sound of a boat in the distance turns my reflections to fear. I start running toward the woods. Could it be Bob returning to make sure no one finds me? I know the truth about Idona's disappearance.

Oh God, I think. Is he going to kill me?

Terrified, I claw my way through limbs and brush not caring about scratches or direction. I hear the boat stop at the shore I just ran from. Tearing my shirt free from a thorn, a searchlight crawls through the shadows around me. I hear someone shout my name, but it isn't Bob.

"Winnie! Winnie, where are you? It's Tim Carson. Please Winnie, if you can hear me, let me know where you are!"

Tim Carson? Why is he here? How does he know Bob left me?

Tim calls out again, "Winnie, please answer!"

Not having any reason to trust him, but afraid not to, I make my way back toward the water. Once I reach the edge of the bank, Tim jumps into the water and swims to the ferns below me.

"Can you make it down to where I am?" he asks.

Wobbly, I assess my strength and answer, "I think I can, if I take it slow."

When I'm close to Tim, he reaches for my hand to help me into the water. Together, we swim the short distance to a boat where an elderly man helps us onto the deck.

Too weak to ask questions, I wait for someone to speak.

"Winnie, I'm sorry I was so cold to you when you asked me to bring you here. This spot, with its rumors of a scarlet lady, dredge up too much pain.

There hasn't ever been any proof Idona was ever at Blue Tail Point. After I sent you away, I went over every detail I could remember of that night. Then, something struck me I hadn't considered before.

When I drove away from the school, I saw Bob Dupre in the school parking lot. I knew it was odd because he never attended anything at the high school other than classes. I brushed it off because I was still aching from Idona's refusal to be my date. I wasn't sure if it meant anything when the memory resurfaced.

The man who helped us into my boat is, Trey Fontain. He is a retired police officer. He was a young cop assigned to assist in gathering information when Idona disappeared. He knew the case well, so I called him to find out if my observation meant anything."

"Miss McCleary," Trey said, "Idona's case has haunted me since I was first assigned to it. I had a strong suspicion whoever did it was local, but every lead I was given was a dead end. My biggest regret when I retired from the department was leaving without solving her case. When Tim called me, I jumped at the chance to see where this would go. You don't have to worry about Bob Dupre. There are police at the dock waiting for him. Do you have anything you can share about what happened?"

"I hired Bob to take me to Blue Tail Point. As a result of seeing my mother's red dress, he admitted he had abducted, assaulted, and left Idona Winston to die here. He had the same plan for me."

"Red dress? Where is it?" asked Trey

I am too tired to even attempt to answer that question. I ask Trey, "Can I go home and change into dry clothes?"

Trey quickly answers, "Sorry, Miss McCleary you can't. I must take you to the police station, so you can give a statement. The sheriff needs to get as much information from you as he can so Bob Dupre can be charged with your abandonment to cause harm and the disappearance and death of Idona Winston. Plus, Tim told me the story about the red satin dresses. This just might lead to solving the murder of Tim Wilson. Red satin is part of the evidence collected from his body. I am beginning to believe Idona wasn't Bob's only victim."

All three of us are silent as we travel back to the dock. Ironic or by chance, fog begins to form on the swamp. When we turned the curve toward the dock, flashing police lights turn the mist red.

Tim broke the silence with a question, "Why does the air smell like cinnamon?"

I smell it also. Granny is here. She's letting me know she's proud of me. I'm sure Granny had her suspicions about the lady's identity, although she couldn't prove it. The town and its people had as many questions as my family did. May we all find peace with the answers.

The End

About Susie Clevenger

Susie Clevenger is an author, poet, and amateur photographer. She was first published at the age of fifteen in *Missouri Youth Write*. She is author of the poetry collections, *Dirt Road Dreams, Insomnia's Ink,* and *Where Butterflies Pray.* Her work has been featured in, *The Creative Nexus, Poetry & Prose Magazine, The Brinks Gallery, The Global Twitter Community Poetry Project, Journey of the Heart,* and *Poetry as a Spiritual Practice.* She is a member of the Academy of American Poets and The Poetry Society of Texas. Susie resides in Houston, Texas with her husband, Charlie.

https://www.susieclevenger.com
https://www.facebook.com/surie.clevenger
https://about.me/susieclevenger
https://www.amazon.com/Susie-Clevenger/e/B00AQNQWTO%3Fref=dbs_a_mng_rwt_scns_share
https://twitter.com/wingsobutterfly?lang=en
https://www.goodreads.com/author/quotes/6863345.Susie_Clevenger

PARANORMAL HORROR

As we have mentioned, paranormal, beyond the normal, directs us to observe and record phenomena and events, which are not part of our customary scientific understanding.

Horror is the attempt by the writer to disturb the reader, shaking them from their everyday existence and allowing them to step into another.

The combination of both is generally associated with the occult, demeaned by churches, and treated as something demonic.

Here we have tale of those things that do go bump in the night but may be more than our imagination.

James William Peercy

PARANORMAL HORROR: STORY 1

WAKE

by Miracle Austin

*W**hat a cruel and disrespectful teen girl!*

That's probably what you'll think in the beginning. Go ahead and judge me, but I bet you'll think differently in the end.

Lucille Night, my great-aunt, died twenty-four hours ago and ruined what would've been the best weekend of the year—my thirteenth birthday celebration.

My name is Judee Lee Tucker.

Six weeks ago, I won a school contest where I scored two, all-access passes with photo-ops of choice for *Garga-Con*, the biggest comic convention in Texas. This was the year I thought I'd finally meet Henry Cavill, a.k.a *Superman*, my favorite superhero, with my bestie, Sadie Hightower.

On Thursday morning, I decided to break the bad news to Sadie before class. She was sitting on the steps near the library reading *Superman Vol 5: Under Fire* by Scott Lobdell. I took a few deep breaths as I approached her to sit down, while slipping my fuchsia and black *Smallville* backpack off my left shoulder.

Sadie placed her book facedown next to her.

"I'm so excited about Saturday. We're going to make the most epic memories," she shouted while tapping her feet in a rapid, rhythmic beat on the concrete and whistling the *Superman* theme song.

Lowering my head, I said, "Yeah, about that. We need to talk."

"Why?" She clutched the top of her backpack and stopped.

Staring down at the cracked pavement for a few seconds before looking into her eyes, I mumbled, "Something happened."

"What? . . . Are you okay?"

Sadie's eyes didn't move until I shared why I had to bail on her.

"I'm fine," I continued. "It's just my great-aunt died, and my mom is making me attend the funeral, which happens to be this Saturday."

"Oh, . . . Sorry about your aunt." She bowed her head toward her chest.

I finished, "Just hate that I won't be attending the con with you and meeting you-know-who."

"I understand, Judee," she said, releasing a long sigh.

Leaning in closer to her, I asked, "Hey, you're still going to have an awesome time and post pics, right, Sadie?"

"No, it won't be the same without you. I'm not going."

"You have to! When will you get another chance to meet Superman?"

"Never, but if you're not there, what's the use?"

"So, you're going to let the tickets just go to waste?" I screamed out. Other kids started staring in our direction.

Sadie shrugged her shoulders. She dropped her book inside her backpack, stood up, and said in a low tone, "I guess."

"Seriously, Sadie! You gotta be kidding me." I took a few steps back.

"Nope. Just wouldn't be right going without you." She started to walk away.

I grabbed her arm. "Hey, would you just go for me?"

Her eyes focused on the ground for a minute before she said, "I don't know."

"Think about it."

"Okay."

We went opposite directions. I watched Sadie head to her science lab, and I shuffled, almost in slow motion, off to my computer class.

***

During our lunch hour, over a greasy burger and cheesy fries, I finally convinced Sadie to attend and take her younger brother. She promised to take a photo of Henry by himself and get his autograph for me.

My mom contacted the school office later that day to share I would be out of school on Friday, due to the funeral services.

I tried to focus in my classes all day but couldn't. Instead, I daydreamed of Superman's eyes locked on just mine, out of everyone in the crazy crowd, as he levitated several feet in the air in his lit suit. Before his boots touch the main stage floor, I noticed a huge Kryptonian bouquet of plum, turquoise, and tangerine Surrum Blossoms—singing flowers. A few Oregus flowers with golden, glittery tips were mixed in. He flew down to my height. Then, he handed me his gift with a light kiss on my right cheek.

That night, dinner was super quiet. I rolled my peas around my mashed potatoes with my fork and stared down at the pile of food.

"Can I be excused?" I asked, making no eye contact with my mom.

"You haven't eaten two bites off your plate. Judee, I know you're upset," my mom said.

"Not hungry. I really need to get some reading done for my history class next week."

Mom inhaled and pressed the glass of red wine against her chapped lips. "Okay, go ahead."

Grabbing my plate off the table, I scraped the food in the trash and washed my dishes.

Before I left the kitchen, my mom said, "Judee, you know family comes first."

I yanked my body around to face her.

"Why do I have to go to this stupid funeral, anyhow? I only met Aunt Lucille a few times. She always gave me the creeps," I barked.

"First of all, you're being very disrespectful. Second, you're going to pay your respects, young lady, and that's final! Make sure you're ready to go by 8:30 in the morning because it's about a seven hour drive."

Rolling my eyes with a deep sigh, I spurted out, "Don't worry, I'll be all ready. Will Dad be there?"

"I doubt it. He never gave my family a chance."

"Can't blame him on that, and Dad wouldn't force me to go, if he was still here," I grumbled under my breath.

"Excuse me, what did you say?" Mom asked, squinting her eyes at me and slamming her glass down on the table, causing all the dishes to rattle.

Grinding my teeth, I said, "Nothing at all."

I stomped off to my bedroom, slammed the door, and slid down the wall to sit on the floor facing my bed. A white, eleven-by-seventeen box with a loosely-tied, pink bow rested in the middle of my bed. I crawled over to pick it up. I slid my orange and black, polka-dot nail under both sides of the box and sliced the tape. The cardboard cover fell off, and I peeled back the tissue papers.

Once I uncovered it, I gasped. I then noticed a small card underneath, which read, *I know it won't make up for you missing the con, but I thought it might help a little. Happy birthday, Buttercup. Love Dad.*

It was a genuine Superman cape. I pulled it out of the box and flung it around my shoulders. Kal-El would be very proud of this glistening Superman logo on the back.

Standing in front of the mirror across the room, I saw it perfectly fit me, not too long or short. It barely touched the top of my ankles.

I spun around and around until I collapsed to the floor and giggled to myself.

I grabbed my cell to text Dad.

J: I love it! thank u so much! I wish u were here

After fifteen minutes, he responded.

D: Hey there, Buttercup! Glad you like your gift.
J: will u be at Aunt Lucille's funeral on Saturday?
D: No
J: why?
D: Long story. Sorry about you not being able to attend the con.
J: ur the only 1. Mom only cares about the funeral, not my feelings
D: Your mom has always had that tendency.
J: no kidding!!
D: Hey, what if I make it up to you?
J: what do u mean?
D: I've been researching some cons and found a few where Henry Cavill will be making an appearance in a few months.
J: really?
D: Absolutely, my treat.
J: ur the best! luv u
D: Love you too. Get some sleep. Long drive to your aunt's place tomorrow.
J: don't remind me. goodnight

Once the texting ended, I packed my suitcase with my toothbrush, toothpaste, socks, tennis shoes, pjs, jeans, Superman T-shirts, and a black dress with matching flats. I folded my cape and placed it on top, before zipping it up.

I brushed up, read my chapter, closed my eyes, and fell asleep.

**

The alarm on my phone went off at 7:15AM. I snoozed it just once before I got dressed. I opened the front door and carried my stuff out to the car.

Upon re-entering the house through the front door, I saw Mom at the kitchen island.

"Want some cereal?" she asked, pouring milk in her bowl.

"I'm good. Ready?" I snatched a protein bar out of the cabinet and a bottle of milk from the fridge.

As she crunched down on the cereal, she said, "It's not even 8:30 AM, yet."

Throwing my empty hand up in the air, I shouted, "The earlier we can get on the road, Hillary, the better, right?"

"Let's talk, Judee." Mom stopped eating. "Please address me correctly or not at all."

"You know, I'm just going to grab my phone and wait for you in the car." I jammed my hands in my front pockets and started heading back to my room.

"Look," Mom continued. "I'm doing my best here. It hasn't been easy at all for me. I've been working late shifts at the hospital, because I used up all my vacation time for meetings with my lawyer and court. I know you think your dad is a hero, but he's not even close."

I stared at her for a minute, and then retreated into my room to grab my phone, charger, and earbuds.

Tears filled my eyes. "See you outside, Mom." I went to the car, wiping my face with the back of my sleeve.

Mom said as she slid into the car, "Sorry, I unloaded on you back there. I shouldn't have said that about your dad."

I placed my earbuds inside my ears. On my phone, I scrolled down to my New Kids on the Block, Lizzo, Pitbull, Pink, and Janet Jackson mix playlist.

Mom reached over and jerked out one of my earbuds.

"Didn't you hear me?" she asked with a huge scowl on her face.

"Yeah, I heard you. Let's go, already."

As Mom backed the car out of the driveway, I replaced the dangling earbud in my ear and texted Sadie.

J: u at school?
S: yes. u on the road?
J: yep, lucky me
S: hope funeral goes ok
J: rather be there with Henry and u, tomorrow
S: I don't have 2 go
J: Sadie, u gotta go for both of us. anyhow, I talked 2 my dad last night and he plans to take me to another con soon.
S: that's great news!
J: u have a blast and post pics, ok? talk more later
S: k

The hours drifted by. We stopped to get gas once and at a restaurant to eat lunch. The conversation was minimal.

We were almost thirty minutes out from late Aunt Lucille's place when I turned down the volume and asked, "Why isn't Dad coming down for the funeral?"

"It's just best this way."

"Mom, it's been almost three months since you and Dad divorced."

"Judee, please, there's just a lot of things you don't know, and I plan to keep it that way. Drop it! By the way, I'll be glad when your dad starts buying you more mature birthday gifts."

I hollered out, "Whatever! I know your family never liked Dad because--"

"Say it!" she shrieked, squeezing the steering wheel tight. I could see a few fingerprints on the soft leather whenever she moved her hand out of the way.

Pulling one bud out, I said, "You know why. I don't need to spell it out for you. I've been dealing with kids snickering behind my back at school and making jokes of how I look, since first grade.

First, it was the nasty comments from the kids at school about my curly hair, and then, how I look like I have a suntan year 'round. Some of your family has even said similar things to me." Tears streamed down my caramel face as I turned up the volume.

We didn't speak any more on the trip.

Aunt Lucille's house rested on top of a hill. Tall, twisty trees encircled it, casting a darkness over the house. Her house reminded me of the one in that old *Psycho* movie—my dad loved to watch it every Halloween, and I would watch with him. It was Victorian-styled minus the Bates Motel nearby.

I never noticed any flowers growing around the house or near it. Come to think of it, whenever we did visit, there were never any birds or butterflies flying around, only big, biting horseflies. Her house always reeked of mothballs and burnt cabbage. I swear she kept a box in every room, even under the stairs outside.

Mom parked. There were over a dozen cars wrapped around the side of the house. We started up the creaky, wooden stairs. A cockroach, almost the size of my hand, raced down the metal-sided rail. I cringed and jerked my hand back in the nick of time.

"Why are there so many cars here?" I asked.

"Oh, I forgot to tell you. Aunt Lucille's wake is at 7:00 PM."

I stopped on the seventh step and asked, "A wake? What's that?"

"It's when the close family comes together to view the body," Mom said.

I could feel my heartbeat revving up. "Like view the body where?"

"In Aunt Lucille's house, silly girl."

"Mom, you're telling me there's a coffin inside with her dead body?"

"Yes, it's an old family tradition. Aunt Lucille always wanted to have a wake in her home. The funeral home will reclaim her body from here at 8:30 AM, tomorrow. Her graveside service will be held late Saturday morning."

As sweat sprinted down my forehead, I took a few deep breaths.

Mom patted me on my shoulder and walked in front of me up the stairs. "There's nothing to be afraid of. You're safe here. It's not like she's going to get up and bother you tonight." She laughed.

My eyes expanded. I paused for a few seconds. "I'm going to go ahead and get our bags out of the car."

"Okay," Mom said. "Don't take too long. There are a few relatives I want to introduce you to. I believe Beaver will be around."

The last time I saw my cousin Beaver was two summers ago. Beaver was shorter than I and chubby with braces and eyeglasses, which resembled the bifocals old people wear. We were the same age.

He loved to collect weird insects in glass vessels and kept them in his basement lab. Whenever we had to visit Aunt Lucille, he made me feel comfortable with no judgments. He was different, in a good way. Beaver always made my visits way more interesting and less creepy.

Opening the back car door, I slipped my mom's oversized tote bag, which felt like she had packed a couple of bricks inside, over my left shoulder. I stumbled backward and regained my balance. Then, I pulled the handle of my suitcase. Before it dropped to the ground, I heard someone call my name. Heavy footsteps came up behind me.

"Hey, Judee! What's up, girl?"

Blinking my eyes a few times, I refocused. It was Beaver, and he must've morphed. He was a few inches taller than I and slimmer, without any metal or thick eyeglasses. His hazel eyes seemed to sparkle, and his voice seemed deeper, too. My mom's bag slid off my arm, and my suitcase fell over as soon as I let go of the handle.

He came up and swung his muscular arms around me in a hug. I didn't smell the familiar old dirt or a cesspool on him. Instead, a scent of warm pumpkin spice and fresh pine saturated his skin and Einstein T-shirt.

I pushed him away and stepped back. "Whoa, what happened to you?"

"What?" He picked up both bags like he was picking up two pillows and tossed them over his shoulders.

"You know what I'm talking about, Beaver." I placed both hands on my hips.

"Umm, I guess Connie Bosak." He wiggled his eyebrows, followed by a huge smile. "You like?"

"She must be something special," I said smiling.

"You could say that . . ."

"So, you're attending the funeral tomorrow too?" I asked.

"Yep, my mom is making me go."

I rolled my eyes. "We got that in common."

Beaver nodded in agreement.

We made our way through the dry grass toward the house.

"Happy belated birthday, Judee."

"Thanks. Had plans to meet Superman." I pressed my lips tight.

"Bummer you have to be here." Beaver squeezed my right shoulder with his warm hand.

"Tell me about it. I so didn't want to come here."

"If you want, we can hang out tomorrow evening," he said.

"Would like that," I snorted out loud. "Maybe I'll get to meet the girl who changed Beaver."

A huge grin appeared on his face.

We paused for a few seconds before we stepped over the threshold. Ice-cold fingers raked through my hair, close to my scalp. I jumped and bumped Beaver from behind.

"Judee, you okay?"

Bending over, I shook my hair out and ran my hands through it, but I couldn't feel anything. "Yeah, I just felt something funny in my hair."

He stuttered his next words and blinked his eyes a couple of times, until I could understand what he was trying to say. After taking a few deep breaths, he whispered, "She did it."

Glowering at him, I stood up to face him, "Who are you referring to?"

"You know who."

"Aunt Lucille?" I twisted my mouth to the left.

"Yes, her."

"Whatever, it was probably just a draft."

"Sure . . . That's all it was, a draft." Beaver arched his eyebrows up and strolled toward the kitchen.

The wood floors made loud, popping, cracking sounds with every step we took.

A group of adults, mostly strangers, were gathered in the enormous open kitchen. Mom looked up and pointed to her right down the long hall.

An ebony coffin was planted in the middle of the room, maybe a hundred feet from the bedroom where I would be staying.

Beaver leaned next to my ear and whispered, "That's her."

"Who else would it be, Sherlock?"

We made our way into "my" bedroom with its tall, antique, canopy bed. Beaver placed my mom's bag next to the door, tossed my bag near the bottom of the bed, and sat on top of it.

"Hope you don't have to go the bathroom tonight," he said.

"Why?" I asked.

"You don't remember?"

I leaned against the tall dresser to face him and replied, "No."

"There's only one bathroom on this floor, and it's through there." He pointed over to the coffin.

"So? I'm not scared." I slid my trembling hands inside my pockets.

"You should be. Look down."

When I did, I saw several deep scratches embedded in the floor.

"Big deal." I shrugged my shoulders.

Beaver kicked his shoes off and jumped on the bed. He lay with his hands cupped behind his head and stared up at the ceiling for about a minute without speaking a word. He then turned toward me and said in a low tone, "Wanna know how the scratches got there, and why they're all over the house? I bet you never noticed that before."

I flopped down on the bed next to him with my legs crossed and begged, "Please, spill it!"

He turned his head to face me, "Don't wanna freak you out. You gotta stay here tonight."

"Just tell me. You're not gonna freak me out." I felt sweat pooling down my lower back.

"Well, your Aunt Lucille was a *bruja,* or witch, and I heard she was no Samantha Stephens from *Bewitched.* She had these super long toenails, which would claw the ground every step she took. It made an awful sound like someone dragging Freddy Krueger nails down a wet chalkboard during the day. At night, when no one was around, she would float inside her house, practicing spooky, magic spells."

"Okay, you know your story sounds crazy, right? Plus, how do you know all of this?"

"My grams told me about her and how her younger brother saw her floating in the air, one night."

"I don't believe it. Just some stupid story." I swallowed a big gulp of air.

"Judee, you might think different in the morning, if she doesn't drag you inside her coffin and gobble you up tonight." Beaver's bulging eyes locked on mine.

Scanning the room, I replied, "Yeah, right. *Bruja*, if you're real, then prove it!"

"Wow, you're braver than I'll ever be," Beaver said in a low hum. "I would never say that out loud. You just invited her to come out."

"You're nuts." I rolled my eyes. "I don't believe any of this."

"Guess you'll just have to find out on your own."

My mom entered the room and said, "Dinner time. Come on, you two, five minutes."

Before she walked out the room, she turned around and asked, "What were y'all talking about?" She picked up her bag from against the door.

"Nothing," Beaver blurted out.

We both hopped down from the bed. He went ahead of me.

Beaver turned around and said, "Whatever you do, don't go to the bathroom after 3 AM. She likes to roam around the house about that time, especially in there." He glanced down the hall toward the coffin.

I patted the side of his face with my hand and said, "Whatever, Beaver."

He placed his hands on my shoulders and muttered, "You'll see."

Rolling my eyes, I slid out of his grasp.

Several family members were present for dinner. Mom introduced me to second and third cousins who didn't mean anything to me. We all ate, and I drank four glasses of raspberry punch. Beaver stared at me a few times and shook his head.

Everyone left soon after viewing her body–an invitation I skipped.

It was almost 9 PM, and the sun was fading. I opened the door to my room and tiptoed all the way from the bedroom to the bathroom, passing you-know-what, to take a quick shower and brush my teeth.

The coffin never changed on my walk back.

As I opened the door to my room, my mom walked up behind me and touched the back of my neck with her cold hand.

I jumped and turned around to face her.

"Judee, you okay?"

"Of course, why wouldn't I be?" I said, as my eyes jittered around.
"You look nervous."

Faking a yawn while stretching my arms up, I said, "I'm fine, just tired, that's all."

"Well, goodnight."

"Night." I shut the door behind me.

I spotted a lock above the doorknob and turned it until I heard a click. Vaulting into bed, I pulled the covers over my head.

***

A few hours passed. I woke up and noticed it was almost 3 AM according to my phone. I tossed and turned a few times. Almost seventy-five minutes had passed, and I knew I couldn't hold it until the sun came up. The bathroom called my name, so I slid on some fuzzy orange socks and put my cape on.

Unlocking the door, I crept down the middle of the hallway. A bright beam of moonlight illuminated my path.

I looked at the coffin. It was the same as before. I took a few deep breaths, counted to ten backwards, and darted past the coffin into the bathroom. Once I flipped the lights on, I slammed the door, locked it, and did what I needed to do.

When I opened the door, I looked out and noticed the coffin had moved from its center placement, and its lid had opened a few inches. I figured I must've bumped it somehow.

I dashed from the bathroom and slid in my socks across the floor to the open bedroom door with my cape flying upwards. Then, I closed and locked the door. Leaping into bed, my cape wrapped around me by itself, and I fell into a deep sleep in seconds.

***

My alarm went off at 7:30 AM, an hour before the arrival of the hearse to retrieve the coffin from the house. The sunlight peeked through the half open curtain. I tossed the covers off.

Placing my feet down on the bare floor, I felt something cold, long, and sharp pierce the center of my right foot. I jerked my bleeding foot up and covered my mouth with both hands before screaming out loud.

My eyes enlarged, as I glanced down and lowered myself to the floor onto my wobbly knees. The cape billowed out around me in slow, rolling waves.

A ten-inch long, curled up black toenail with razor-sharp edges rested in front of me. I examined it closer. Swiping the nail over to the side with my left hand, I noticed something written on the dusty floor in backward, smoking, squiggly letters, which read,

I almost ate you before dawn.
Lucky, lucky girl with the red cape.

The End

About Miracle Austin

Miracle Austin works in the social work arena by day and in the writer's world at night and on weekends. She's a YA/NA, cross-genre, hybrid author.

Paranormal, horror, and suspense are her favorite genres, but she's not limited to them. *Doll* is her debut YA/Paranormal novel. It won 2nd place in the Young Adult category in the **2016 Purple Dragonfly Awards**.

Miracle is a Comic-Con/Marvel/DC/Horror Fangirl and loves attending cons and teen book events.

She lives in Texas with her family. She looks forward to hearing from her awesome readers, who already know her, and new readers, too.

Website: www.miracleaustin.com
Email: shadesoffiction@miracleaustin.com
Twitter: MiracleAustin7
Instagram: @MiracleAustin7
Facebook: Miracle Austin Author

SCIENCE FICTION

Stories based on future advances generally are classified as science fiction. This can include technology as well as social and environmental changes. The relationship between scientific principles and the story plot are crucial to defining this genre. Whether it is aliens, time travel, or political intrigue the combinations are limitless.

So for those who wish to delve into this entertaining and, sometimes, predictive universe, I bid you read on.

James William Peercy

SCIENCE FICTION: STORY 1

ALREADY DREAMED

by Claudette Stacey Peercy

Sometimes life is a little weird. You look around, and you wonder where that building came from. It wasn't there yesterday. But then, a full ten-story building shows up out of nowhere.

Another time, your significant other, your spouse, or your best friend mentions a gray horse. But while you're nodding in agreement, you've never heard that story, never been in that conversation, never had that thought.

And wasn't that car blue? Now, it's green. You know what I mean. How can that be?

Yesterday, the horse down the road was gray, when my memory says he was brown. And lately, the changes have become much more frequent. It's like being out of phase with everyone. All I want to do is understand whether this is a dream or reality.

BEEP, BEEP, BEEP.

"Aww, it's too early. Make it stop!"

I open my eyes as I grab my smartphone to silence the noise. My dream fades–a dream I can't quite remember.

Starting my morning, especially these days, is hard. All I want to do is sleep: turn my back on the alarm, close my eyes to the light shining through the window, and seal my mind against the constant noise.

Grumpy and out of sorts, I look over and see Reve. He's on his smartphone with his laptop propped on his lap, still in bed.

Moving my tired body, I winch. My muscles scream in agony as I stretch and then crawl out of bed. He turns and watches me with his empathetic, brown eyes.

"Sorry, I woke you," he says as he lowers his voice and continues with his phone call.

I sluggishly walk down the hallway of our old ranch house to the bathroom, listening to the wooden floor creak beneath my feet. It is a very old bathroom, and some may even call it vintage. It has a single sink with an old rust stain which has been there since Reve was a child.

My mind wonders about the faded dream as I use the toilet. I then take a quick bath, wishing we had a shower.

The splash of water on my skin brings back the dreadful floating sensation of the dream I cannot remember. I claw my way out of the tub, sloshing water on the wooden floor.

Grabbing a soft, white, bath towel to dry off, I try not to slip and fall. Sweat drips from my face as if I had never taken a bath. Breathing heavily, I walk blindly back to the bedroom to dress.

The decisions on what to wear are endless and yet so simple. They get harder to make every day.

Do I dress for comfort? For style? Or simply for fun? Clothes always make me feel confident and pretty. Today will be style and comfort. Maybe it will ease the anguish I feel.

As I put on a pair of black jeans and my favorite purple tunic, I contemplate whether it'll be purple sandals or purple Converse. I choose the Converse.

As I start to leave the bedroom, I gaze at my tiny closet, wishing for a walk-in closet and trying to remember my dreams. My dreams reside in the recesses of my mind. It's like they live in a tiny closet but are struggling to reside in a big, fancy walk-in.

I stride into the kitchen, look out the window, and stare into the backyard. The tall stalks of grass are slowly changing from green to brown as summer arrives. It needs mowing. Squirrels run across the yard and chase each other. They scurry up the oak tree.

My mind wonders, once again, about my dreams. Did my mind ever stop wondering?

"I know there have been dreams, but I can't seem to remember," I say in my mind.

Startled, I turn as Reve enters the kitchen. I stare at him.

"Reve, I thought you'd be in the bathroom by now."

He peers at me. "I detoured because I thought I heard you talking to yourself."

Reve has an empathic ability when it comes to me. He's always been able to sense my emotions. I love that about him. He is the love of my life.

"No, I didn't say anything," I continue. "I'm just staring out the window and watching the squirrels."

"Well, all right. I've finished my phone call. I'm heading to the bathroom to get ready for work. Didn't mean to startle you."

"No worries. You didn't startle me."

Reve, the love of my life–without him, none of my dreams would be.

He looks over at me. "Were you thinking about dreams? I had a dream, too. I'll share it with you if we have time." He walks toward the bathroom.

As he leaves, I call, "Hey babe, was it a great dream?"

He comes back and smiles at me. He reaches over and caresses my face with his strong, soft hands. "I know you're having trouble with your dreams. I'll tell you about mine later."

I lean into his embrace, wrap my arms around him, and listen to his heartbeat as he sighs into my hair. At last, he releases me and heads to the bathroom.

Staring after him, my heart is wildly beating. I wonder who this man is who loves me. For just a minute, he seems a complete stranger. Everything around me shimmers, and then I'm back.

"He's Reve, and he is the man who makes all my dreams come true. He's the love of my life. I know that. I know him. I love him," I say out loud.

With a deep inhale, I continue with breakfast. The bacon sizzles in the skillet. The eggs are waiting to be mixed and scrambled once the bacon is complete. It'll all be ready when he gets out of the bathroom. I wonder what he dreamed. I hope they were happy dreams.

Reve comes back to the kitchen and leans toward me for a kiss. I allow myself to once again lean into him and savor the moment. It is perfection. The softness of his hair in my hands makes me want to stay in his embrace all day. I'm lost in his smile and lost in the love I see in his gorgeous brown eyes.

"I really want to tell you about my dream," he says, "but I'm going to be late. How about we meet for lunch, maybe come back here, and then I can show you what my dream was about?" Reve laughs as he grabs me for one last, lingering kiss.

I pull away, giggling. "Sounds like a plan. Now, eat your breakfast and then go to work before we're both late."

Once breakfast is finished, he runs down the gravel driveway to his truck, unlocks the door, and jumps in. As he starts the engine and drives down the road, he leans out the window blowing kisses at me.

I stand in the driveway, laughing as the dust from the gravel settles. My love for him takes my breath away.

Turning toward my vehicle, I admire it. I love driving my SUV. It's got power. It's got speed. And it's safe. It's the vehicle Reve purchased for me. He said he wanted me to be protected, and this SUV would protect me. It is red, my favorite color.

I turn on the radio app on my smartphone. I should have done this before I started driving, but I had other things on my mind. Reve, he's always on my mind.

I love listening to the oldies station, the one playing the music of our parent's youth. This usually distracts me, but not today. I can't stop thinking, "Why can't I remember my dreams?"

My red SUV smoothly handles the curves, but the bumps on the road are rough. I bounce up and down in my seat. It's a good thing I'm wearing my seat belt.

After one particularly rough bump, the glove box on my SUV pops open. With one hand on the steering wheel, I lean over to close it, struggling to keep one eye on the road.

With each mile, I pass the different cattle ranches: cows, cows, and more cows. On the right side of the road, two miles after crossing the creek, is a field with a solitary horse.

"What a beautiful horse," I say. "Next time, I need to make sure my camera is with me so I can stop and take his picture. His coat is the color of warm cocoa. Or should I say it's brown? Yeah, it's brown." I pause. "Here I go, talking out loud to myself again."

Passing the horse, I speed up, trying to get to the highway before I'm late for work. I follow the last curve in the road, hit another bump, and hope the glove box doesn't open again – although, the distraction would help drown out my thoughts.

A question reverberates in my mind. *"What was my last dream?"*

Not remembering my dream is driving me crazy so I think, *"Maybe if I increase the volume of the music, which is playing from my cellphone app, it will finally divert my thoughts."*

I turn onto the highway and reach over to the holder where my smartphone is anchored. Attempting to adjust the volume, I knock the phone out of the holder onto the passenger side floor.

For a brief moment, there is nothing in my head, and then the thoughts return with a vengeance. All I hear is the constant refrain, *"Dream, Dream, Do I dream?"*

I reach for my smartphone on the floor, struggling against the thoughts, when the refrain changes.

"Are you asleep? Are you alive? Are you asleep? Are you dead?"

The sky grows darker. The wind howls. Rain thuds against the SUV, much like the refrain does inside my head. A storm rages in both worlds.

My head aches. As I wipe sweat from my brow, I realize I'm hyperventilating. There is darkness around me. I drift through an endless void of no stars.

"Should there be stars?" I ask myself unsure of how I can hear my own voice.

Waves of energy enter the void and surround me. There are flashes of light. A crackle of electricity feeds the energy.

A scream echoes in my head. It roars like waves of a sea whose water crashes around the fear embedded in my mind. And then, there is silence.

In the middle of the highway, a large, brown and white panel van has stopped. The brake lights are dark. There is no time to think. I tap my brakes as I look to the right and turn the steering wheel hard.

I cut into the tall, spiraling grass beside the road next to a driveway. The steering wheel jerks right and left as I fight to maintain control.

My mind is a void, filled with electricity, energy, and the sound of my scream. I swerve across the top of the driveway. My SUV runs over the reflector at the end.

I steer along the edge of the yard and tear though the brush. My vehicle bounces through a ditch and skids sideways to a stop, parallel of the van. I stare at my hands, gripping the steering wheel.

"Am I dead?" I think. *"Did I really hit the van?"*

The words echo in my head as my heart pounds and blood pulses through my veins. The question gets louder with no way to make it stop.

I look to my left and notice I'm beside the van in my blue SUV. And yet, a red SUV has struck the back of the van, but I cannot see the face of the person inside.

Everything goes quiet, and the red SUV fades from sight.

"Did I die?" I wonder. *"Did I fall asleep?"*

I hear my own short, rapid gasps followed by long, heaving breaths. All the heavy breathing makes it hard to focus. The highway looks the same, so I put my blue SUV in gear.

The van starts forward. I drive onto the road. Ahead is a big tractor-trailer crossing the highway. This is why the van stopped with no warning. It's disconcerting to think I could have crashed into the back of the van.

"But I didn't, did I?" I whisper. That was someone else in a red SUV. My SUV is blue, my favorite color.

As I arrive at the office, I drive into the parking lot located at the back of the building. I exit the blue SUV, grabbing my backpack, which I usually leave in the car overnight, and struggle not to trip on the poorly repaired parking lot.

As I get ready to use my key to open the backdoor of the office, the door swings out. I jump back. It's Vu.

Vu works for me. He is my go-to guy for all things at work and has been with me for years. He knows a little about a lot of things. Maybe he can make sense of what happened.

"Vu, come help me check out my vehicle. I almost rear-ended a van."

Vu walks over after putting his briefcase into his car. "I was heading to a client, but I guess I can take a look. What did you do?"

Slowly walking around the blue SUV, we find a scratch on the front license plate where I struck the reflector. There is a small dent on the passenger side where I hit something during my skid onto the road.

"You were lucky," he says. "You need to keep your eyes on the road. It could have been much worse."

I sigh and then think, *"It's not like I did this on purpose."*

Vu looks both familiar and unfamiliar. When I peer at him, I see the name Rich, not Vu, as if Vu should not be his name. Shaking this feeling off, I say, "Yes, it could've been worse."

He continues as if not hearing me, "Everything appears all right, so I'll get to my next job. See you later."

Turning away, I glance back to see Vu staring at me. He then walks toward his car.

Entering my office, I put my keys in my backpack and set the backpack on the old, wooden chair in front of my desk. The chair once belonged to Reve's grandfather.

I stop and admire the chair, rubbing my hands over the wood, feeling the indentions beneath my fingers. These indentions represent the past: the journey of Reve, his grandfather, and now me. They are my past and my present.

Sitting down at my desk, I sort through the files and soon discover a report which was sent to me. It is a discussion on what happens to an insomniac, and how their inability to sleep can lead to a variety of psychoses. This study talks about how people could eventually die if they don't sleep.

As I'm reading, I think, *"Am I dreaming? Am I awake?"*

I put the report down and grab the next one.

The light in the office blinks, and my eyes grow dim. The world around me spins, but I struggle to hold onto my reality, my sanity.

The spinning stops. I look around and notice I'm still at my desk. I start to read the next report.

This one was written by a popular psychologist who writes for our local paper. This report states there is a difference between déjà vu and déjà rêvé.

It says, "Déjà vu means already seen. While doing a task, you feel as if you've already done it, not dreamed the experience.

Déjà rêvé means already dreamed. It is an awareness that a dream you have previously experienced occurs in the waking world and you may feel as if you're dreaming it now."

Reading this passage brings back the question in my head, *"Am I dreaming now?"*

I get up and walk to the front of my desk to gaze at the windows. The street sounds have stopped. The ambient noise that normally fills my ears is gone.

The outer office lights are off. There is still daylight coming through the blinds, but the silence suffocates me, filling my head with chaos.

"Does silence make a noise?" I muse. "Maybe in my dreams."

The reality hits me. I am alone.

I stride to the middle of the room looking out through the glass front door. The whole block is now devoid of people.

The phrase, *"Am I dreaming?"* vibrates through my thoughts as I fight to rationalize what is around me.

I go out the front office door. As I walk down the street, I notice cracks in the sidewalk. A newspaper blows from across the road, lands on my feet, and rustles in the wind.

All the historic buildings are empty and rundown. I continue to look into each building but see nothing and no one.

Turning the corner, the street brightens as if the sun landed at my feet. I close my eyes tight. I see bright red behind my eyelids.

"Did the sun fall out of the sky?" I say inside my head.

The heat radiating against my body is unbearable. I must get away from it. I stumble on the sidewalk, my hands covering my eyes.

"My eyes, they're on fire," I sob.

The heat recedes. The light dims. Laughter and voices assault my ears. The street is filled with people who, earlier, were not there.

"What is this? What did the fire do? Am I awake?" goes through my mind.

As I rub my sore, tear-filled eyes and aching head, I sigh in relief.

Vu rushes to my side and helps me up. "Hey, are you all right?"

A crowd of people hurry past. Some look, but most ignore us.

Vu's concern changes to frustration. "What is wrong with you? You ran out of the office. You didn't even hear me when I called."

He steps back to glare at me, worry written on his face. But he is forced to sidestep to avoid the crowd.

Frowning at him, I say, "What do you mean? You had gone to a client. I saw you walking to your car. No one was here, not even you."

Rubbing my eyes again, I peer at the people around me.

He chides, "I don't know what you're talking about. I arrived back at the office, and you rushed past me. Maybe you should go back in, sit down, and rest. It's almost lunchtime. You should eat something." Vu places his hand on my back and tries to guide me to the office.

"Hey, stop that." I slap his hands away. "I'm not going inside."

Vu stares at me as if I've lost my mind. "Okay. Maybe you should go home and get some rest. Perhaps you should take the rest of the day off. I'll close the office."

He slowly walks back, glancing over his shoulder at me.

"I don't care what he thinks. I need to get out of here," I mutter to myself. *"I'll deal with his bossiness later."*

I hurry around to the back of the building. As I get to the parking lot, I realize I left my backpack with the keys inside the office.

I go to the backdoor, hoping Vu left it unlocked. He did. Slipping into my workplace, I grab my backpack before he notices I'm there.

I head back to the parking lot. Outside, everything seems overly bright, with each color exhibiting an illumination that blinds the eyes. The greens are as shiny as an emerald. The yellows are as bright as the sun.

A couple from the neighboring building is outside unloading their van. An old man from another building walks his miniature schnauzer. A teenage boy rides his hoverboard near my green SUV.

All the historic buildings appear well maintained and operational. There is a café open in the building next door. A dry cleaner is across the street in a painted, white brick building. The parking lot has new concrete. Frowning, I remember when the concrete was old and cracked but cannot tell how long ago.

I get my keys from my backpack and start to unlock the door of my green SUV. Staring at my vehicle, something seems different. Shaking my head, the moment passes. I settle inside and close the door, heaving a long, heavy sigh.

It's nice being inside my pretty, green SUV. It's the only thing I seem connected to. Next time, I'll get a red SUV, my favorite color.

As I drive home, I realize its only lunchtime. Wasn't there something I was supposed to do at lunch?

I notice the solitary gray horse along the road home and wish I had my camera to take his photograph. Oh well, next time. I'm going home to take a nap.

Later in the day, as I lay in my bed trying to sleep, I realize I'm still out of phase with my life. I've had times when my dreams are so real, they last for days. Other times, I can't remember them at all. It's like I've never dreamed or have already dreamed.

I live in this adorable ranch house by myself. Someday, I plan to marry a wonderful man, with gorgeous brown eyes. He will be the love of my life.

"The love of my life? Where is he?" I murmur as I draw the covers over my head.

My life is repetitive, like I have lived it more than once. Throughout the day, I catch sight of a brown-haired man. He seems familiar along with Vu, or is it Rich, but they are not where they were.

Maybe they are watching me. Maybe they are in the house with me. Maybe this is all a dream.

***

The sky turned to dusk, and the stars winked on one-by-one above an abandoned town. It was the perfect place for Reve to work.

He turned a corner and walked to one of the old, run-down buildings to locate Vu, his partner. Only he and Vu could see the town was abandoned. Anyone else coming into the town would get the sudden urge to leave, despite it appearing as a thriving community.

The two partners came to this town to perform their revolutionary Reality versus Dream study. They interviewed over fifteen women and found only one who could survive the experiment. They immediately hired her.

It was sad to have to eliminate the unsuccessful interviewees, but it was of no consequence. They would never be found. The research was the only thing that mattered, and someday they would be rich and powerful, more powerful than they were now.

Upon entering the building Reve said, "I heard what happened today. We need to make a few modifications to her dream. It did not hold as her reality for long."

Vu asked, "Are you sure we need to continue? We have the basic data." He viewed the surveillance cameras at the ranch house.

"Yes," Reve answered. "We must do it for her sanity. If we correctly reset her dreams, she will get the peace she needs, and we will have all the results we require." He moved next to Vu as they both stared at the cameras.

"There is no room for failure," Reve stressed as he grabbed Vu's shoulder and squeezed. "Do not let me down, dear friend."

Vu stared at his partner's hand. "Don't threaten me, Reve. This project is as much mine as yours. We both need results."

Reve relaxed his grip. "I apologize. I'm just anxious for this to work. Of course, you're right. Tonight, we will let her reality be her dream. But tomorrow, when she wakes, we will start her dreams once again. After all, her dream will become her reality."

The End

Inspiration for Already Dreamed

As a member of the Authors Round Table Society, I've watched and listened to the various members discuss their reasons for writing. I also listened to people at different shows talk about how they could be writers. They present ideas the authors should use, because they are unable to write their own stories.

The thing I realized is if these writers, with all the ideas, can't write for themselves, then they will never be an author. We have authors who write books, poetry and articles for our *ARTS* magazine. They all utilize their craft, their passions.

After spending time with the Authors Round Table Society, I decided it was time to write. It took several false starts before I landed on the idea that would become my first story.

Initially, I barely could make 1500 words of a 2000 word minimum. However, as I learned and studied, I managed to end the story with just over 3900 words.

My take-a-way from this exercise is that everyone has ideas, but writers write. I wanted to take an idea and turn it into something more, to create what I hope is a cohesive and interesting tale people would want to read.

About Claudette Stacey Peercy

As a child, my mother read bedtime stories to me, and I never wanted her to stop. My love of words and books began.

From then on, there was no stopping me. I read about *Curious George* and eventually graduated to reading *The Bobbsey Twins, The Hardy Boys,* and *Nancy Drew.*

I started a journal. Using this, I wrote down my thoughts and observations. Words kept me grounded and kept me in flight. As poet Maya Angelou says, "There is no greater agony than bearing an untold story inside you." We all have a story to tell.

Claudette S. Peercy

Links:
Facebook: https://www.facebook.com/claudette.peercy
Instagram: @claudettepeercy
Twitter: @ccscweb

SCIENCE FICTION: STORY 2

DREAM PHASE

by John M. Moody

The sign on the door of the second-rate, one-room office read:

>Dream Phase Readings
>Reliable – Economic
>Let Science Do All the Work
>Randolph Marston, Certified Dream Phase Technician

Randolph knew it was all just a lot of bull, but hey, lately it paid the bills. Yes, he performed dream phase readings, whatever they were, and as for the science behind it, he didn't particularly understand or care.

The old guy who sold him the equipment had assured him it worked okay. The fellow even said he had tweaked the power cells and—how did he put it?—he had "boosted the sensitivity." The aging guy might have been a good salesman, but he claimed to have been one of the inventors of the device. At least, he spoke a lot of technical jargon like he had once been some sort of engineer and knew what he was talking about.

Randolph's main concern was to keep the equipment running smoothly for as long as possible. He hoped to pay off the loan and make some money on the service before the fad lost its current popularity. With the engineer having recently passed away, fixing the contraption after a breakdown would be prohibitively expensive. Randolph crossed his fingers each time he turned on the juice. So far, so good.

The color hardcopy wasn't his idea, either. It came as part of the set up. Randolph normally gave potential clients the standard spiel.

Strong crimson in the spectrum signifies passion. Different shades of green show a willingness to compromise to varying degrees. Blue meant calm or mellow tendencies, with the richer, wider, and stronger stripes indicating "Florence Nightingale" personality traits. Yellow and purple? Who could say? In any case, he always came up with believable interpretations, which were presented to clients with enough of a poker face, so they believed him.

A Dream Phase Wave was an invisible, natural phenomenon with colors added for visual representation and nothing more. Even so, researchers had published a lot of speculative research on the subject using the colors as guides. The printout was a great sales tool, and it wasn't actually a scam.

The waves really existed. The machine really did read them. That thought brought a little calm when his conscience said he was little better than a used car salesman.

As for compatibility interpretation, Randolph always left it up to the client. Some people believed similar spectrum-balance readings meant *soul mate*. Others believed *opposites attract*, the more diametrically opposed the better. Which side was right? Randolph could care less so long as they paid him.

The chase for a few extra bucks had brought him to the back of an old building on this cold and rainy night. As he guided his car into the dark alley, he thought about the circumstances which brought him here.

Most of his clients were young couples who came to his office all moon-eyed. After he gave them the basic sales pitch and showed a few sample scans, they willingly signed the individual permission forms and noted the addresses where he would later capture the readings.

Then, he outlined the proper rules to follow. It would work better if the consenting client slept and dreamed while in a familiar environment. In order to capture the data, a client must be completely alone.

During one early attempt to capture a reading, Randolph inadvertently used the device outside an apartment, and it gave a rather colorful composite spectrum consisting of his client plus another man, the man's wife, and his two children from the apartment next door. Who knew? There might have been a sleeping dog or a cat mixed into the mess.

He had to ask the client to move into another room for a second, free attempt the following evening. That was the last time he made such a mistake! Although the equipment wasn't expensive to operate, the time lost set him off schedule for a week.

His latest client, a man who claimed his name was "Gary," giving no last name, had been cast from a different mold. That same afternoon, the shabbily-dressed, middle-aged man entered the office alone. Randolph usually had no opinion about his clients, but one schemer can spot another a hundred kilometers away. While "Gary" didn't at all fit the other man's looks, "Shady" appeared to be his middle name.

As Randolph searched for the best place to park behind the building at what he estimated to be the proper address, he recalled the earlier encounter:

"So, Gary, will this reading be a double for you and someone else?" asked Randolph.

"No, it will only be a single reading ... on another party," said Gary.

"I'm sorry, but the law says I can't perform a reading on anyone without that person's explicit, written permission. The Supreme Court has said performing a dream phase reading on someone without permission is as bad as breaking and entering . . . into someone else's mind, that is."

"Isn't there any way you can fulfill my request? I can't find anyone who's willing to do it, and it's very important," Gary pleaded behind shifty eyes.

"You probably won't find anyone else who'll agree for the same reasons I gave. I could get into serious trouble for doing something like that," Randolph replied.

"I assure you, Mr. Marston, I'm not involved in any sort of law-enforcement sting operation."

Gary lowered his voice and continued, "And I can also assure you, I'll make it well worth your while."

Randolph had remained silent as he considered how much money *well worth your while* might represent.

How much money would it be worth to risk going to prison, especially if the chances were slim I would be detected?

Gary apparently viewed Randolph's hesitation as a possibility of acceptance. The man spoke again in a low voice to make an emotional plea. "Please, I really need the information. And besides, it's not like it's going to hurt anyone."

Then, Gary simply stood there.

Randolph's darker nature took its course. It was a common practice utilized by the best professional conmen. You cut up the meat and potatoes, you add a little water, then you step back and let the pot cook slowly as the aroma fills the room and the mark gets hungry. Gary was among the best, that is to say, the best of the worst.

At one time, Randolph had also utilized this technique. Now, he didn't especially enjoy being on the receiving end, but the carrot of temptation had been close enough to his nose to smell.

After another moment of silent consideration, Randolph Marston quietly enquired, "What's your angle?"

"I can't tell you that," the client sheepishly said as he diverted his eyes.

Then his voice hardened again. "Do you want to deal or don't you?"

It was a take-it-or-leave-it ploy to apply pressure.

After another half minute, Randolph nodded to agree to at least hear the deal. He had already drawn the line in his head. Anything under ten times his normal fee would be unacceptable.

The guy offered twenty. Cash.

Randolph didn't even think about negotiating. He put out feelers for full payment up-front, but they ultimately settled for half and half.

Then Gary gave him an address in a sleazy part of town. "Your target will be near the back. Is there any problem if the location is below ground?"

"How far down?" Randolph asked.

"The basement," Gary answered.

"It shouldn't be a problem provided it's less than 20 meters. The waves will travel through any substance with a density less than that of silver. But, the precision requires a clean reading over the collection period." Randolph tried to sound like an expert but was only repeating what the old engineer had told him.

Gary's eyes lost focus for a second as if he performed a mental calculation. Then he said, "No problem."

Gary didn't have the money on him but returned with the fifty percent within the hour. "You'll get the other half in exchange for the hardcopy reading. Do you need anything else?"

Randolph asked as he counted the cash, "Do you want a name on the hardcopy?"

"No. No name." Gary turned to leave, once more projecting a hint of guilt.

Randolph continued, "Remember, the person must be asleep and dreaming before I can capture the reading. And there can't be anyone nearby, absolutely no one. Otherwise, the machine won't know who's who."

Randolph's final instructions caused the guy to pause before he reached the door. "Yeah, I get it. I'll be back tomorrow."

***

The multi-storied, dark brick building looked ancient. It was probably a twentieth century apartment that developers hadn't gotten around to leveling, the same as its neighbors on all sides.

It appeared to be abandoned. Randolph didn't see a single light. It crossed his mind he might be in the wrong place until he double checked.

He didn't like being there. He didn't care for the darkness of the place, the cold rain, or the fact it was an alley in a bad part of town, this late at night. Most of all, he felt sorry his weakness for money had put him in such a position, doing something he knew to be completely wrong.

Why wasn't I stronger? He thought. *I should have sent the guy packing straightaway.*

Then, he remembered why. The money would get him that much closer to paying off the loan before the contraption had a chance to break.

Well, now that I'm here, I might as well get it over with. And maybe I can get out of here before a policeman happens along.

Randolph removed the machine's protective, plastic cover and lifted the bulky, wedge-shaped device onto his lap, feeling its weight pressing down on his legs. With the flip of a switch, he started the warm-up process. The colored readouts on the screen appeared remarkably bright and familiar in this unwelcoming place.

The actual setup and run was simple. He only had to perform a few quick checks to see if the circuits were functioning and the output reader was calibrated. He would have never admitted to a client that a trained monkey could do this.

When the readouts showed it was ready, he directed the cone on top of the device toward the brick wall three meters away. Then, he angled it slightly downward while studying the left-hand scale. When the scale peaked, Randolph knew he was focused on a higher lifeform well within range.

The rich, multicolored glow from the second readout on the right side of the screen confirmed the strong presence of Dream Phase

Waves. The preparations went flawlessly, which gave Randolph another feeling of guilt. He was about to delve into a person's inner workings without permission, but thoughts of the money in hand and the money to come gave him little choice.

Okay, he thought, *here goes!*

The machine began to collect and sort the produced waves. He settled into the seat of his car to wait.

Three minutes later, he heard the chime. Surprised, he glanced at the screen. The completion light was on. A reading usually took twenty minutes.

What happened? Did I doze off or something?

Concerned, he sat up to compare his watch to the device's built-in clock. It wasn't a mistake. The reading had ended less than three minutes after it started.

Something must have gone wrong.

When he brought the spectrum onto the screen, the surprises weren't concluded. The entire spectrum displayed white: no reds, no greens or blues, not even a hint of yellow or purple.

Damn! What a time for my equipment to foul up!

He started from the beginning and checked all his initial readings. They seemed to be fine. He reset the machine.

Once more, he located the lifeform and found the optimum position for the cone. The results were the same as before, waves . . . and plenty of them. He set the screen to display analog readings as digital data as they entered the machine.

Then he carefully held the machine motionless and pressed the button. Astonishingly, the wave data started flooding into the machine, but the numbers simply weren't possible. Each column of data scrolled by showing 999.99 with only a handful of exceptions. The dream phase waves were there, but they were too high to display individual colors.

The readings ended in less than *two* minutes—again, with a completely blank spectrum.

Now, what do I do?

He stared at the screen. He had never before cared about who produced what sort of spectrum. For the first time since he purchased the equipment, Randolph felt something sparking his curiosity.

Who could produce such a strong flow of Dream Phase Waves?

For several moments, Randolph searched his surroundings for any sign of the police. Parking in the dark behind an abandoned building was suspicious enough for them to ask the wrong questions, which could lead them to finding out he *was* doing something illegal.

Then his mind drifted off as he pondered his predicament, until something snapped him back to reality. It was like coming back from a daydream because someone next to him cried out. He glanced around again but saw no one. He was not sure if he really heard a cry or not.

Is this some sort of trap?

Or is someone, perhaps the client, watching me? He then remembered the best way to find out was in his grasp.

The machine was still on. He stored the data, reset for another pre-scan, and carefully directed the cone in all directions, shifting his position enough to ensure 360 degree coverage.

He repeated the process, raising the cone high enough to cover all surrounding buildings. There were no significant lifeforms nearby other than possibly a cat or a couple of rats huddled together. He only noticed the same person as before, only this time the Dream Phase Waves were missing.

He made a strange decision, strange at least for Randolph. He turned off the equipment, removed the peripherals, and slipped the plastic cover over the machine. He stepped out of his car and locked the equipment in the trunk.

Randolph walked through the drizzle to reach the door into the back of the building. It wasn't locked, but he hesitated.

How will I be able to see?

Even so, a strange feeling urged him to open the door. He stepped inside and listened. Everything was remarkably silent after stepping out of the rain.

What next?

After a moment, Randolph was drawn forward by an urgency he couldn't explain. It was like someone cried for help even though he saw and heard nothing.

He carefully stepped into the dark, unsure if the floor might give way or if he might encounter obstacles. As rapidly as he could, he walked forward one step at a time, frequently waving his right hand in front of him while running his left hand along the wall. The space seemed to be a hallway. The floor under his feet remained firm.

With his right hand, he encountered something solid directly in front of his face. It angled down away from him. He realized it must be the back of a stairway heading up, but he wanted to go *down*.

As his eyes adjusted, he noticed a faint light surrounding him. He saw a banister and beyond it, another staircase heading down. He descended. The same desperate urgency pulled him down the stairs, and with each step, the light increased

The basement hallway was easier to navigate. He avoided a stack of old boxes along one side as he made his way toward the rear of the building.

He couldn't see any light source. Instead, it was like he had developed the ability to see in the dark. The walls, the floor, and objects in his path were distinguishable, but they appeared strange, like they lacked shadows. His newly-acquired ability grew the farther he walked underground.

What the hell's happening to me?

"I am helping you," said the musical, female voice in his head. Though startled, he continued to walk.

"Who are you?" he asked aloud to the woman he could not see.

She responded, "You may call me Theta, but please, you must hurry. He will be back before long." Growing ever stronger, Theta's voice pleaded.

"Who?" he asked, but the answer entered his mind without her direct answer. She feared Gary, his client.

Randolph turned a corner and reached a door after a couple of dozen steps. In some way, he knew it was the right place, but he found it tightly locked. He tried it with his shoulder, but the door was too solid for his thin frame.

Theta's voice shouted out in his head, "Please, I feel him coming!"

Randolph searched his surroundings and spotted a long, metal bar, which stood in the corner at the end of the hallway about four meters away. He ran to the bar, which was a loose piece of scaffolding. The bar felt heavy when he lifted it. Both ends were flattened with bolt holes passing through them.

He ran back to the door carrying the bar as he might a weapon. Repeatedly, he pounded the bar against the door directly next to the lock. Each impact made a loud crunch, but every swing caused a new dent to appear in the old wood.

Within less than a minute, the bar punched completely through the door with a splintering crack. He paused to look through the hole, but he couldn't see anything other than a faint orange glow—actual light this time instead of his see-in-the-dark capability.

Randolph went back to work making the hole larger. At one point, he asked, "How am I doing?"

"There is still time, but not much." Her voice was in his head and faintly in his ears this time.

He hit the door three more times with strength he did not know he had. With the third strike, a large piece of wood splintered with another loud crack. The hole which resulted measured wide enough for his hand to reach the lock. Randolph tossed the bar to the floor, where it landed with a loud, ringing clang.

Within seconds, his right hand flipped the tab on back of the lock. He reached for the knob. The door opened.

His ability to see through the darkness remained, but it was mixed with true sight. The scene he found astounded him. He hesitated.

The skin of the marvelously-beautiful creature in the center of the room appeared as blue as a baby boy's blanket. It glowed with a faint aura. Long hair hung straight on both sides of a heart-shaped face. Her hair also appeared light blue, although with a silvery hue when compared to her skin. The eyes were especially striking and reminded him of a person who had been suddenly startled. They never changed. The centers of her eyes were cobalt blue. She stood the same height as him. Her face was that of a young woman.

A simple, white dress covered her entire body except for her hands and neck. Her body had enough resemblance to a human female for him to want to stare, but there was no time.

She made up only part of the spectacle. Theta stood in the center of a cubic, metal cage about three meters wide. The structure of the strange cage, both the bars and the woven-metal covering, faintly glowed orange.

"He approaches the building from the front. He is only two streets away now." Randolph heard her voice with his ears only.

"How do you know?" he asked.

"I just know."

He stepped forward to examine the cage, but she warned him, "Do not touch the metal."

"Why not?"

"It is . . . ," she struggled to find the proper word, ". . . electrified."

He walked two-thirds of the way around the cage and spotted a dark cable, which snaked across the floor toward the nearby wall to connect the cage to a gray fuse box. The fuse box was locked, but he retrieved the metal bar. One quick strike downward took care of the problem. He switched off the breaker switches connected to the cable. When he glanced toward the cage, the metal no longer glowed.

Half a minute later, another lock on the cage made it easy to locate the door. Randolph popped open the door using one of the flattened ends of the bar. "I think it's safe for you to pass through now."

"Yes. Thank you." The way she said it made Randolph feel like he had done something heroic. Maybe he had.

"Can we get out of here without Gary seeing us?" he asked

"I think so. Let us try."

Theta led the way. His eye's light receptors had grown stronger as he had traveled deeper into the basement, and they remained strong as he followed her back along the hallway. He could clearly see everything, although none of the details he saw earlier appeared especially bright.

She stopped and held up a hand. Up close for the first time, he noticed her hand possessed five, slim fingers. Her entire hand was a little longer than most human hands.

From just around the corner, he clearly heard someone descending the stairs. The person carried a flashlight because its beam illuminated the floor at the next corner.

Near the corner, she turned to face him and placed her extended fingers over her mouth. Randolph took it to mean he should remain silent. He nodded. Then she surprised him by extending her arms outward as she pressed him back against the wall with her entire form.

He felt her slim body against his. He noted her scent, like some unimaginably-fragrant flower, only no flower he could identify. He sensed her warmth. He saw and felt nothing other than the creature standing there against him. Her touch made him feel remarkably exhilarated despite the approaching peril.

Is she causing me to feel this way?

Randolph didn't believe he would ever forget the experience.

The footfalls were nearer, but as soon as the sounds turned the corner, they continued past where Randolph and Theta stood. Although he never saw the person who passed, Randolph assumed he was the client. He couldn't understand how Gary had failed to see them, especially if the intruder carried a flashlight.

Did she do something to him, too?

When the footfalls became faint again, Theta backed away–to his disappointment. Then she turned and silently led him around the corner.

He saw the stairs ahead leading up. Halfway to the stairs, an anguished cry sounded from around the corner behind them. She increased her pace, taking fewer precautions about moving noiselessly as they ascended the stairs.

Randolph whispered, "This way."

He led her straight to the rear exit, which then he could clearly see. He dug out the car keys as they passed through the door, electronically opening both car doors as soon as they were in range. Theta stepped around to the passenger's side without him having to tell her. They both got in, and he started the engine.

The car purred to life. He drove away from the building without lights and without doing anything else to call anyone's attention.

After rounding the corner onto the street, Randolph turned on the car's headlights. He glanced over at his passenger as he drove. Once again, Randolph felt euphoric, like experiencing a wonderful dream where everything ended in a triumphant climax. The feeling persisted.

He suspected he might never know the full story, but he still decided to ask, "Can you tell me anything about what just happened?"

"You rescued me," she said.

"Yes, but why did he have you there? . . . I mean, in that cage."

"He built the cage to hold me securely and to diminish my power."

"I think I figured that much out already. But why you, and what was he going to do with you?"

"He studied me with the hope of finding the others."

"Others? There are more like you?"

"Yes. And now, I wish to ask for your help again."

"Sure." At this point, Randolph would have done almost anything for her.

"I felt that device you used. I felt it as I slept. We have been trapped here for a long time, but we have managed to stay hidden. In recent times, however, your people have been toying with many such devices, making it more difficult for us to avoid you.

"I believe you collected information with your device. Please, that man must never see the information. By using the information, he will be able to search for my companions and me whenever and wherever we must sleep. Others like him would like to enslave us," she said.

"I'm just happy I was able to help. Don't worry. I'll get rid of the information." For some unexplained reason, Randolph had lost all fear of running into the police. With someone like Theta beside him, nothing would be a problem.

"Your device brought me out of my slumbers so I could call out to you. And you answered my call. You are the first who has willingly come in response to our call.

Once again, I am thankful you came. It gives me hope that we might someday meet again and discuss many subjects. There are so many things my companions and I do not understand."

She smiled and then said, "I look forward to a day when we might live among you without hiding, but much has to be considered before we might safely take this step. If it ever happens, I believe we can learn much from each other. Perhaps if the signs are favorable at some later time, you might consider asking questions of your people to see if they would like to meet with us."

Randolph felt honored she would make such a proposal, and based on his continued elation, he thought he might be willing to give it a try. "This is all new to me. I never thought about being an ambassador, but if you need my help, just let me know. Are you sure you'll be able to find me again?"

"I am sure, Randolph Marston."

He imagined she would because he had never told her his name. According to her, he couldn't pronounce her true name, but she said Theta was a word he could understand that represented roughly the same meaning.

He drove her out of town following the route she gave him. Although it was still dark, Randolph no longer thought about the police or anyone seeing a blue woman in a white dress riding as his passenger. In some way, he knew she had the ability not to be seen once she left the confinement of Gary's "electrified" prison.

They talked along the way about all sorts of things as the rain stopped falling. She asked a lot of questions, which he tried to answer as simply as he could. Sometimes, it wasn't easy. How do you explain in simple terms the "purpose" of daytime soap operas or why manufacturers specifically make their products *not* last forever?

He asked some questions too, such as, if life is common throughout the galaxy. According to Theta, it was, but most of it lacked the ability to share conversation, such as they did while he drove.

About an hour before sunrise, Theta requested he let her out near an empty field. He was sorry to say goodbye. They had shared some special moments, despite how different they were. Toward the end of their time together, he even noted touches of subtle humor in her most pleasant personality based on some of the things she said. He looked forward to seeing her again, someday.

A few minutes after he started back to town, Randolph remembered something important. Since it wasn't raining, he pulled off along the side of the road and opened the trunk. He fired up the device and erased the data in its memory. Then, he had an idea.

With the car parked next to another open field, he pointed the cone in search of higher lifeforms, but the first readings showed no Dream Phase Waves. After the second reading, he found one and spent about twenty minutes collecting a proper sample. He immediately printed out a colorful spectrum to examine as he briefly wondered what kind of animal was asleep in that field.

A cow? A horse? An alligator?

Soon after Randolph opened his office the following day, Gary stepped in, looking like he hadn't had a good night.

Gary sat and asked without preamble, "Did you get something for me?"

"Yeah, as a matter of fact, I did. But there seems to be a problem. Here, let me show you," Randolph responded as calmly as he could.

He knew he was about to take a pretty big risk. He needed the money from the job, but after his experiences the night before, some additional misleading was in order. Maybe Theta would thank him for it, when they could see each other again.

Without letting go of the hardcopy, Randolph waved it under the client's nose as he explained, "Just look at these colors! I feel sure the machine must have messed up. These readings don't even appear to be human!"

Randolph watched as the guy started to get excited. He continued to explain, "I don't feel comfortable taking your money under the circumstances, so, here." He opened his desk drawer and extracted the bundles of cash the client gave him the day before. "I'm giving you a full refund." He tossed the printout into the still-open drawer and closed it.

"But . . . ," Gary began.

"No, you don't have to thank me. It's just my way of doing business."

Gary jumped in as soon as his mind caught up. "Hey, but at least tell me what happened."

Randolph said in perfect calm, "I followed the usual protocol. I arrived on location by about two." It had really been closer to three.

"I set up and ran my initial screening. I located the subject, the *only* subject, I might add. There was no one else in the area. I ran my DP scan.

When I saw it, I knew right away something was wrong. I set up and ran a second scan, but the results were identical. I'm sorry, but there was nothing else I could do. I packed up immediately and got out of there. I didn't care much for the neighborhood, you understand."

Most of it hadn't been a lie. The best misdirection includes plenty of truth.

"But why won't you let me have your results?" Gary asked.

"Because they're garbage."

Gary seemed to force his mind to work faster. "Listen, I appreciate what you did; I really do. I know you did a lot of work. I'd like to pay you half but on one condition; I want you to give me that printout."

Randolph had expected to hear something along those lines. "I can't do that. After all, I have a reputation to uphold. If you started showing this hardcopy to people, it could do my business a lot of harm."

"What if I give you the entire amount in exchange for the printout? And I promise that if anyone ever sees it, they won't know it came from you. I'd just like to have it as a souvenir."

Randolph pretended surprise. "You mean you're willing to give me the full fee for this worthless printout? Why would you do that?"

"Out of the goodness of my heart."

Yeah, sure, Randolph thought.

Gary continued, "And I know you went to a lot of trouble. Besides, maybe we'll do business again sometime. So, what do you say?"

Randolph hesitated and stared back with his best blank face.

Wait for it, he told himself. *Wait for it. Now.*

"Well, okay. If you insist."

Behind the client's eyes, Randolph detected gears meshing. The client pushed the bundles of cash to him from across the table. Then, Gary opened the small sack he carried and dumped out the other half.

Acting reluctant, Randolph opened the drawer and extracted the hardcopy, passing it around the bundles of money to the other side of the table.

Now who's the better con? Randolph thought.

"I'll be seeing you around, sometime." Gary immediately stood up, appearing like a man impatient to be somewhere else.

Smiling, Randolph countered, "Not if I see you first." He knew his comeback sounded rude, but Gary wasn't listening, anyway.

It's the best money I've never earned, Randolph said to himself.

The End

Inspiration for Dream Phase

"The idea for this short story 'Dream Phase' came to mind immediately following a spell of delirium due to a high fever."

John M. Moody

About John M. Moody

North Texas, independent author John M. Moody has presently published eighteen books, including romantic adventures, mysteries, and "future history" novels. Moody has held a variety of jobs, among them geologist, paleontologist, railroad worker, and writing instructor. Work continues on his fossil discoveries in Venezuela.

John M. Moody has been a member of the Author's Round Table Society since its initial meeting, bearing the title Knight. One of his mysteries, *Shards of Time*, is set in Denison, Texas, the town where ARTS meetings are held.

Based on his experiences, Moody often incorporates actual places, emotional situations, and true-to-life characters to produce his unique and imaginative stories. Critics have described themselves reading late into the night to finish his books. His fans return again and again in search of more.

https://www.amazon.com/John-M.-Moody/e/B072MB4FJL

SCIENCE FICTION: STORY 3

ILLUSION

by J. J. Aarons

. . . Ruby Hanson's breath came in ragged gasps as she pushed her body harder than she had ever done before. Her red, satin dress billowed around her, making it impossible to move as quickly as she needed. The humidity in the air did not help and neither did the heavy, garbage stench in the alley.

They just had to find us at the banquet, she thought, *not when I was wearing clothes suitable for running.*

If there was one thing she'd learned from recent events, it was that things never happened when it was convenient.

A man's deep voice boomed behind her. "You can't hide!"

But he was wrong. She could hide. She and Nate had been hiding for months. They hadn't even known she was alive until three weeks ago. If they managed to outrun them this time, they could finally disappear for good.

She'd found the perfect hiding spot for their most valuable asset, the lynchpin in the plan which would bring their organization crumbling to the ground. Even if they did catch her, at least it was safe.

A deep boom filled the alley, and Ruby cried out as a bullet ripped through the flesh of her bicep.

"I'm hit," she yelled to her partner. "Faster, Nate!"

He ran in front and slowed to help her.

She thought, *You can't help me now.*

He needed to keep running, so she shouted, "No, keep going!"

Light called to her from the end of the alley, and she knew beyond that exit was their freedom, if only they could make it.

"I can do this," she murmured to herself. "Almost there."

Red light surrounded Ruby, and she screamed as the ground beneath her disappeared. She began to fall. Arms thrashing, she fell, down, down, down, until everything faded to black. . . .

She sat up panting, her body covered in a layer of thick sweat.

"It's not real, not real," she said aloud to her empty apartment. Pressing a hand to her chest over her thundering heart, Ruby forced herself to breathe.

She could not remember when the nightmares had first started: the running for her life and being shot. All of it, repeating itself over and over again, was like a twisted merry-go-round.

It was strange. She'd never run from anything. And yet, everything about these dreams seemed so real.

Ruby touched her bicep where the bullet had ripped through. The unmarred skin was smooth beneath her fingertips, but her arm still ached.

Sighing, Ruby stretched her legs and put her bare feet on the floor, letting the cold of the tile seep into her body. It chilled the heat still pulsing through her veins.

The phone rang on her nightstand, and she answered without checking the caller ID.

"Hello," she croaked, voice raspy from sleep and lack of coffee.

Her boss's angry tone was apparent even through the phone. "Hey, can you come in early? Janet skipped her shift."

"Yeah, I can be there in thirty."

"Great." He ended the call, and Ruby made her way into the kitchen to make coffee. The call center where she worked was a twenty-four-hour-a-day operation, and she was already scheduled to work tonight. Not that she'd complain, extra cash always came in handy.

The scent of brewing coffee filled her lungs while she dressed. Her hands shook as adrenaline from the nightmare wore off.

The dreams always left her in such a foul mood. The feeling that her brain was trying to remember something never left her, which of course was impossible. All in all, she'd lived a boring life.

Walking into the bathroom, she studied her exhausted face in the mirror.

"Smile Ruby, it'll be a good day, if you let it."

Pulling out her bag of makeup, Ruby went to work covering up the physical proof of her rough night.

No sense in scaring the neighbors when I go outside, she thought.

Finally finished, Ruby rushed back into the kitchen. The clock on the coffee pot read 3:15, which meant she had another fifteen minutes before she had to be at work.

Since it was only a five-minute walk, Ruby cracked open the cover to *Cemetery Tours,* an awesome, new paranormal series by her new favorite author, Jacqueline E. Smith. As she lost herself in the ghost story, the nightmare faded to nothing but background noise.

***

Ruby made her way into work smiling at those she passed, even though she couldn't say she *saw* anyone. After all, when you work in a cubicle eight hours a day, seven days a week, it is hard to make connections with those around you, not that she'd want to.

The anxiety she suffered every day kept her from socializing. It was hard to trust anyone when you felt as if everyone was out to get you.

It made for a very lonely existence.

Sitting down at her desk, Ruby set her backpack on the floor. On the desk next to her keyboard, she put her travel mug of coffee.

As she booted up her computer and got everything ready for her shift, Ruby caught a glimpse of something slipped beneath her keyboard.

Lifting the keyboard, she spotted a red envelope. She reached for it.

Agony exploded in her brain sending tiny spots swimming into her vision. Ruby dropped her keyboard and clutched the sides of her head as the pain continued to radiate down through her neck.

Images flashed through her mind in a continued assault as the pain intensified.

She was running, hiding. . . . They can't find it. . . . Keep it from them. . . . A man with brown hair and dark green eyes appeared. Love, passion, anger, and betrayal filled her thoughts. . . .

She wasn't sure what any of it meant, but the last word stuck out, *betrayal*. He'd betrayed her.

"Ruby."

Without looking up, she recognized the voice, her thoughts continuing.

"Run, Nate," she thought. *"Faster!"*

In front of her, images of a dark-haired man pushed into her conscious mind, beating back the pain.

Cautiously, she looked up and directly into familiar green eyes. She recoiled, the back of her chair hitting the wall of the cubicle behind her.

"Ruby," he said her name again. The sound sent her heart thundering in her chest. "Do you know who I am?"

"Nate?" His name came out as a whisper while she continued to stare at a man she hadn't known existed until seconds ago.

He smiled and nodded. "Yes, that's me. I, I need you to come with me." He reached a hand out to her.

She frantically shook her head. "I don't know you."

Looking away, he muttered a curse before turning his attention back to her.

"Yes, you do. You may not remember, Ruby, but I promise you know me. I won't hurt you. Please come with me."

Ruby shook her head again but was unable to dismiss what he'd said. She did know him. She just wasn't sure how.

"I need to work."

He urgently said, "They are using you. Please come with me."

"I can't."

Quick footsteps thundered from down the hall, and Nate peered out of her cubicle.

Looking back at her with wide eyes, he reached down and touched her hand. The contact sent another jolt of recognition through her mind.

"I'll be back for you, Ruby, I promise. Please stay safe."

He pressed a button on his watch and disappeared into thin air.

Ruby stared at the now empty space and thought, *What happened? AM I going insane?*

Two men dressed in security uniforms stopped at her desk. One said, "Ma'am."

Ruby thought, *Since when do we have security?*

The officer continued, "Are you all right?"

They glanced into her cubicle and into the ones beside hers.

She offered them her best fake smile. "Yes, just woke up with a mild headache this morning. It doesn't seem to want to leave."

He peered at her and said, "You were talking to yourself?"

Ruby laughed, though there was little humor in it. "I do that sometimes. It is so embarrassing someone heard me."

Both men continued to stare as if determining whether she was lying. The one to her left finally smiled and said, "If you need anything, please let us know."

"I will. Thank you."

The feeling of emptiness left behind by the green-eyed man made no sense. When he'd touched her, it had been almost as if she remembered, briefly, what he meant to her.

What did he mean to her? Why was she dreaming of a man she had no memory of?

Ruby covered her face with shaking hands and rested her elbows on the top of her desk, wondering, *What is happening to me?*

***

Nate cursed under his breath as he materialized in the alley across from the call center. He'd been so close, so close that he literally had touched her.

He could have grabbed her and run. Yet, he was man enough to admit that was a terrible plan. They were watching, and the chances of the two of them making it out alive were slim to none.

So, he would sit and wait until she was alone. He would convince her to trust him, no matter what it took.

Her life depended on it.

***

Ruby all but crawled into her apartment at seven the next morning. She was exhausted, more so than usual, and all she could think of was falling into bed and sleeping for the rest of her life. Of course, sixteen hours with a mind-splitting headache would do that to anyone.

She dropped her keys and purse on the counter. At the sight of the red envelope she had retrieved from under her keyboard, she cringed as a fresh wave of pain rushed over her.

She thought, *Why does my mind reel every time I see it?*

She'd kept it hidden in her backpack, afraid of what might be inside. Between finding it, her strange reaction, and the man disappearing in her cubical, she wasn't sure she could take much else.

Don't be a chicken, Ruby, she told herself. *It can't be much weirder than your day already has been.*

Closing her eyes, Ruby took a deep breath and slipped the note from inside the envelope. Discarding the envelope without looking, she read the note in her hands.

The words read, *Trust him.*

Those two words scrawled on a notecard had been stuck under her keyboard.

She thought, *Who is 'him', and why should I trust 'him?'*

In her dark living room, against the curtains, Ruby saw a shadow move. She dropped the notecard, walked to the window, and threw open the curtain.

The man from her cubicle, Nate, stood on the fire escape eyeing her warily as if she might run away.

I might, she thought. *He disappeared right in front of me, and now here he is, standing outside my open window.*

His presence was both disconcerting and oddly comforting.

He put his hands up. "I won't hurt you."

"Did you leave that note on my desk? Under my keyboard?" she asked, desperate for answers. She undid the screen from her window and stepped aside, allowing him to duck through into her apartment.

"What note?" he answered.

"The one in the red envelope."

"Red," he said. "Have you ever seen that particular color prior to today?"

"Of course, I have." She looked around. Surely there was something in here that was–her search stopped as awareness dawned on her.

Nothing, not a single red thread existed anywhere in her apartment. The only thing red was the envelope.

"So it was from you." She pressed her fingers to her throbbing temples as images bombarded her thoughts.

He betrayed me, betrayed all of us.

Who had betrayed them? she thought.

Ruby's mind screamed at her, begging her to remember, but everything was so mixed up. Nothing made sense.

"No, it wasn't from me. But I've noticed they have eliminated that particular color from this world." He looked around the room as she'd done only moments before.

"Excuse me? From this world? Eliminated a color? Who are you?"

He took a step toward her.

She stepped back.

"Don't you recognize me?" He moved closer. "Other than just knowing my name?"

This time she held her ground: deep green eyes, kind, loving, passionate, short beard, and gentle hands.

She knew him that much was true, but how?

"I recognize you, but I don't know from where," she said, not willing to tell a stranger she'd been dreaming of him.

He continued, "I need to tell you some things, but they are going to sound insane. I need you to keep an open mind. Please try to believe me."

She hesitated. If he were going to kill her, now would be a perfect time. She was home alone. And since it was the middle of the day on a Tuesday, chances were that no one would hear her if she screamed.

Still, he hadn't made a move to cause her harm. She took a deep breath. "Okay."

He gestured to the light brown couch in her living room. "Can we have a seat?"

She nodded.

He sat on the couch.

Ruby turned toward the kitchen. "I'm going to grab some water, are you thirsty?"

"No, thank you."

She could feel his eyes on her as she moved around her space, before taking a seat beside him on the sofa.

Laughing nervously, he continued, "Okay, I suppose we should dive in. My name is Nate, as you already know. My last name is Hanson."

She said to him, "That's my last name."

"I know," he answered.

She tipped up her water, letting the coolness of the liquid slip down her throat and then asked, "Are we related?"

He smiled. "Something like that. We're married."

Ruby coughed, choking on her water.

"Married? I'm not married." She gaped at him, confused as to why he would tell such a lie. *Surely,* she thought, *I would remember being married!*

His jaw tightened. "Not here, you aren't." The humor from moments ago vanished under the barely leashed rage he wore all over his face. "You were taken three months ago by a company searching for an asset we stole. It is beyond important they do not discover the location of it. No matter what torture they put you through, you refused to crack. Their last hope was that you would reveal it to them in a dream."

"A dream?" she asked and thought, *Was he serious?* Had she allowed a crazy man to sit on her couch? Unable to restrain herself, Ruby scooted away. Her need to be close to an exit overpowered her manners.

If he noticed, he didn't show it. "Yes, that's where we are now."

She repeated, "We're in a dream?"

"We're inside your mind," he continued. "They have you trapped. And to be honest, I'm not quite sure how to get you out."

"Let's say for the sake of argument that I do believe you. Why are you here? Why not just wake me up?" she asked.

"I can't. If I were to pull you off the machine before your mind was released, you would die."

Ruby sat quietly staring at her hands and thinking, *What he is telling me is crazy! Absolutely impossible, even. So why do I believe him? Why is my mind saying he's telling the truth even as it is fighting against the idea?*

She asked, "Then why come here now?"

"I was hoping you would know something, anything that might help us get you out."

"I don't even know if I believe you." She got to her feet and walked back to her entry table, where she'd discarded the envelope.

"And if you didn't leave this, who did?" She looked down at the envelope. The splitting headache returned along with another wave of images and fear so strong it nearly sent her racing out the door.

Run, she heard inside her mind. *They're coming for us. Can't let them have it. Have to hide it. They will kill him.*

"Aghh!" She clutched her head and fell to her knees.

Within seconds, Nate was next to her. His scent filled her lungs and caused tears to build in the corners of her eyes. She thought, *He has always smelled like cedar, hasn't he?*

He asked, "What is it? What's wrong?"

"The envelope," she said. "Every time I look at it, I get this pain and flashes in my head."

"What kind of flashes?"

"I don't know—words, images, and feelings."

"You don't recognize any of them?"

"That's the thing, I recognize them all, but it doesn't make any sense!"

He pulled her into his arms.

She leaned against him. This man was a stranger to her, yet she felt as if she knew him better than herself.

Both of their heads snapped up at the thunder of footsteps outside her apartment.

He said as he got to his feet, "I have to go."

"No, not yet. I have more questions."

"I will be back."

"But I . . ."

He put his hands on her shoulders. "I will be back, Ruby. There is not a force in any world, dream or otherwise, which could keep me away. I know you don't remember, but I love you." He pressed his lips to hers, and a shock of electricity zapped through her. "I'll always come back for you," he whispered against her mouth and disappeared in the blink of an eye.

Stunned by the responding buzzing in her blood, it took Ruby a few moments to hear the knocking on her door.

Still in shock, she slowly opened it.

"Can I help you?" she asked the uniformed police officers on the other side.

"We are checking all the apartments. A man has escaped from Jackson Penitentiary and was spotted in this area." The officer pulled a photo out of his pocket, and Nate's face stared at her from the photo. "Have you seen him?"

Ruby pretended to study the photo, ignoring the alarm bells going off in her head. "No, I'm sorry, I haven't."

A second officer said, "You haven't seen this man? He is incredibly dangerous, ma'am."

Ruby tore her gaze from the image to stare at him. "I haven't. If I do, I will call."

The officer narrowed his eyes, his mouth pulling into a tight line.

He doesn't believe me.

The alarm bells in her head rang louder, making the pain from her lingering headache seem obsolete.

"Miss Hanson, we need you to focus."

Ruby's eyes widened. "How did you know my name?"

The first officer shoved the image back into his pocket. "We checked the building residents list before we came up."

She told herself, *Lie!*

Her mind screamed at her to shut the door, to run away from them, but she held his gaze knowing that if she did either, they would no longer be polite.

"I told you, I haven't seen him."

She started to shut the door.

The officer stuck his foot in the door and gripped it with his hand. "We aren't done talking to you."

"Yes, you are."

She slammed her body weight against the door, but he pushed harder, sending her flying back into her entry table.

The second officer said, "We need you to come with us." He reached for his handcuffs.

Dazed, she shook her head.

"We can do this the easy way or hard way," the second officer said.

She growled, "I suppose we're doing it the hard way then." Grabbing the envelope and notecard, Ruby bolted for her window and climbed out onto her fire escape.

Bullets flew, missing her by inches. When she should have panicked, Ruby became calm. Every single move she made was deliberate as she escaped down into the bright street.

She dodged traffic, ignoring the screams of the people around as the two officers chased her through the streets of New York, a city she'd called home for as long as she could remember.

Not really home though, she reminded herself, *not if Nate was being honest with her.*

She turned a corner and hid behind a dumpster.

The two officers stepped into the alley.

Ruby held her breath.

"You might as well come out, Ruby. We know you're in here."

She didn't say a word, and silently prayed they wouldn't know where she was.

One of the men laughed and said to someone else, "Nice of you to show up."

Nate's voice was a welcome sound as he answered, "I don't think you'll be saying that for long."

She peered around the dumpster to see him standing between her and the officers.

One charged. Nate ducked, narrowly avoiding a fist before planting his own in the officer's gut. He lifted his knee and slammed the officer's face down into it. The first officer fell to the side. The second officer roared with anger and attacked.

Nate spun, slamming his fist into the second officer's side. He dropped enough so Nate was able to tackle him to the ground. Nate hammered his fist into the officer's face.

When it was clear the other man was not getting up, Nate stood and wiped his knuckles on his jeans.

"Are they dead?" Ruby asked.

He turned toward her. "That's the trick. We can't actually kill each other while we're in here. It's a failsafe. If we could, it would risk killing off part of your mind. They know that."

A part of my mind? she thought.

Shoving her fear to the side, she asked, "Why were they after me? I told them I didn't know you when they asked."

"Well, honey, you may be great at keeping secrets, but you're a terrible liar."

For the first time since this all started, she smiled at his joke. "I suppose I must be. Thank you."

"No need to thank me, Ruby. I'd do anything for you."

Their eyes held, locked together. The connection between them turned electric.

"We need to move. There will be more."

"How will we hide?" she asked. "If they're watching my mind and monitoring what's going on, they will be able to find us no matter where we go."

"They can't watch your mind like a movie. When you picture a place or thing, that's when they can see it."

She closed her hands into fists.

If this is true, she thought, *I've been living a lie for who knows how long. How much time has passed while I've been trapped in my mind?*

She said out loud, "They will still be able to find us. I can't not think."

He thought for a moment and then said, "True. Do you trust me?"

Her answer came without hesitation, sealing her feelings for the man in front of her. "Yes."

Nate pulled a bandana out from his pocket. "I'm going to cover your eyes and lead you somewhere. If you don't know where we're going, I should be able to get us somewhere safe."

Despite her nerves about being blindfolded and led around the city by a man who might as well have been a stranger, she nodded. "Okay."

He stepped toward her and lowered his mouth to hers. "It's going to be fine."

The feel of his lips, pressed against her own, was not alien like it should have been, but rather, familiar. It sparked a longing she remembered but couldn't place.

"I missed you," he whispered, "more than you could imagine." He covered her eyes with his bandana.

Ruby adjusted her mind to the dark. "Let's go."

***

She wasn't sure how long they walked, but it was afternoon before he removed the blindfold.

Ruby blinked, the sudden light an assault on her senses. "Where are we?" Before he could answer, she shook her head. "Oh, that's right. I can't know."

"We're safe." He smiled, and lightly squeezed her bicep.

The studio apartment she stood in had seen better days. The kitchen boasted a mini fridge, faded, peeling countertops, and a single burner plugged into an outlet. A bed sat on one wall, and a door led, to what she guessed, was a bathroom.

"So, they are after me now because they know I saw you?" she asked.

He nodded. "They had to have known I would come for you. I just bet they didn't count on me finding you." He chuckled, but there was no humor in it. "It took me a lot longer than I thought it would."

"Are you with me now? I mean, your real body."

He stepped close to her, his eyes darkening. "I assure you this is my real body, Ruby. But as far as in the actual world, no, it is not. I actually have no clue where they are keeping you."

"Then how are you here?"

"Our employers have some technology that allows you to tap into someone's subconscious, even if you aren't physically next to them. The trick, though, is you have to be emotionally connected to the person. This prevents someone from entering a strangers mind."

"Is that how these people got into my mind?" she asked.

He shook his head. "They possess your body. They used a different machine to submerge you into a fictional reality they control."

Ruby closed her eyes and searched for a memory, which would gleam light onto her real life, but got none. "What have they done to me?" she whispered, looking down at her shaking hands.

Nate stepped forward and grabbed them, wrapping them in his much larger ones. "Everything is going to be okay, Ruby. I promise I'll find a way to get you out."

She looked up at him, tears in her eyes. If everything she knew had been a lie, how was she to know if she could trust herself?

"Tell me about your day," he said, pulling Ruby from her thoughts.

"What do you want to know?" she asked.

"Everything."

"Okay. I woke up yesterday afternoon and got a call that I needed to go into work because Janet couldn't make her shift."

He stuck in, "Janet is our employer's name. What happened next?"

"I read a book until it was time to leave."

"What book?"

"Cemetery Tours," she said.

"Your favorite series, you actually met the author once."

"Really?"

He nodded. "Go on."

"I went into work, and you were there. I was on edge because of my nightmare, and when you showed up it freaked me out because I had dreamt of you."

He straightened. "Tell me about the nightmare."

She recounted it, being sure to include every detail.

When she finished, he was staring at her and said, "That was the night you were taken. The flashes of red and black were the flare I shot up before they fired on us. We were supposed to be airlifted out, but I learned a week later Janet left us cornered so our enemy could get their hands on you."

"Why would she turn me in when I had information about the asset?" she asked, remembering her thoughts from the nightmare: *protect the asset, at all costs.*

"Because she knew you wouldn't break. No matter what you were put through, she knew you would keep the secret. Having you taken would serve her other purposes."

"Which were?"

"We'll get to that, I promise. All you need to know is she's been dealt with."

"What does that mean?" Ruby asked.

He ignored her question. "Listen, we will find a way to get you out, I promise."

"What happened to her? To Janet?"

Nate sighed. "I did what I had to do to find out what she knew." When Ruby didn't respond, he continued, "So, tell me about the red envelope. What did it say?"

"Trust him."

"Hopefully, that means me." He was silent a moment. "You haven't come into contact with anyone strange recently? Someone who didn't fit in?"

She shook her head. "Not until you. I actually can't remember what I did yesterday. I know I did something, but it's a fog. I wonder if it's always been like that."

"Probably, they restart your mind, resetting the world when you fall asleep."

She panicked. "Does that mean they will make you go away? Will they erase the memories from today?"

213

His jaw tightened. "It's possible, if you fall asleep, they can do it. But they would risk erasing everything permanently if they tried to do it while you were conscious." He squeezed her hands. "If they do, I'll just try again and again until I find out how to rescue you."

"So all I have to do is stay awake and remember anything that might help figure out where they are keeping me. Easy peasy."

Nate grinned at her.

"What?" she asked.

"You used to say that before every mission. I've missed it."

Ruby blushed, and their eyes held for a moment. "So what's the red have to do with it? Why erase that particular color?"

"It's your favorite. Perhaps they were worried it would trigger a memory."

"It does: pain."

"Anything else?" he asked.

"Blurry images, thoughts, but nothing that makes any sense."

"Did you happen to grab it?"

She reached into her pocket and pulled out the envelope, careful to not look directly at it as she handed it to him.

Nate studied the handwriting on the notecard. A slow smile spread across his lips. "Come here." He searched the kitchen drawers until he found a pen.

He handed the pen and notecard to her, turning the card over to the blank side. "Write 'trust him'," he instructed.

She did.

Nate studied it before grinning widely. "I knew it!"

"Knew what?"

"There is a part of you that's aware of what's happening. Look." He turned the card over to show her both sides. Her writing was the same.

"So, you're saying I wrote this? Is it possible they've erased even my own handwriting from my memory?"

He nodded. "Which means, you might know where you are!" He lifted her and spun her in a circle.

"I don't know. I can't remember anything prior to today."

"Let's start with red." He held up the envelope.

She avoided it.

"There's a reason you put it in this color envelope. I know it hurts, but you have to look at it."

Ruby turned her head and forced herself to look at the envelope. Pain assaulted her senses as she rubbed her eyes with the palms of her hands.

Emotions came to her. She desperately tried to grasp onto one: a*nger, hatred, betrayal, and love.*

Her mind settled on a memory and willed herself to focus.

"You have to give me another chance, Ruby. I swear to you nothing happened," Nate pleaded from where he knelt on the hotel floor.

"You expect me to believe that nothing happened between you two? You took an assignment to seduce her, Nate. Even after we talked, and I asked you not to."

"We needed that information. We have to keep the asset safe. She was our ticket to learning what they had on us."

Ruby shook her head as tears formed in the corners of her eyes. "You whored yourself out for information, Nate, and I can't forgive you for that. There were other ways."

He got to his feet. "First off, I didn't whore myself out. We didn't sleep together. I didn't even kiss her! We flirted for a little while so I could stroke her ego enough to get her to open up."

"I don't believe you."

"We've been married eight years, Ruby. Ten full years of partnership, and you're willing to throw that down the drain because I took an assignment you don't agree with?"

"You promised me!"

The memory faded. Ruby's hands shook. This was more painful than she could have imagined and seeing the agony on Nate's face was tearing the heart out of her chest.

She knew he hadn't done anything wrong, but like Janet had given him an assignment, she'd been given one, too. She had to follow through with it. Their lives and the life of their asset depended on it.

He moved toward her. "Ruby, please. I'm so sorry."

It took everything in her power to not rush into his arms. "Just go."

"Ruby."

She shook her head and he stepped back.

"So that's how it's going to be?" he asked. He swallowed hard; his bottom lip slightly quivering.

"Goodbye, Nate," she whispered. She bit back tears at the look of complete disbelief and brokenness that crossed his face.

Knowing her mind was made up, he turned and left the room.

Ruby fell to her knees and pressed Janet's name on her phone. Putting it up to her ear, she spoke into it as soon as the other woman was on the line. "It's done."

"Good, now he can finish his job," Janet said.

"Was this really necessary?" Ruby choked out, her heart completely shattered.

"The asset comes first, Agent Hanson."

Ruby ground her teeth together and focused on the painting behind the bed. Splashes of red covered up gold, and she knew in that moment, her life would never be the same. . . .

The memory faded.

"We were divorced?" Ruby looked at Nate who stood intently watching her.

Pain flashed across his face. He shook his head. "No, not yet. You ended things a week before you were taken. By the time I realized what was happening, it was too late."

"What do you mean?"

His jaw tightened. "Our employer was using you to take the fall. She wanted you captured because she believed it would make me focus more on the mission and less on you."

"That's why she wanted me to end things."

"Yes, and when I didn't go through with the mission she'd given me, she took matters into her own hands, knowing I would do anything to find you."

"What is our asset?"

"You've blocked it from your mind, so if telling you makes you remember where you've hidden it, they would know. We can't chance that."

She nodded.

"I think I may have an idea to get you out, but it's risky."

"What is it?"

He turned away and paced, before returning to stand in front of her. Nate took her hands and pressed his lips to the back of each one. Looking into her eyes he said, "I think you are going to have to die."

Her mouth fell open. She stared at him. "What?"

"Not permanently, only long enough for you to come out of the machine. I believe that if you were legally dead for at least thirty seconds, your mind would be free of the machine. Then, we can start your heart again. In theory, you would wake up."

"In theory?"

"That's the best I've got, unless there's a 'wake her up' button on the actual machine."

"You don't even know where I am!"

"I know," he said. "We have to figure out where you were taken the night after your abduction."

"How do we figure *that* out?"

"I think you need to go to sleep."

"But you said earlier I can't sleep. They could reset me. They could reset everything."

"It's a possibility," he continued. "But you said that's when your dreams of that night come to you."

"If I wake up back in my apartment, I won't remember you."

"I'm a stubborn guy, Ruby, you can't shake me that easily." He winked at her.

She relaxed.

"Besides, maybe you will wake up here, and we will have worried for no reason. Minds work strangely. You may have to repeat the exact routine for their process to function. They don't know where you are because you don't know. Maybe that will keep your mind safe from tampering."

"So if I lie down and sleep, how can I be sure I'll have a dream?"

"You can't, but if you focus hard on the night you were taken, we may get lucky."

She considered. The logic made sense, as much as logic could be applied to their current situation. Looking up at him, she smiled despite her nerves. "Easy peasy, right?"

He returned her smile with one of his own. "Easy peasy, Babe."

She sighed before walking over to the old bed and lying down on the dingy comforter. It smelled musty. She tried to ignore thoughts of who might've slept on it before and how long ago that had been. They were in her mind, so germs didn't technically exist, right?

"I'm here," he assured her, "and I will do my best to be here when you wake up. As long as they don't find a way to pull you, I will be."

Ruby closed her eyes, willing herself to think about the night she was ripped away from the man sitting beside her, and the dream began. . ..

Ruby ran through the dark alley as fast as she could. Her lungs burned, but she pushed on.

A man's deep voice boomed behind her, "You can't hide."

For months, she and Nate had managed to stay undercover. She wasn't sure how they had found them tonight, but the asset had been hidden. That was all that mattered.

"Nate, faster," she screamed to her partner who was only two paces in front.

He turned his head long enough to look at her. When all this was over, she was going to tell him the truth: Janet had forced her to end things with him because she'd wanted him to complete his mission with Malco's twenty-two-year-old daughter.

Life wasn't worth living without Nate, and if that meant they had to quit, she was just fine with an early retirement.

She could see the end of the alley, knew that beyond that exit would be freedom, if only they could make it there.

Nate shot a flare to signal the helicopter which would lift them to freedom.

A blast of pain exploded through her, and she screamed falling to her knees. She pressed her hand to her stomach and pulled it away to see blood dripping from her palm.

Nate stopped. He turned, his eyes widening when he saw her on the ground.

"Ruby!" He started to move toward her.

She put her hands up. "You have to go!"

"I'm not leaving you!" He dropped to his knees beside her and lifted her into his arms."

"You can't carry me, Nate."

"I will."

"No. If they find you, no one will be around to watch over the asset. Please, you have to let me go."

He frantically shook his head. "You come first."

Tears filled her eyes. "I love you, Nate. You have to know I didn't want to leave you."

"Then why did you?"

"There's no time. You have to put me down and run."

"I won't leave you."

She reached up and cupped his face with one hand, lifting her gun with the other. Pressing it to her chest, she looked into his mossy, green eyes.

"You have to. I'm not worth risking everything we've fought for."

"Ruby, you can't. Put it down."

"I will pull this trigger; you know I will. If you escape, we might stand a chance. I know you will find me, but you must get away first. It will do us no good to both be captured."

"Ruby—"

"There is no time," she said.

Tears streaming down both their cheeks, Nate stopped and set her on her feet.

"Go baby," she continued. "I'll be right behind you. Easy peasy, right?"

He choked up. "Easy peasy, babe."

The images faded away, replaced by more memories. . . .

She lay on a gurney and was being wheeled into a warehouse.

Searching the room, Ruby focused on every detail, looking for anything that might give her some clue as to where she was.

"Ruby Hanson, I have to say it's an honor."

She looked up to see a middle-aged man standing in front of her, looking particularly smug. His dark eyes looked upon her in both wonder and excitement. It was Malco Ramirez.

Her dream-self took control of her voice as it replayed her own memory.

"I certainly wouldn't," she sneered.

"Spunky, too," he laughed. "You know I can have them remove that bandage and let you bleed out."

"Then do it."

"We'll save that for later."

She demanded, "What do you want?"

"I want to know where my daughter is," said Malco.

"Your daughter? I assume she's clubbing it up with all of her male suitors."

"Not Melanie." He ground his teeth together. "I want to know where Andrea is."

"You don't have another daughter." The words left her mouth, and Ruby tried to hide the lie in them.

His face turned red. "Yes. I. Do. And you and your husband took her from me!"

Ruby didn't respond. He was only using her to get an answer. His words were lies. Janet wouldn't have had them kidnap someone's daughter, would she? She told them the little blonde girl had been a prisoner, and that they were saving her.

"Look." He held up a photograph.

Ruby refused to look at it. She would not be manipulated.

"Fine," he said. "Hook her up. You don't want to give me the answer? I will rip it from your brain."

She internally panicked as wires were attached to her chest, neck, and the sides of her head.

Ruby winced as the gurney she was lying on was hoisted up, sending pain shooting from the wound in her abdomen. They wheeled a giant TV into the room, placing it directly in front of her and turning it on.

The entire screen was red.

***

Ruby sat up, her heart threatening to beat right out of her chest. Relief flooded through her. She smiled as her eyes locked onto Nate's. "I know where I am, and what we have to do."

He sat on the edge of the bed, "What?"

"You have to bring Andrea to--"

He interrupted, "What are you doing? They will know!"

"Nate, Andrea is Malco's youngest daughter. We've been played."

He looked at her with disbelief. "What do you mean?"

"I saw him. When they took me to the warehouse to hook me up to the machine, he asked me where his daughter was. He showed me a photograph of them together. He's her father."

"He's playing you," Nate insisted. "They have to be playing you."

She shook her head. She remembered everything.

"It wasn't a game. Think about it. Janet had us sedate her before we took her, remember? She said the girl had to be sedated to protect herself. What if that was really because she didn't want her telling us that Malco was her father? Remember when she woke up? She was asking where her dad was, and we assumed she was talking about someone else."

He listened to her, his jaw tightening as she spoke. She knew he heard the truth in her words.

Yelling, Nate slammed his fist into the wall. "She played us," he roared. "I'll kill her."

"Nate, we need to focus."

He took a deep breath and turned to her. "So, what do we have to do?"

"You have to take her home."

"Won't he kill us both?"

"I don't think so. He only wants his daughter back. We can explain everything to him later."

"All right." He stood. "Will you be okay?"

She nodded. "Go and get me. I'm still in New York in a warehouse on the docks. It has a large, faded 'M' on the door."

"I'm coming for you." He stepped to her and pulled her mouth against his in a kiss Ruby prayed wasn't goodbye. She had no assurance Malco wouldn't kill them.

Nate disappeared.

***

Ruby paced the room. Nate disappeared four hours ago and still nothing had changed.

Walking to the window, she looked out at the darkening street.

Had Malco killed him? Had he even managed to get Andrea home? Why had Janet tricked them into kidnapping a child? So many questions and not nearly enough answers.

"Wake up." A male voice filled the room.

She turned around, but no one was there.

"Wake up," he said.

The room spun out of focus. She closed her eyes, unsure if she was being woken or dying. Either way was better than this continuous loop of dreams.

She heard the voice again, closer this time.

"Wake up."

Ruby opened her eyes. She was in the middle of the warehouse, a red screen in front of her.

A woman removed wires attached to Ruby's head. When the woman moved out of sight, Ruby smiled.

Malco and Nate stared at her. Both appeared exhausted. Andrea was in her father's arms.

Nate stepped forward, reaching down to help Ruby from the gurney.

"Easy peasy, huh?" he asked.

"It was for me, I've just been pacing for the last four hours."

Nate laughed and wrapped his arms around her. "I love you, Ruby Hanson."

Her memories restored about Nate, Ruby returned the gesture. "I love you, too."

She released him and gripped his hand before turning to face Malco. "I'm so sorry about your daughter. We didn't know"

Malco held up his hand. "Your husband explained everything, Mrs. Hanson. We have Janet in our custody and will be dealing with her accordingly."

"Why your daughter? Why have us take her?" asked Ruby.

Malco looked down at Andrea. "Janet has been trying to get her hands on my tech for years. Perhaps she believed if she used Andrea as leverage, I would turn over my latest prototype."

"But she already has a machine like this, doesn't she?" Ruby asked Nate.

"That's not the prototype she wants," he responded.

"What is it she wants?"

Malco set Andrea down but clung to the little girl's hand.

"I recently developed a machine which I hope will allow us to travel freely throughout history. We would be able to observe monumental moments firsthand."

Ruby crossed her arms. "Time travel?"

"Yes," said Malco.

"Well, that's not hard to believe," she sarcastically responded.

Sarcasm dripped from Nate's voice. "We just pulled you out of your own mind, yet time travel is hard to believe?"

Ruby grinned.

Malco said, "Thank you, both, for bringing her back to me and for turning Janet in." He looked to Nate. "I understand setting your own revenge aside was difficult. If you need jobs, I will find a place for you in my company."

Nate squeezed Ruby's hand. "No thanks. I think we are looking to retire."

Malco laughed. "I understand. Still, if you change your mind." He grinned while turning toward a group of suited men standing behind him.

One waved and Ruby recognized him as the officer who'd shown her the picture of Nate.

Lifting a hand in return, she put all but one finger down.

The man laughed loudly before following his boss out of the warehouse.

Together Ruby and Nate walked toward the exit.

"What do we do now?" Ruby stretched, grateful her wound no longer hurt. "How long was I out?"

"Three months. And we're taking a long vacation. I'm thinking Fiji."

"Three months? Seriously?"

He nodded. "Longest three months of my life." Nate pulled her against his body and kissed the top of her head.

She smiled at him. "So, Fiji?"

He agreed, "Fiji."

"What's after Fiji?" she asked as they stepped out into the early morning sun.

"Anything we want." Nate kissed her.

Ruby relaxed as her world fell back into place.

The End

About J. J. Anon

J.J. Aarons mixes romance with high-powered tech to give you an incredible journey into endless possibilities.

Follow them at https://www.facebook.com/authorjjaarons for more information on upcoming books!

SCIENCE FICTION: STORY 4

RED EAGLE

by Thomas Fletcher Grooms

The red eye flight to Red China had just come from Red Square in Russia and landed in a pineapple grove. What was of most interest in the cargo bay was a package of red algae being transported from the red planet. The algae became an intergalactic cash crop grown on the star Red Giant, known for its low temperatures. It had been smuggled aboard the last interstellar flight and sent to earth for a high definition assignment.

The young man on board Flight 36 at 3 a.m. was a dead ringer for a late night television talk show host. He could have been mistaken for a movie star. He had the allure of a suave, persuasive politician. Having been financed by the Red Baron of Europe, he was being groomed to become the next President.

His code name was Red Eagle, and his two mentors were Red Cloud and Red Deer. They were considered to be the masterminds behind the power center of the capital. This was called Operation Red Jacket.

This project originated in the land of red roses, the source of the red algae, which was no bed of roses, whatsoever. The climate was hot and dry near the birthplace of Red Eagle in the forested hilly areas to the West. His parents had taken him to a new land, a new country, where his exceptional rhetoric came to the attention of the Red Guard, a secret intelligence organization.

The Red Guard was the muscled arm of the rulers of the World Council on Earth. Their mission was to keep an orderly balance of power over all governments. To do this, they had to stoke the coals of war.

The operation needed absolute control over the person who sat in the highest seat of power. This would allow them to determine the currency of every government. It would not matter what anyone thought after this was accomplished for they would be neutralized into submission.

Red Eagle caravanned to a safe house in the red target country for programming. He had two tutors.

Red Cloud had served in past administrations. He wrote foreign policy and acted as the closest advisor to previous presidents in areas of foreign affairs.

Red Deer leaped about the world negotiating foreign treaties and tying diplomatic relationships together, mirroring Red Cloud. They worked as an orchestrated team which played the same red vocal symphony.

Their job was to instruct and become the guiding influence for the next president, Red Eagle. They were to indoctrinate their protégé as instructed from Europe.

The teachings of Marx were important to set the tone for the subtle preparation of collusion. Eliminating the last island of independence was necessary to gain control of the world.

Red Cloud and Red Deer mapped out the steps necessary for the protégé to move from obscurity to prominence as the next president. There was a strong red line of ascension designed to complete the

Red Circle of the World Council. This meant operation Red Jacket would produce one of the world's greatest orators.

Operation Red Jacket was a symbol of the best, the best minds and talent which would control almost every red cent in circulation. This was red hot power.

After the education of Red Eagle was complete, he was moved for safe keeping and minimum exposure to the public. The area was famous for its Red Orchard's hallucinatory drink. This combination of herbs and plant-based potency was the most sought after high on the planet. It left no traces of usage, but it was no morning after cure for an aching headache.

Red Eagle entered public service to gain age in order to qualify to run for public office: the Executive Office of President. He spent his entire life grooming for this one office. The promise of unlimited power and wealth was reassuring to forever keep him out of the red.

There was no way anything could go wrong. All was in place. Everyone who was anyone was onboard.

It began with the idea for permanent, neutral, volunteer societies in all countries. They were organized in peacetime for safekeeping.

A committee of five Swiss called an international conference that met in Geneva, and the Red Council, Red Society, was established. The convention was signed by five governments. Later, twelve more countries joined.

All countries, except one, signed. The one exception challenged the Red Society for control of the world.

Red Jacket wrapped around the arrogant rogue country. The elders referred affectionately to this country as the Red Hairs.

With the next stage, a nomenclature of Redfish Society established themselves in all countries, subservient to the now ruling Red World Council. The doors to council membership were closed. To join the club, it was by *invitation only* from select members, and only those in government could join.

A Red Alert was issued, the code for the third stage of operation Red Jacket in the pre-election years. During the campaign, the press was silent about Red Eagle: who he was, from where he came, and how he got here. The fix was in, and there was no dissent.

When the political convention was over, a new name was nominated for president, Red Eagle. He was so powerfully persuasive, supported by the national media, that no one questioned his credentials. As though hypnotized by a magician, the last dissenting country became spellbound, seeing red, and the entire world lost all borders: one world made up of one country controlled by one government.

On election night, the red-blooded countrymen voted Red Eagle in as the new president. The Red Circle of the World Council was now secure. It was only a matter of execution to continue to stage four of operation Red Jacket.

On the day Red Eagle was sworn in, an action list was given to his staff to make required changes. This was to fulfil his obligation for this ceremonious moment.

The persons responsible for seeing the orders carried out were Vice President, Redford, and the Chief of Staff, Redgrave.

The capitol was located on the Red River, which flowed into the Red Sea. The grounds were lined with redbud trees. The Redheaded Woodpecker was the national bird. The background of the national flag was the color red.

The World Council now had control of the treasury. It controlled the purse strings and military. The direction to be taken would destroy the currency and deplete the military, bankrupting the country. By doing this, the circle would be made complete and stage five could begin.

The president had in place his preplanned supporters. He controlled his entire Cabinet, all agencies, and all levels of government. He controlled the Red Empire.

But like any well laid plans, all did not go as expected. Someone started asking questions. Questions that would not be answered and could not be covered up. All members reported to their battle stations. Red Alert. Red Alert. Red Alert.

One should not be embarrassed upon realizing an entire country had been hoodwinked. Less than a year later, the dismantling was disrupted.

The Red River Rebellion broke out. It was a group labeled as revolutionaries, hatemongers, unpatriotic discontents, and terrorists.

These citizens, who sought answers to questions that could not openly be answered by the Red Circle, were silenced. It was like stirring up a hornet's nest. The more the red pepper was shaken on the situation, the more volatile the entire country grew.

This red gum was disgusting to the capital elite's shoes. They were being threatened by those who wanted their country back. This was never going to happen. The red die was cast.

The Red River of the North separated from the Red River of the South matching the dividing geography of the world. This happened when the Red Circle government separated from the people. The separation was like a moat around a castle.

The red line of contention had no advantage, no chance. The people were supposed to be programmed by the media so this would never happen.

But some people will not do what they are told. Instead, they started thinking for themselves and asking questions. This had to be stopped: by inference, by intimidation, or by force.

These citizens were making the country a lawless nation, a divided country. They were the problem. They could not be trusted, especially to vote.

The red news syndicate was supposed to control all minds and actions. No one was permitted to escape, but something went terribly wrong.

It happened one night, the Red Scare. People started openly protesting, demanding transparency. They demanded corruption throughout the capital and government be brought under law. They demanded insider trading and open bribes be investigated. They demanded Red Eagle prove his citizenship and legal qualification to hold office.

The Red Circle of the World Council broadcasted these people were nuts. They had no rights, and certainly no right to question anything about or in the capitol castle. They were causing a tear in operation Red Jacket.

As the shift grew daily, it was an ever-rising threat. In the minds of the people, the doubt of government legitimacy grew. It shook the entire world.

According to the Red Circle, the capital was the country, the only country. The capital was a nation unto its own, and its citizens should have understood this.

To the Red Circle, the citizens did not seem to have any patriotism. Because of this, to those in office, they had to be the enemy, an enemy to all that is good and pure and right in the Red Circle's eyes. After all, the president and the capital know what is best for the country, not the people.

Leadership is the color red. Everyone must accept it. There should be no dissension.

If anyone else had been as smart as the Red Circle, they would be the government. They would have been given select citizenship in the capital.

But they were not and never would be. They are not royalty red citizens of the country of the capital. They were not members of the club.

Red Eagle came prepared for the dissenters. It was the sixth stage of operation Red Jacket.

Like any takeover of another country, planning far in advance anticipates what might happen. The president and all in the capital were confident. Soon, the whole incident would fade into the annals of history.

The solution to such a threat was prepared before operation Red Jacket ever started. It was time for Redemption.

Red Eagle had been promised complete protection for executing a doomed country, not the oath of the Executive Office of President. It was time for operation Red Tide to commence, the final stage of operation Red Jacket.

Order would be restored. Absolute control would be taken. After this, there would be no question as to who was running the country–no more questions ever.

The permanent solution was simple. The program of Red Tide was eloquent. The Red Circle's involvement would easily remain invisible. Only the chosen few would know of its resolve.

The president ordered the red algae, transported from the red planet, to be quietly disseminated into the Red River. The red algae, which signified the red rose, would spread in marine and freshwater environments unencumbered. Its scientific formula was Sunlight + Chlorophyll (in their cells) + Carbon Dioxide + Water = Glucose + Oxygen. This form of red algae from the red planet contained some additional factors which distinguish its properties–mind-numbing properties.

The time it takes for the extraterrestrial red algae to make its way through the entire water supply of the country and into the cells of unsuspecting citizens is about ninety days. Within one year, it would affect the entire world.

The Red Circle of the World Council made sure everyone approved had installed a special water filtration system. It was designed to neutralize red algae in the red blood cells. The Red Circle was part of the designated few allowed to keep their right minds.

After all, they were the only ones who could make decisions for the whole world. They were the only ones who knew what was best for everyone. They were the only ones continually living reality, their reality.

As for the rest of the world, those who drank the red algae, red Kool-Aid, would live forever in bliss. The world had finally come under complete control. As all stories must come to an end, we might *finis* this one by saying, "All is good in La La Land."

The End

About Thomas Fletcher Grooms

Dr. Tom Grooms, commentator with unparalleled expertise on world affairs and international business, earned two PhDs and a JD for teaching. He was a former laborer, entrepreneur, manufacturer rep, corporate executive, full professor, and United States Congress House Page. Tom taught the first international business course in Texas, helped with the accreditation of the first international business degree in Texas, and created the first international business card in the world. He is a full-time author in Denison, Texas with his wife and enjoys reading everything, world travel by cruise ship, long walks, and a comfortable rocking chair.

Where to Find the Author
   Https://www.TomGrooms.com
   Https://www.linkedin.com/in/thomas-fletcher-grooms-46487211/
   Https://www.facebook.com/tom.grooms.35
   Https://youtube.com/w2efkyxPSlg

SCI-FI HORROR

Stories based on future advances generally are classified as science fiction. This might include technology as well as social and environmental changes. The relationship between scientific principles and the story plot are crucial in defining this genre. Whether there are aliens, time travel, or political intrigues the combinations are limitless.

Combined with horror, the writer attempts to shake the readers from their everyday existence allowing them to watch the skies. It can be appalling, macabre, or simply the worst side of human nature. It can be used to wake people up to the reality of what could happen if we continue down our chosen path.

Together, these two create a genre of dark futures, predictive warnings, and wakeup calls perhaps we can avoid.

James William Peercy

SCI-FI HORROR: STORY 1

FLYING BROKEN

by Gabrielle DeMay

It's a funny thing how an audience never realizes how closely they are watched. I have been watching their chiseled features for six years, since my first night in The Window after four years of instruction on How To Be An Angel. On my debut night, I was terrified, but it was my eleventh birthday, the year of womanhood, and I was expected to act like a woman.

I didn't feel grown-up. I felt sick and naked, and I would have been sweaty if they hadn't powdered me like a pastry. I was sure every eye in the living world, and some from the grave, was fixed on me, willing my skin into stone so I could be perfect forever. But we Angels cannot stay on earth long. We are not stone, but ice sculptures, as perfect as snowflakes and just as temporary.

I think again of that night and wish I could laugh, but my tethers will not allow it. I content myself in the familiarity of the fixed steps of my dance and the strangeness of the new faces seeing it for the first time. They are too enraptured to notice I allow my amusement to crack my lips for the barest moment. They do not notice they are the observed. Watching us, the audience forgets they exist. I know this because I am their audience, and by watching them I can forget my existence, too.

I am not their only observer. I can see the House Master's assistants in the darkest folds of the little theater, scribbling demographics. They are counting the young boys in the audience, there are more of them than usual tonight, and I wonder if they will bring out Lyra and Ara more often because of it.

The House Master, himself, scrutinizes each face for signs of disinterest, for the barest excuse to end my act, but I am not afraid. My performance is perfect, as always. I look at them again, the neat rows of faces unaware of their audience. The House Master sees billfolds . . . I see people.

I finish my routine, neck and back arched, head lowered, toes in perfect form. It seems as though my toes are the only force securing me to the floor to keep me from drifting up and floating away. Achingly beautiful: a phrase which must have been invented as a subtitle to ballet, for how else could it fit as naturally as a breath fits a set of lungs? The music fades.

I cannot leave. A morbid suspense holds me hovering offstage with the other Angels hiding in the wings where we can see the stage, but no one can see us. It is the first time for the youngest generations to see the Leap, and I can taste their curiosity like bitter flowers . . . but I cannot hate them for it.

These girls were never told. The older Angels do not speak of it. Now as I watch their untainted eyes, I remember I was once like them. I ought to leave, as I have every time since, but this time the horror is personal. I start when the Stage Master booms out a greeting to our patrons. I hadn't noticed him take the stage.

"You enjoyed the dancing of all our little Angels, yes? Ah, but tonight you are here for something special. On this night, our Ceremony of Stars, you have come to bid farewell to a favorite of ours here at Heaven's Window. Tonight is the farewell performance of Angel Sagitta.

But do not be sad! She is leaving to join her sisters. She is going home to the constellation from which she descended to grace us with her mesmerizing dance. If you look closely, you might see her constellation wink a little more brightly at you, happy to have her home. Here tonight, she will give us one more performance worth remembering her by.

Well, I know you did not come to see me, so I will not delay any further. Watch her, memorize her, and don't forget! When she leaps, make a wish!"

On the happy side of the soundproof glass, the crowd obediently claps and cheers. They look like mimes performing on cue, their eternally-empty hats held out for review after doing a trick. This is their reward.

The lights dim. The Stage Master has vanished, leaving the glossy floor to dully reflect the gathering mood. I think I see a few ghosts there, too. Sagitta has appeared onstage from nowhere through a trick of lights and mirrors. Behind me, an effects engineer is berated by his superior for a trivial mistake in the execution. He shouts, knowing the audience can't hear anything this side of the glass.

I fix my eyes on Sagitta, obediently memorizing her as the Stage Master commanded. I won't remember her graceful position, her lightness of foot, or anything else artificial. I want to see the opinion in her eyes.

The music begins as she unfolds herself from a deceptively simple recline, growing and spinning out of the ground like a carved doll in a music box. She may well be, I muse to myself.

Her features are painted over into someone's ideal, and her hair for all its stability could withstand the real angels, if they came down in their fire and fury to shake it. I track her across the stage.

The Dance Mistress worked on the choreography for this set for months. She calls it "The Flight of the Lunatic," but I cannot see why. She says true genius cannot be comprehended by anyone save its originator.

I disagree. Genius is the discovery of something so obvious everyone else wonders why they had not thought of it before.

Sagitta's soft breaths set a beat separate from the music. The unscheduled flash of her eyelids breaks the carefully crafted tension of the performance.

I imagine I can see her quick pulse under the layers of makeup. These traces of humanity form a dance of their own, and I wonder if I would be hailed a genius for pointing them out.

See here, I might say, *these Angels you worship and admire walk in the mud, not above it, and their toes are stained the same as yours.*

But I doubt they would believe me enough to recognize the mortal truth.

The Ceremony of Stars has two purposes. The first, as advertised to the masses, is to celebrate the Return of an Angel from Heaven's Window to the constellation for which she is named. The second, known only to the Window's collaborators, is to reap the profits of a limited-time product.

When I was a child, I was as innocent of the second purpose as the other celebrators flooding in around me to the glass-partitioned theater. I remember how men and women packed themselves so tightly in they could not tell, of the clothes pressed to their skin, which were their own and which were their neighbor's, while the children slid between bars of legs like birds escaping from a cage.

The signs in those days bore hand-painted stars and the occasional poorly-programmed marquis. Yet, enough metal poured in every night to plate the Window with political armor. By the time the odd rumor surfaced to question the ethics of the business, the Window was untouchable.

The draw then was the novelty of it all. I remember the dances, though I had not yet learned the mechanics. The Angels were dressed in flowers and were dancing out the fables of fairies and gods.

The final Angel wore a wool shawl and cloche. She was meant to be a lamb and told a story of freedom from her shepherd. All the Return dances have a set theme of liberty.

I had never seen the Angel before, yet the Stage Master's eulogy had me weeping that I should never again witness such talent and passion. As she rose in the Angel's Leap, I lifted my tear-streaked face to her flawless one…and wished for something petty.

I didn't bless her, as I hope now someone did. I didn't think Angels needed wishes. I know they do now.

Like other little girls, I was mesmerized. Like other little girls, I wanted to be an Angel. Like other little girls, I was chosen.

It was then I learned the Angels of Heaven's Window are only human. But it wasn't until my next Ceremony on the quiet side of the glass that I learned what really happens to Returned Angels.

I blink back into the moment as Sagitta finishes her routine with the brisé volé or "flying brisé." "Brisé" means broken. It is an advanced move that the Dance Mistress has made Sagitta practice over and over for weeks, always chiding her on the finish.

"It's all about the landing," she would say.

I don't know why she said it. Sagitta's final flying brisé doesn't touch down but seamlessly becomes the Leap. It is a slow, magical process where her initial momentum is caught like a leaf in a stream.

She is drawn upward, wingless, toward the invisible ceiling of Heaven's Window, which viewers assume doesn't exist. She is lifted by the pinions which rupture her abdominal organs even while they hold her limbs in motionless perfection.

It isn't until the Stage Master is bowing to silent applause that I realize I have been standing fixed the whole of Sagitta's trip. As though I had ridden it with her, I don't move until she is gently set backstage and the pinions released, ready for reuse, allowing her to drop softly to the floor.

The lunatic is free.

The youngest Angels around me shuffle and gasp. I am distantly aware of their good sense not to scream.

We are herded to our quarters while a few attendants quietly soothe fraying nerves with hushes and gentle touches. They mean to prevent crying and the destruction tears wreak on delicate faces, expensive faces.

Almost to my dressing room, I notice a fleck of that taboo substance, the last evidence of Sagitta's life, dark on my hand. An attendant sees and hurriedly wipes it away.

See here, your Angels bleed, I think. *They dance like a fish on a string, caught by the throat for your delight. See here, your Angels die.*

***

My dressing room is quiet. I sit with my back to the mirror. I am undone as only a handful, outside the Angels, have seen me: hair shapeless, skin scrubbed raw, loose shawls drawn on only for warmth. Alone, in moments like this, do I feel a portion of myself detach from who I was trained to be, raise its head, and sniff the air for danger.

This is not Virgo, Wingless Angel and Maiden of the Stars, my painted facade. This is the forbidden whisper, Individuality, which cackles on for all it is suppressed. This is Defiance, worthless for all it cannot inspire action, and must soothe itself with a righteous inner tirade that dies, muffled by its own echo in so small a space. This is Fear, or the source of it, because for Fear to work there must be something worth losing with the potential of being lost.

Here I sit, then, me and my temporary self. I rub the skin on the back of my hand where the blood had been, hoping, rather than fearing, there is any left.

My thumb rolls over a pinion. It's too small to be felt, but I know it is there, hidden. The magnetic bead is powerless here, so far from the stage. Here, I can do as I please.

I rub harder. Here, it cannot force my movements, as it has done every day since I began my training, a terrified seven-year-old covered in stinging pinpricks where hundreds of pinions had been injected beneath my skin.

I was told they were to teach me to dance until I learned the muscle memory, but they are used in every performance to guard against deviance and mistakes. I dig in a nail, and a perfect sphere of blood wells up. I lift my hand and tilt my head until I can see its reflection in the mirror then wonder if the blood on other side of the glass is real. The blood slides leaving a tear streak and then shatters on the floor.

Art Mistress opens the door. Perhaps she meant to prepare her workstation and found me instead. She stops, then starts, then flutters like a bird when she sees the blood. She scolds and wipes it from the floor first, then from my hand to prevent further dripping on her precious floor.

Art Mistress is very protective of her floor, and her creams, and her cakes, and her brushes. Even her paint obeys her, never daring to drip anywhere she has not authorized.

I don't apologize for the mess. Art Mistress tells me my punishment.

"No dinner," she snaps, and then after a pause, "and no breakfast!"

Angels are never struck as punishment, for fear of leaving a mark even Art Mistress cannot hide. Meals are subtracted instead. It doesn't matter whether we have the strength to dance. The pinions will dance for us. However, only a great displeasure can induce one of the Mistresses to take away two meals for one offence. Art Mistress is *very* protective of her floor.

I call to Art Mistress. She fusses over her brushes but cocks an ear toward me. I ask her why we wear pink.

"Pink is pretty."

She doesn't sound angry anymore, but she isn't ready to be nice to me, either. "Pink is . . . unreachable and temporary, like the clouds at sunset."

The only pink sunsets I see any more are permanently glazed into frames, but I don't say so.

"Angels must be pretty, pure, and unreachable. Temporary, yet immortal. You would do well to act like one."

I tell her we die.

Art Mistress pauses but doesn't look at me.

I tell her Sagitta is dead. I wait.

"We are all immortal souls." She says it like a mantra, liltingly, as if convincing a child of a truth she only half believes.

I don't answer her. I don't know how.

***

Ara and Lyra are the youngest Angels performing at Heaven's Window. I pass them in the dormitories long after midnight as I return from my dressing room. Libra is with them, comforting them as well as her hardened nature allows. Ara has been crying. They are afraid of pinions, of punishments, and of the Ceremony of Stars. They should be. I want to turn away, as I have always turned before. Yet, I pause.

Ara's hair: it is wild and heavy and defiant. Pins go in knowing they will be rejected or lost forever. It is so red, it is gold. It reminds me of Sagitta's hair, before they bleached it an acceptably neutral strawberry-blonde, pink.

I can see at the fringe where they have already begun the process on Ara, and I can imagine her five years from now, levitating too early to fill seats with poor admirers. It was not Sagitta's time to Return. Perhaps, this is what bothers me the most. She was too young, sacrificed early to boost income in an economic recession. We are out of the barest comfort with which the promise of time once graced us.

We are already dead.

Sales run high the night after a Ceremony. When an Angel is retired, the population remembers a radical love for the remaining performers which transcends poverty and a steep admission, at least temporarily.

Tonight the crowd is thundering, or I imagine they are, behind the muffling wall. If only noise could be something other than invisible. Then perhaps, they would know by my sobs what we endure.

But an audience does not know those sobs exist. An audience sits and smiles and supposes everything is directed as someone else. If they heard me cry for help in an Angel's Leap, if they really knew the danger, they would worry their brows and wait for someone else to do something.

But they will never hear me, only see. My routine begins. I don't want to rise to my death bound and gagged, shamefully disguised by the gathering shadows, and released into their clinging embrace. If I must be murdered, I would rather make an event of it.

Gracefully, I dip and bow and melt. Funny how an audience never notices when something goes wrong. Until it does. Gracefully, I twirl and sway. Gracefully, I disobey.

It is only a sweep of the arm up instead of across, so casually it could have been scripted. Even the Stage Master might not see the deviation, if not for the miniature eruption which sends a thin ribbon of blood spiraling past my elbow.

The pinions are not supposed to come out. They are designed to pull and direct and incur pain when ignored. But so sudden and massive a departure from routine rips one away from me forever.

I imagine it quivering against the wood-paneled magnets behind me. I wonder if they clean the pinions before injecting the old ones into new Angels, or if my blood will someday beat from a stronger heart.

I turn and continue as usual, and no one appears onstage to escort me away or calm the audience. They do not need calming. As far as they know, it is all part of the show. Heaven's Window wouldn't alarm its esteemed and paying patrons unnecessarily.

But the power of the magnets is increased. I can feel the tension in the pinions. Heaven's Window isn't taking any chances.

Perfect, I think.

I wait. The adagio cocoons me like a tired muscle, eight steps, nine . . . I lull them while my arm stains my drooping skirt.

Now an illegal spin, terrible and beautiful, clashes with the music. I dance to my pulse, my eyelash, my sigh. I shake off a cloud of pinions in orbits like so many moons. The pinions clutch at me, stronger, yet there are fewer. I wonder if that means there is a little more of me than before.

I think so. I see it, rivers of myself cutting tracks through my makeup and blossoming across my bodice in a color more feral than the sickly, sheltered pink.

I see it. The audience sees it, too. It is me in liquid identity. It screams and weeps in a thousand wordless languages, shedding profundity and truths with every drop that strikes the stage as it calls, "Pain! Flaws! Life!"

The color twists and curls like a parasitic vine choking out its enemy and building a home upon my corpse. It is a color so familiar, yet so fascinating, it cannot belong to Heaven or Hell, but pools mesmerizingly on Earth.

It tastes of broken chains.

It is red.

The audience is unsure of itself. They look around, wondering if they ought to be uncomfortable and do nothing. But I don't need them. I send a shower of red across the Window: freckles for their innocent faces. I laugh.

This is the Individuality, shouting from the rooftops. This is the Defiance, manifest in action. Of Fear, there is none. That I leave to the Angels. Red slicks the stage and smears my face until real features break through.

Still I dance. I try every unpracticed maneuver Dance Mistress forbade and giggle at the imperfect attempts. The brisé volé comes to mind, and I lift to embrace the pattern. As I touch down, I think of Dance Mistress and her instruction, "It's all about the landing."

She must be watching and crying for the butchered set. I will butcher it all: dance, face, stage, and perhaps even House Master's precious projected income.

I have no aversion to the blood. More pinions fly. A knot of them clenches in my gut, but I refuse to cry out. I am done with their manipulation. I am flying broken. I am string-less.

Pain plays a new tune in my body, its rhythms like tremors and its tempo wearying. My energy is red on the floor, finally spent. I command my limbs a little longer, still heady from my newfound control, and drift into a slow spin. Somehow, my hair is loose, warm and wet, as though I had been baptized. But I am not as holy as that.

I wonder why no one has taken me away. Perhaps, I inspired an Angelic revolt. Perhaps, I will be played off as an experimental performance and business will continue as usual. But I won't be here.

When I am too dizzy to stand, I sit, and mindlessly arrange my red-soaked bell skirt around me on the stage. I wave at the audience.

They look startled.

If I wave at the audience, it means they exist again. It means I know they have spent money to stare at a beautiful girl. I don't think they like the idea. No one has ever waved at them before. I laugh, then cough, then find myself too dizzy to sit up.

How funny, I think. *Didn't I stop spinning already?*

I lay down, watching the audience. They look sad, as if I made the Angel's Leap, but I didn't. I know I didn't because I can still see them.

See here, I whisper in red, *your Angels bleed. See here, your Angels die.*

The End

About Gabrielle DeMay

Gabrielle DeMay has been writing poetry and short fiction for over a decade and has been published in the online magazine ArtAscent, in various newspapers, and is working on completing her first novel. While working at a restaurant in north Texas, Gabrielle is putting herself through college to become an English and literature teacher. She spends her free time writing and reading anything she can get her hands on. Her style involves nature and the flickering absolutes that establish the complexities of the human heart. Her favorite genres to work with are fantasy and historical fiction.

ABOUT THE AUTHORS

All authors in this anthology have participated in the Authors Round Table Society. They have donated their time and expertise to helping others. As a living, vibrant group, we constantly seek to learn new ideas, realizing the world is a living, changing entity. As all things in life, we must grow to succeed.

May you succeed in all your endeavors.

James William Peercy

Made in the USA
Columbia, SC
08 March 2020